Rejecting the Future Moon Goddess

Rejection Series, Volume 2

Alana Dyer

Published by Alana Dyer, 2023.

The characters and events portrayed in this book are fictitious. Any similarity to real persons, living or dead, is coincidental and not intended by the author.

ISBN-13: 978-1-7381004-4-6
Cover design by: Elizabeth Korosaya

Table of Contents

Dedication

This book is dedicated to all the people who have been used, cheated on, and hurt. Remember that Rejection is a new beginning!

Chapter 1 - Once Upon A Time... Yeah, Right!

Have you ever heard about the stories of Werewolves?

Do you know the legends and stories about beings forced to shift from human to wolf only once during a Full Lunar Cycle on the night of a Full Moon?

Has anyone ever told you about those who have no control over their instincts or nature when in full wolf form and can attack anyone, both friend and foe?

Do you know about the beings whose Mates are destined to them and them alone by the Almighty Moon Goddess who created them?

If you said yes to any of these, would you believe me if I said these are true stories? That werewolves are real and walk amongst you? Well, everything but the forced shift on the night of the Full Moon is real. The truth is us werewolves can shift whenever we want and stay in control.

Now you are wondering who I am, and that's understandable so let me introduce myself. My name is Geminie Starlight. I thought I was Geminie Blake of the Hidden Claws Pack and future Theta—also known as third-in-command— to my pack. It was supposed to be my birthright since the Beta would be my brother, Alex. But things changed when I was a child, and I soon learned how fast blood was not actually thicker than water. That at a moments notice my life can become worse than it already was and I was demoted to an Omega, a slave within the pack. It soon worsened on the night of my eighteenth birthday and life seemed to have a different plan for me, my world turning upside down when rejection forced me into an early shift, and my true birthright came to be known.

I guess you're interested in my story since you've made it this far, so I'll tell you. But I need to start from the beginning...

Chapter 2 - The Thief of the Night

Eighteen years ago...

The Harvest Moon's emits a soft, orange glow over the land, bathing the forest and surrounding meadow in an ethereal light. The soft breeze carries the scent of fall on the wind towards where two wolves sit in waiting, hidden amongst the tall grass and wildflowers that cling to life before the winter frost can hit.

As the Harvest Moon slowly climbs to its apex, a mirage slowly appears on a crystal clear lake in the shape of a crescent moon. This mirage will soon be a lush green forest only visible during two events. The first is the ascension of the new Moon Goddess, who will take the place of the current one once she is old enough. The second is the birth of the Moon Goddess' pup. The latter is only if the Moon Goddess has met her Mate after becoming the next Goddess, and is a rare occurrence, happening only once in a blue moon.

Today is the latter event.

The current Moon Goddess is due to give birth to her child after many years and hoping and waiting from the wolves she watches over. This is also the day for the two wolves to strike. The Goddess took their daughter from them just after the two heard their child's one and only cry. Took away their hope of raising her with their only son and having the perfect family.

Tonight they plan to take her newly born child as revenge and make her face the suffering they have gone through as well. The time soon comes for the wolves hidden in the shadows to strike as the lush forest comes to life. With only a twenty-minute time limit from the moment the forest materializes to the moment the full moon begins its descent, the two wolves spring from their hiding spot, their paws thundering against the hard dirt.

The guards are sure to patrol the forest while the Goddess gives birth, forcing the two thieves to take as much caution as possible while they slink like shadows along the trees and underbrush of the forest, the orange moon providing enough light to see but also enough shadows for them to hide in. Their snouts are to the wind, sniffing the air to avoid any wolf who may block the way to their goal—the centre where the weak Goddess will lay after childbirth.

"The Goddess' mate is on his way to retrieve the pup." The thieves freeze, their heartbeats picking up, as they catch low voices conversing. If the Goddess' mate arrives earlier than expected, their plan will be foiled.

"We have orders to take the Future Goddess to him outside the forest before this forest vanishes." The voice continues. The two guards continue to converse, planning when to bring the new born pup to her father. The thieves wait as patiently as they can until the guards move on and silence resumes.

With the coast clear, they continue moving from shadow to shadow until the soft wails of an infant reach their ears. They have finally reached their destination. Slinking out of the shadows, the two wolves bare their teeth at the woman sprawled across a bed of moss, her white hair fanned out behind her and her complexion waning from the hardship of childbirth. Beside the weak woman— the Moon Goddess —is a wooden stump carved into a bassinet where the sound of wailing comes from. A child with white hair and prismatic eyes protests her birth and the cold she is facing outside of her mother's womb. The future Moon Goddess is just within their reach.

Suddenly, a twig snaps, alerting the resting women to the thieves' presence, but no one - not even a single guard - is there to stop them. "Please, leave." She whispers weakly, her hand reaching towards the pup who has now settled down. The larger of the wolves growls menacingly, stopping the weak Goddess from moving in fear of her newborn being harmed. The smaller of the two wolves steps forward, her eyes trained on the newborn.

The girl lays there so innocently, swaddled in a black wool blanket with small curly wisps of her white hair peeking out of the fabric. The smaller wolf knows she has come here to kill the infant pup, but instead of closing her sharp teeth around the little one's neck and ending her life as the two had planned weeks before, the smaller wolf picks up the blanketed bundle and gingerly carries the pup away.

Confused, her partner follows suit and they scamper away. The heartbroken wails of the Moon Goddess follow their retreat and the guards are quickly ordered to find Baby Geminie.

Chapter 3 - Family

Seven years later...

I giggle happily, eyes following my brother Alex as I stumble around the yard, chasing his brown wolf form and reaching for the fluffy tail he wags before me. Alex stays just out of my reach - as always - his tongue lolling from the right side of his muzzle. He gives me a wolfish grin with a mischievous twinkle in his eyes when I finally manage to grab the fluffy tail before me.

"Geminie, leave your brother alone." My father, Bastian Blake, Beta of Hidden Claws, orders. His stern, angry eyes bear down on me, making me stop in my tracks as a small spark of fear buds inside me. Alex nudges my hand gently, whining lowly as he wraps his furry form around me protectively.

"Alex and I are playing, Father." I answer quietly, leaning into Alex for comfort while trying to avoid the glare my father sends me. At seven years old, I have never been able to understand why my parents are so strict with me, why I feel like they hate me. With Alex being only eight years older than me at fifteen, I always felt like he is the favourite of the two of us. From the food he receives to the gifts given, I am nothing but a second thought to my parents. No matter how close Alex and I are and how much my brother adores me, in my parents' eyes I am nothing compared to my brother and the pups of our Alpha and Luna.

"Gem, as always, your brother is the future Beta. Mika will be his priority as Mika will be our next Alpha. You are just a she-wolf who will have to move the moment you find your mate." My mother Jasmine Blake states, rolling her eyes and standing next to my father. Alex lets out a sigh and licks my face, motioning towards the house and silently telling me he is going to shift and put on some clothes before returning to help me with our parents. Alex, thankfully, never agreed with our parents and always stood up for me whenever he could.

"As Alex's little sister, he should protect me too. We are family, and it should be his job to protect his family." I argue back, upset at feeling like nothing to my parents once again. I just want their love and affection too.

Within a blink of an eye my body is falling sideways, and the sting of flesh hitting my cheeks brings me to the reality my mother has just slapped me. Anger radiates off of both of my parents as their eyes glare daggers at me.

"Geminie Blake, Mika will always be more important than you, and that is final." She yells. My father stands silently behind her, disappointment mixed in with his angry gaze as he continues to stare down at me. I hate both of them. I hate their unfair treatment and reminders that I am not important, that I will be nothing but a mate to some wolf one day and must be an obedient lady.

Without another word, tears falling down my chubby cheeks and the stinging sensation on the left side of my face, I take off to the woods behind me and rush towards where I can feel safe and loved. My father's shouting for me to return, along with fear of any punishment they will give me if I turn back, fuels me to run even faster towards the river, where I can hide my scent from anyone who tries to follow me.

Alex taught me this trick where if you enter a river until it is up to your knees and walk in either direction, the water washes away any scent a werewolf can follow and allows you to get away safely. My direction is the waterfall north of the pack territory's boundaries. My safe spot lies just beyond the flowing water.

Wading into the shallow part of the river, I wipe the tears still falling from my eyes to help me see as I make the two-hour trip to the waterfall that falls from the large mountain our pack sits in front of. I soon find the vines that climb up the side of the rocks that I easily slide behind. Keeping inside the small stream that flows into a hidden cave, I let the glowing moonstones guide me toward my destination. The stream breaks into two and a light at the end of the cave indicates sunlight. A lush meadow greets me, my short legs hidden in the tall grass and wildflowers as I walk towards the weeping willow tree, wiping angrily at my tears. This is my happy place; I refuse to cry here.

"Gem, who hurt you this time, Little Wolf?" A soft, melodious voice fills my ears as I lean against the tree where she waited.

"My parents, as usual," I whimper, feeling strong arms pick me up and hold me gently to a warm body, one who smells like the wildflowers here.

"What happened this time?" Lizaria, the elf who guards this hidden meadow, continues, her long black hair blowing in the wind as she comforts me.

"The usual. Alex and I were playing but I was told to leave him alone. I will never be important to them, will I?" I answer, my voice growing quiet as I look into the elf's green eyes.

"You are bound for remarkable things, Little Wolf. I can see it," She says instead, always dodging my questions. I pout, tears flowing down my chubby cheeks once again. Lizaria sighs, carrying me from the comfortable shade under the willow tree towards the small lake where unicorns drink and frolic around.

"Little Wolf, one day I may not be able to protect the unicorn. Witches and werewolves, especially Soulless, hunt them for the magic hidden in their bodies and their blood." Lizaria sighs out, playing with my hair. I nod, understanding that the unicorn population has dwindled, only a few herds left and under strict protection.

"Do you know why I let you come in?" She asks, her eyes holding pride at the hidden home she protects. I shake my head no after thinking, my white curls bouncing with the movement as a light breeze brings the scent of flowers closer to us.

"Because you look at them as friends." She answers, surprising me as I look at the unicorns once more.

"I was wary that day I found you here, curled up amongst the foals, fast asleep. Always sending you back home every chance I could, but you would show up without failure every few days, tears staining your cheeks as you cuddles a foal." Lizaria smiles at me, her slender fingers wiping away the tears from my face as she kisses my forehead. That was last year after a fight father and I had. I followed a comforting scent up the river and that's where I saw the unicorns.

"One day, I hope you can take up the mantel and protect these creatures. You respect and love them as much as I do." Lizaria finishes, my eyes widening for a moment.

"Do you mean it?" I ask quietly, hiding my face in the crook of her neck.

"Of course, Little Wolf. I know this herd will be in good hands with you. Now, go to sleep, it's late. You'll wake up at home soon." Lizaria's voice soothes me to sleep, my eyes closing and my little body exhausted from all the crying and being held safely by the elf I think of as my mom.

"Gemmy, is this where you have been hiding since the argument?" A hand shakes my shoulder gently awake, and my eyes slowly open to see Alex looking worriedly at me. His hand touches my face, causing me to wince, and his eyes harden in the dim light. I most likely gained a bruise from that slap earlier today. I am in Alex's closet, lying on a teddy bear two times the size of my small body, as the clothes hanging above me hide me from view in case anyone comes looking for me. This is the same place Lizaria always sends me to keep me safe, she knows that Alex will protect me from our parents.

"Yes, I fell asleep crying." The lie comes easily as Alex ruffles my hair and carefully scoops me into his arms with a sigh. Silently, my brother carries me into my room and tucks me into bed, a look of sadness in his eyes that I have never seen before.

"I always tell them that you always hide in my room when you run away, but they never listen. You're my little sister, and I know you, Gemmy." Alex starts off, running his hands through his hair and staring outside my window at the Full Moon shining down on us, a warm glow from the white orb in the sky bringing me a sense of peace.

"I know, Alex." I yawn, giving my brother a sleepy smile at his concern.

"Go to bed, Gemmy. You have a big day tomorrow with the Alpha Family, hopefully that bruise fades by then." He bids me goodnight and flicks off the lamp beside my bed before getting up and leaving me to sleep under the comforting glow of the moonlight.

Chapter 4 – Bloody Picnic

"Now you know the rules, Geminie. Be polite and don't eat too much. You're a lady, not a Rogue." My father warns, and I nod, my curly white hair bouncing with the movement. Mother and Father set lofty expectations for me the moment I was old enough to hold a fork. Sit with your back straight and hands folded in your lap. Never rush to eat your food, and only eat what is on your plate—never ask for more. Never speak unless spoken to, and if I do not follow this rule when out in public around other pack members or dignified visitors, then Father will punish me.

I learned quickly what a leather belt felt like against my skin the first time I asked for more food when I was hungry. After that, I obeyed each rule without a fuss, even if my back hurt from sitting straight for so long or if my stomach protested for food in the middle of the night.

"I understand, Father and I will behave properly," I answer quietly as I catch Alex clench his fist and glare at our father from behind him. After my first and only punishment for not following these rules, Alex and our cousin Gracie helped me with moving around and cleaning the wounds caused by my father's rage. I know that my brother is thinking about those long and painful four weeks I spent last year.

I can tell both my father and mother, are about to say something else in warning to make sure I am a well behaved lady, but the front door behind me opens, revealing the easygoing smiling Alpha Sorus as he walks in and ruffles my curly white hair. A tall man with black hair and tanned skin, Alpha Sorus always has treated me like one of his own, letting me be a pup and enjoy myself to the fullest. I feel safe with him and always wished that he had been my father and not the man who yells and threatens me whenever I do something displeasing to him.

"Sorry I'm late, Bastian. Mika was trying to find his new toy car to show Gemie here. You know how kids are." Alpha Sorus explains, looking down and winking at me.

I know that Alpha Sorus secretly wishes for me to be his son's mate, to bond our families together. I had overheard my father and him talk about it one time when waking up in the middle of the night to use the washroom and I remember how happy the thought of being related to Alpha Sorus made me.

"It's fine, Alpha, I understand." My father answers, smiling warmly. Mother stays quiet, giving me one last warning look to behave before excusing herself and heading into the kitchen. I can never understand why my parents always warned me to behave. Can't they see that I'm a good girl?

I stay silent as the Alpha and my father talk about pack matters, Alex giving me a reassuring smile.

[Remember to tell me all bout your day when you get home tomorrow.] Alex links, giving me a wink and quietly slipping out of the room after I agree happily, watching as Alex heads up the stairs to what to his bedroom. Being the next Beta, I know Alex has been given work from our father to look through on the weekends as a way to train him. Alex hates it as my brother has little to no freedom to go out on the weekend like a normal teen, something he complains a lot to me about when ever Alpha Sorus takes me out along with his family.

"Well, we should be heading out now before it gets too late. Bastian I will bring Gemie home tomorrow safe and sound, so have a good night. You ready to go, Gemie?" Finally, the conversation ends between the two grown wolves. I grin, looking at the out-stretched hand offered to me after picking up my bag that contained some clothing and a sleeping bag for the night.

"Yes, Alpha." I answer Alpha Sorus, taking his hand and skipping out the door as I leave without a glance backwards or saying goodbye to my parents. The excitement of getting away from this house and from my parents makes me extremely happy.

The walk towards Mika, Lace, and Luna Reena—the blonde, fair-skinned wolf who Lace takes after—is filled with Alpha Sorus asking about my school life and what I've been up to since I last saw the Alpha Family. The pathway through the pack leads us closer to the dense forest on the west side of Hidden Claws.

I love the smell of our forest, the scent of wildflowers mixed with tall Canadian maple trees and sturdy pines. I'm almost done telling the Alpha about the book I'm reading when I'm tackled to the ground, and a giggle fills my ears. Lace's scent fills my nose as her blonde hair brushes against my cheek.

"Hi, Gemmy!" She greets me, the two of us giggling as we sit up and start chatting about our trip today. Alpha Sorus chuckles as Lace and I jump to our feet excitedly, my friend pointing to where Mika and Luna Reena stand waiting for us. As usual, Mika is holding a Nintendo DS in his hand, the sounds of a video game blaring from its speakers. I frown in the direction of the twelve-year-old. I know that it's not his fault my brother is forced to spend more time with him than me and that my parents make his future more of a priority than mine, but I couldn't help being slightly resentful and jealous of this future Alpha of mine. Even if he is cute.

Lace pulls my attention back to our conversation as she babbles on about the full moon tonight and how, under the full moonlight, the Unicorns will appear and bring their foals out to play in the pink crescent moon-shaped lake. I pretend to be surprised, but Lizaria has already informed me about this.

The Unicorns will be celebrating the foals gaining their own powers, blessed by the Moon Goddess. The pink water in our Pack is filled with magic that only the unicorns can absorb, and when foals come of age, drinking the water will help their powers manifest. I had heard stories from Lizaria about her overseeing this event and how years ago, she made a treaty with the first Alpha of Hidden Claws to protect the unicorns during this event. It is the reason Alpha Sorus takes his family and me out for the picnic and camp out tonight.

Of course, what no one else knows is that a small stream flows from the lake into a small cave and out to the hidden valley where Lizaria and the unicorns live and into a small pool that mixes with regular water from the river; Lizaria calls it a moon pool. Sitting on the edge of the pool whenever I visit Lizaria, I always watch the foals play and run around the pink water, mesmerized by the shimmer of the small traces of magic in the air, each drop twinkling like diamonds. To say I'm excited to see this at the pure pink lake instead of the small moon pool is an understatement.

With a nod from Mika and a hug from Luna Reena, the five of us set off toward the lake. Lace and I chase each other around the trees giggling. Alpha Sorus reminds us to stay in sight and takes away Mika's Nintendo D.S., forcing him to play tag with us. Now that I'm "it," I chase Lace, planning to keep away from Mika as much as I can, when she suddenly stops in front of me, causing me to crash into her.

"Gemmy, I see the water! It's so pink," My friend squeals in excitement, causing me to cup my hands over my ears and wince. But in front of us, just visible past the trees, is the lake. With a call in unison of "Last one there is a Soulless," the three of us race to the water's edge.

We happily spend the day splashing each other and eating the delicious picnic packed by Luna Reena herself. I have a day free from fear of my parents and instead just pure happiness. As day turns into night, Lace and I huddle under a tree, our sleeping bags blending into the background and hiding us while we wait for the Full Moon to reach its peak and the unicorns to come out.

"A few more minutes," I jump at Mika's voice as he rolls out his sleeping bag, sits beside me and wraps his arm around my shoulder while grinning. I can't help but blush and nod before looking out at the lake, my eyes blurry with the need for sleep as I manage to catch a glimpse of the creatures I love to watch begin to come out and frolic in the water.

◆◆◆

Geminie wake up... please, my love...

A soft voice flutters through my ears and I yawn, looking around the night, my dream of watching over the forest and some blurred faces now gone.

Feeling dizzy, I look around at the still-pink lake and the eery silence of the forest, causing goose bumps to form. Soft snores from my left and right alert me to Mika and Lace still fast asleep, but the Alpha and Luna are missing.

That's when I hear it.

The sounds of growls and howls echo everywhere. Scared, I turn and decide to wake up Mika, hoping that the twelve-year-old will be able to help. Shaking the sleeping boy awake, the growls and howls get closer, fear closing in on me. What if they are Soulless?

"What is it, Gemie?" He asks as he swats me away.

"Wolves and lots of them." I whisper-sob with fear, watching him bolt up and silently slip out of his sleeping bag while motioning to Lace. I quickly shake my friend awake, wondering how the blond-haired girl can sleep so heavily.

"I smell blood," My friend says as she rubs her eyes, and she is right. The iron tang of blood hangs in the air and we both look in fear knowing who exactly this scent belongs to.

"Where is she?" A screech echoes across the area surrounding the lake, and all three of us freeze.

"I don't know who you're talking about." The Luna is crying... But she never cries. Her answer is filled with fear, fear she has never shown any of us. Luna Reena is strong, always taking on a problem with calm and grace. But the way she sobs now is something I will never forget.

"The Future Moon Goddess! Your wolves took her from our Goddess as a newborn." The voice rings again as a loud smack rips through the air.

"I don't know anything about this." Luna Reena wails. Mika and Lace are frozen in place, but I slowly crawl forward. I see wolves in both human and wolf form standing around the lake, but I can't see Luna Reena or Alpha Sorus. A dreadful feeling fills me, and the thought that this night will not end well has me shaking with fear.

"I do not believe that you know nothing about the kidnapping of the Moon Goddess' pup, stolen the night of her birth. We have searched everywhere, and the only pack whose wolves gained a new pup that same night is this one. For your insolence in this incident, you will die, just like your husband." A cold voice shakes the trees as the sounds of something tearing and the Luna's screams fill the air. Then all is silent with a thud of something or someone falling to the ground.

The strange wolves leave the lake, but Mika, Lace and I are too terrified to leave our hiding spot. The Alpha children are curled up by the tree sobbing while silent tears fall from my face. I know what that tearing sound means, having heard it while my father slaughtered Soulless in front of Alex and me. Someone was beheaded without a second thought.

The sun finally rises but the three of us stay huddled together under the tree, refusing to leave the safety of our hiding spot. It isn't until the sun begins to set when wolves from the pack come calling our names and looking for us, my parents being the first to find our hiding spot.

"Thank goodness you're alright, Mika and Lace." My mother exclaims the moment we are found. My parents coo over the Alpha pups, helping them from their hiding spot and ignoring me, each one holding onto one of the siblings and forgetting that I, their daughter, also need comfort right now.

Alone, I slowly crawl out to see the pack crowding around Lace and Mika, some Omegas already cleaning the mess caused by the intruders as the rest block the sight of the lake from the sibling pair. But, unfortunately, I see everything.

The lake is dyed red in spots where the bodies of wolves with the scent of those last night lay, the ground holding small puddles, but not of the lake water. What hurts the most is seeing the Alpha and Luna both missing their heads, both lying dead just at the edge of the lake, where the water slowly laps at their fallen forms. This is a sight that Mika and Lace are forbidden to see and are protected from, while I stand apart from everyone.

Chapter 5 – No Longer a Beta

"Do you remember much of what happened?" My father asks, the tension in the air so thick, making me feel as if the walls are closing in on me. Mika and Lace, with tear-stained faces, sit to the side on a small couch while my parents force me to stand.

Today, we buried Alpha Sorus and Luna Reena. The idea of dealing with my parents after everything that's happened in the last three days is not something I want to do after their neglect the night they found us pups huddled together in fear. Instead, I keep my gaze towards the window, watching the raindrops pitter-patter against the glass wondering if I can melt away and be free.

"I don't remember much. We fell asleep watching the unicorns play. Geminie woke me up because she heard something, then woke Lace up." Mika answers, his voice wavering. I turn to look at the older boy to see my mother comforting him she sends a seething glare my way.

"Geminie, if you woke them up then why didn't you come get help!" It isn't a question, but an accusation that Mother throws my way. I can feel her hatred where I stand halfway across the room.

"I woke up and got Mika up right away, then Lace. There were too many wolves and if anyone of us tried running, we would have been caught and most likely killed, too." I answer plainly, meeting her gaze with a pleading look hoping my own mother will listen to reason.

"That's just an excuse!" She snarls at me, standing protectively in front of the Alpha pups and staring at me with contempt, a look I know all to well.

"It is the truth. They killed the Alpha and Luna because they were looking for the Moon Goddess' lost pup and believe that they were hiding her in this pack. If we came out, we would have been in danger, and if I left Mika and Lace there, they would have been in dan-" I stop mid-sentence, flinching as my father slams a fist onto his desk, causing me to jump in fear. Anger radiates off of him in waves and my attention turns to him.

"Enough of your lies, Geminie. You're the reason our Alpha and Luna, Mika and Lace's parents, are dead!" His voice bellows, the bookshelves rattling from the power. I stand frozen in shock and fear.

"Since Mika won't be of age to take over for another twelve years, I will be in charge as acting Alpha and my wife as acting Luna. You, Geminie, will be nothing but an Omega, a slave to this pack for your insolence and failure to protect our leaders." He continues, his words a finality on my fate in this pack. I turn to look at my friends, knowing that their words would help me keep my status as a Beta female. But Mika glares at me with hatred before turning away and Lace stares at the floor, clearly not listening to a word. I know at once that in this room I am alone.

Alone, disowned, and an Omega. Beta Bastian dismisses us, my face now sporting a bruise from the slap he had given me just moments ago when I tried pleading my case and calling him "Father" one more time reminding me that I am to now address him as Beta Bastian. An Omega with a car waits for me outside, his job to drive me to the Beta's house, a place I can no longer call home, and leave me there to pack up whatever can fit into a single duffle bag. After that, I will have to find my own way back to the pack house and to the small room that will be assigned to me. The car ride is quiet, and the Omega gives me a look of sympathy, his eyes too large for his sallow face.

"We know it's not your fault, Geminie. The Omegas know what happened was a freak event. We believe you," He reassures me before we return to the quiet drive. It feels nice knowing that the Omegas have my back now that I will be one of them. I have a sinking feeling that Beta Bastian will make our lives worse for it.

The car stops in front of the house, the Omega giving me an encouraging smile and telling me to be brave while handing me an empty duffle bag as I step out of the vehicle and head inside. The house feels cold and empty, a forbidden place to me now. Heading past the living room and up the stairs, I make my way to my bedroom and stop in the doorway. I see everything is gone except for five duffle bags sitting on the bare mattress of what used to be my bed.

"Thank the Goddess you're okay, Gemie." Alex's voice sounds from behind me and I turn to see him holding a bundle in his arms and pushing past me to fill another duffle bag.

"I heard them talking last night, mom and dad. They already planned to make you an Omega, and when they left me here after the Funeral, I asked an Omega to bring me a few bags to fill for you. I have everything, including your blankets and toys." He states, pulling me into a hug.

"Do you think I could become a Beta again?" I ask in a whisper, tears threatening to fall.

"I don't know, Gemie, but you have to be strong when they come back." I nod, giving my brother a reassuring smile and handing him the empty duffle bag I held. I help him pack a few more items, taking some food from the kitchen and pantry. A car pulls into the driveway and my heart skips a beat, thinking it's the Beta couple, but it's the Omega who dropped me off.

"Liam here said he would drive me to the pack house. They are on their way home now, but I texted them the excuse of checking up on Mika and they bought it. Liam is going to help me take your bags your new room. Just pretend to finish packing up the last one I leave for you, okay?" I only nod at my brother, letting Liam into the house as he and Alex carry six of the seven bags down and into the car. I wave to them before rushing upstairs and double-checking to see if we left anything before doing my best to carry the bag downstairs just in time for Beta Bastian and Mrs. Jasmine to burst through the door.

"You should have been gone by now." Beta Bastian growls out. I keep my head down, looking to the floor to hide my fear.

"I was just leaving, sir." I answer quietly, staying in my spot and waiting for the two wolves to walk past me. Instead, a hand grabs my hair and I cry from the pain, the Beta's face inches from mine.

"Well get the fuck out, you stupid pup," He screams at me, dragging me to the door and throwing me off of the front porch and into the mud-soaked lawn. Mrs. Jasmine just smirks, her arms crossed over her chest.

"You know the way to the pack house, you bitch, so make your way there." With that, Beta Bastian growls again, turns and slams the door, leaving me all alone. The rain stops suddenly, clouds clearing and the full moon shines down on me. I feel like the Moon Goddess takes pity on me while my small body slowly walks back towards the pack house where my life as an Omega will begin.

Chapter 6 – An Omega's Life

I groan while going through the laundry, nearly gagging at the smell left on the sheets from a particular room while the heat of the dryers in the brightly lit basement room intensifies the smell emanating off of this particular basket I am stuck with.

Visitors from Forest Paw had just left and their Alpha, Alpha Leo, the biggest sleaze I have ever met left a mess in the guest room that I had the unfortunate luck to be in charge of cleaning. He came to negotiate an alliance with our pack and I watched as Mika and Beta Bastian accepted this man openly while I cleaned the foyer of the pack house.

Alex managed to keep me as far away from the visiting Alpha as possible after the first night where I was forced to serve dinner. I could feel his eyes on me throughout the night, knowing that if he spoke one word to the Beta, he could have his way with me— a fourteen-year-old child. It wouldn't be the first time the Beta tried to use my body for his own advantage, but thankfully Alex has a friend in the medical wing who handed him a highly potent sleep drug and before anything could be done. Leo, the wolf in question, would be safely passed out in his room at any time if I were ordered to tend to him.

My hope to become a Beta Female again in this pack has been all but dashed by the many bruises that paint my skin and the scars that linger from punishments that were unnecessary, in my opinion. But at least I was not offered as a play thing to the visiting pack like some Omegas were for the last seven days.

"Someone got the raunchy sheets left by Alpha Leo," Lilly fake gags as I throw the white sheets with bodily fluids I refuse to think about into the soaking tub. I would rather incinerate them, but if Beta Bastian finds one sheet missing by the end of the day, then I will become the scapegoat as usual.

"Honestly, I am just glad Alex kept me in the cleaning rotations and not the serving rotations," I groan with relief, throwing the rubber gloves into the trash bin and washing my hands with scalding water and the strongest soap I can find. I feel dirty just touching anything of that nature and can feel the panic attack rising inside me.

Mumbling to Misbah that I am going to get air, I rush up the Omega staircase and burst into the garden, the frigid winter air a refreshing welcome to my lungs. I find a corner free of snow and take some deep breaths, hugging my knees to my chest and doing my best to keep the tears at bay. I found this spot thanks to Alex, a place to be weak between the walls of the pack house and the evergreen shrubs that leave a sharp pine scent in the air. No one comes to this part of the garden, not even Omegas, leaving me alone and feeling safe.

After an hour passes and my panic has settled down, I make my way down to the basement and put on another pair of rubber gloves, intending to finish those sheets. To my surprise, the sheet in the soaker tub is gone, and Lilly gives me a sympathetic glance while I go fold the dry clothes. She is one of three people who knows what happened, knows the night that officially killed my hope of being a Beta Female again.

I keep an eye on the time, working hard and keeping to the basement or the kitchen helping with meals for the day. When Lace comes in and lets the Omegas finish for the day and enjoy the rest of the night off at 7:30, I sigh with relief, finish folding the laundry fresh from the dryer and hand it off to a waiting Omega for him to deliver to its respective room.

Being the last to leave the laundry room and climb the stairs closest to the pack kitchen, I take a deep breath at the top of the stairs and confirm that no one else is around. Many are most likely in the dining hall, with the smells of freshly baked bread, stew and cupcakes lingering in the air. I see the goods sitting on the stove and counters, my stomach grumbling with hunger pains at the thought of being able to fill my stomach.

Since Beta Bastian and his wife took over, Omegas have become nothing more than tools, only deserving of enough food to live and nothing else. No extra food, no treats, and no drinks other than water. I've spent countless nights trying to fill my stomach with water in hopes of calming the hunger pains since my first week as an Omega. I think about all the tears falling from my eyes as I cried from the cramps an empty stomach brought when Beta Bastian took away my food privileges for some reason or another. I spent days trying to make it through another day until Alex could sneak me something small enough to eat. I learned quickly how to steal in order to keep on living in hopes of finding my own mate one day.

With a deep breath, I scan the area for any lingering scent of pack members. As I thought, most seem to be in the dining hall, with only a few upstairs. My scent will be gone by the time dinner is over. With a grin, I quickly grab the tote bag I stashed earlier in the day in the small broom closet beside the basement stairs and quickly fill it with the bread, easy-to-store goods from the pantry and a thermos of the still-hot stew. I leave the cupcakes with a reluctant gaze, knowing there is only enough for those dining in the hall, and quickly run up the stairs with my stolen goods towards my room in the attic.

Seven years have passed since my demotion to Omega, and in those seven years, this small room with bare wooden walls, a daybed, a desk, and a dresser slowly became home. A lock on the door handle was added two years ago, as well as a deadbolt that I locked each and every night since that incident a few years ago. Alex put in place this safety measure in case a visiting wolf needed a "Bribe" from Beta Bastian.

Placing my stolen goods on the desk beside my laptop, I sigh and take a seat on the worn wooden furniture, the damp cold only associated with an attic seeping into my body, causing goosebumps to form and shivers to crawl down my spine. Flicking my laptop open, a prize I won for a writing contest in school, I reach into the bag of goodies and pull out the stew as I wait for it to power on. With school still ever-present in my daily life at fourteen, I have no choice but to comply and do the homework needed for the following Monday.

After many bites of food and multiple assignments later, my tired eyes glance at the time and sigh. It is midnight, and I am finally done. With a groan and a final sip of the stew, I stash the remaining food I stole into an airtight container hidden in the walls and climb into the small bed for much-needed sleep.

Chapter 7 – For Days, Years, Death is a Wish

I groan as every step leading to my room causes a wince of pain. *I hate life!* is the thought that floats through my head while I slip out of my worn-out clothes and into some plain, comfortable black sweats and a black long-sleeved top.

Alex is still helping me every now and then, protecting me from Beta Bastian and Mrs. Jasmine as best as he can, the only other ray of hope I have to survive as my eighteenth birthday rolls closer. The thought that I will meet my mate, break free from Hidden Claws, and never see this pack again after graduation and the eleven years of hell I have suffered makes me smile as I lock the door to my room and open the window.

It's midnight, and the moon shines down on me while the wind brings a much-needed breath of fresh air. The leaves of the large sugar maple tree next to my window rustle in the breeze, bringing the delectable smell of maple inside.

At this time, the chores in the pack house are done and the Beta couple are most likely snuggled safely in their house. Now is a great time to relax and make my way to my sanctuary.

With a grin, I silently slip out of the window and onto the sturdy branch that normally scrapes across the glass. This tree is a luxury, one Alex managed to convince the Betas I keep when they realized the room I was put in almost eleven years ago had a means to escape. His excuse was I was too terrified to try to sneak out and run away. They reluctantly kept the tree thankfully and I gained my freedom through this one act.

I remembered the first night spent in the attic, the tapping on the glass and shadows cast by the sugar maple tree scaring me so badly that I was unable to sleep. I was curled up under the duvet cover, shaking like a leaf in the wind until morning, when I finally gained enough courage a seven-year-old could muster to peer outside and see the tree standing tall and proud with its bright red leaves. Alex promptly taught me how to sneak out once I felt brave enough, using the window and the tree. Beta Bastian and Mrs. Jasmine were none the wiser to their son teaching their disowned daughter how to climb in and out of the attic with the help of a seemingly useless tree. It took some practice every night, almost getting caught by patrols, but by age nine, I had mastered sneaking out unnoticed.

With sure footing, I shimmy down the tree with deft movements and land silently on the grass-covered earth. Blending into the shadows, I look around and listen for a moment, making sure no one is near nor awake. I survey the pack grounds before sprinting towards the safety and cover of the forest.

At the pack house, I may only have a few friends, but outside deep in the hidden valley, I have Lizaria and the Unicorns to keep me company. With a wide grin hidden behind the mask I wear, I make my way towards the river, keeping my footsteps light and body hidden in the shadows. With the calming scent of water and the sounds of the waterfall drawing nearer, I pick up speed, letting the glow of the moon guide me. It'll be the Harvest Moon soon, and my eighteenth birthday is drawing close.

Thoughts of being free from this place again bring a sort of giddiness inside my battered heart as I pass through the hidden entrance and into the tunnel. The magic in the air breathes life into me with each step until I enter the meadow, the scene glowing with the moonlight and wind bringing a sweet scent that washes over me.

"You're late," The musical voice of the Elf reaches me just in time for me to dodge to the right, reflexes having me backflipping away to a comfortable distance. Lizaria chuckles, her eyes mischievous as the Elf and I stare at each other.

"Sorry about that, but I'm here for training like always, Liz," I answer, rushing forward and throwing a handful of loose soil into her face. This gives me an opening, jumping over the ancient one and quickly unsheathing the sword strapped to Lizaria's back. Spinning around just in time to block the blow sent my way, the blades meeting with a clang and the two of us wait for an opening. My body is already sore from the punishment I received earlier that day, and it's a struggle to keep my position with the blades locked against each other and sweat building on my forehead.

With a deep breath, I drop to the ground, bringing my right leg around and sweeping out the Elf's legs from under her and quickly dodging to the left. Lizaria lets out a surprised gasp behind me, but I am too slow as I spin around, ready for the next attack and barely dodging the blade wielded by my mentor but not the punch thrown to my left side. I gasp, my body flying backwards as the punch activates the pain from the large purple bruise made by Bastian himself.

"What took you so long to get here?" Lizaria questions, her slow steps walking towards me. Too focused on the pain, I ignore her question and curl my body in on itself, trying to breathe through the pain and pleading for it to settle down.

“Gem?” The footsteps stop, and the sound of a dull thud hitting the ground alerts me to the sword fight I am supposed to continue with Lizaria, but my body refuses to move. Even when I oh so wanted to keep practicing and fighting. I did not want to be weak anymore, and Lizaria promised to make me stronger.

“Geminie, they beat you again, didn't they?” By “they” Lizaria meant the pack and the Beta couple. I was lucky today that Alex was on patrol when this happened or he would have been forced to watch and partake in handing out the punishment. Neither of us could refuse an order, and a public beating where every wolf but an Omega could partake is a fan favourite amongst the pack.

Warm hands cup my cheeks, and I look into the concerned eyes of my friend, her brows furrowed above me while I force myself to take slow, steady, deep breaths.

“I spilt water while in a rush to serve dinner. They beat me in the middle of the dining room as punishment, then made me drag myself out to the foyer while everyone else ate and chatted away like nothing happened.” I explain, tears forming in my eyes at the pain I felt while fifty wolves surrounded me after Beta Bastien grabbed my hair and dragged me to the middle of the room. His steel-toed boots connected with my rib cage as he screamed at me for being a clumsy, useless idiot that could do nothing right. Everyone mocked me and laughed while I rolled into a ball and covered my head, silent tears streaming down my face. I learned long ago to not make a sound, since the crowd loses interest when the wolf being beaten as punishment is quiet and accepts reality.

"When Lilly and Misbah rushed to my side and helped me to clean and bandage my wounds, it was already late and it took a little longer to finish chores. That's why I was late." I continued, feeling my friend take the sword still grasped in my hand and throw it behind her.

"You don't have to explain everything to me, Little Wolf. Just cry it out," And with her words, I cry. My sobs fill the air while Lizaria cradles my body to her, my hands clutching at the pastel pink tunic she wears, while her hands pull down my hood and run through my curls. She hums a lullaby while my heart twists with pain and grief. Nearly everyone in my pack hates me, blaming me for the death of Alpha Sorus and Luna Reena. That and being a weak wolf who never shifted at age sixteen like the rest of my peers, I became an easy target for their abuse. It's why Lizaria agreed to train me in the Elven way, as a way to protect myself against any sneak attack unjustly thrown my way inside the pack house.

Between my exhaustion, tears, and pain in my heart and body, my sobs soon turn into sniffles, the little energy I have left leaving me even more weak. I hate this feeling. The feeling of weakness and helplessness. My life revolved around this feeling since that day eleven years ago.

"Feel better?" Lizaria asks, worry still evident in her voice. All I manage is a nod, her calming scent wrapping around me, making me drowsy. I felt safe in her arms, something akin to motherly love from her.

"Come on, Geminie. Let's get you into the hot springs to heal, Little Wolf." She sighs, pulling away and giving me a soft smile. She helps me to my feet, her arms wrapping around me while I lean on her six-foot frame for support. The hot springs located fifteen metres away from the entrance are surrounded by moonflowers, the magic within a welcoming warmth. Lizaria frowns as she helps me to undress, leaving only my undergarments on and the multitude of bruises and scars littering my worn-out body in her view. She stays silent, her forest-green eyes giving me a once-over before helping me crawl into the shallow basin and laying me down gently.

A comfortable feeling washes through every pore of my body as the healing effects of the water take hold quickly. My prism-coloured hair floats out around me as I stare at the silver-white moon above. I did not heal the same as normal wolves. Being unable to shift when I turned sixteen effectively left me as a strong human, an even more disappointment in the pack. I have no wolf form, meaning the quick healing every wolf is born with never took effect for me, leaving my curvy body littered with bruising and scarring that took days, sometimes weeks or months, to heal. If I could get to Lizaria and the hot springs, then my body would be blemish-free. Sometimes that took days or weeks to happen if my punishment was severe.

"Gem, when will you leave the pack? We both know you're not safe there, Little Wolf." I look to Lizaria, her statement filled with sadness and her eyes shining with unshed tears for me. At three-thousand-and-some-odd-years-old, Lizaria looks no older than thirty. Her lithe body is filled with muscle meant for fighting, and long hair that splayed out around her made many envious. If it weren't for her long pointed ears, she could be a model in human society.

"My high school graduation and my eighteenth birthday are tomorrow. If I find my mate then, I'll stay. If not, then I... I will leave." Lizaria is right, I have spent eleven years being abused for a situation out of my control. One of these days, I'll end up dead without knowing how. The problem is leaving Lizaria and the Unicorns behind. It's the only reason I was hesitant to leave in the past. But once I graduate, I have no more ties keeping me here. Alex already stated he would leave, and so would Lilly and Misbah. If I could convince Lizaria, then we could find a place to settle down outside pack territory, where the Unicorns will be safe.

"I wish I could watch you walk across that stage tomorrow, Gem, but I have to stay here and protect the Unicorns." Lizaria sighs, holding out a towel for me. I smile at my friend and accept the towel, wrapping it around my body and sitting on the edge of the hot spring as we stare up at the moon.

"If it weren't for the school being shut down for renovations after exams back in June, I would have walked across the stage already." I chuckle. Lizaria will be busy with both protecting the unicorns as well as dealing with the magic the Harvest Moon will provide. Even if I asked my friend to join me for my graduation, being isolated from the world for hundreds of years and returning to the outside world would be a huge culture shock for her. After an hour of chatting and Lizaria promising me a graduation gift tomorrow, we watch as the moon floats across the sky.

When two hours have passed, I dress in my black clothing with a sigh and bid farewell to Lizaria and the unicorns before making my way back to the pack house so that no one notices my disappearance.

Chapter 8 - Planning a Departure

I glare as the small device on my side table rings shrilly in the quiet morning, my alarm clock is one I cannot wait to throw away. With only four hours of sleep after training and talking to Lizaria, I want nothing more than to sleep in, but I have duties as an Omega to perform.

Slamming my fist onto the alarm clock and turning it off, I take in the time of six o'clock in the morning and groan. Today is my day to cook breakfast for the pack, and with only an hour and a half to have the meal ready and on the table or face punishment from Beta Bastian, I will have to quickly get ready and make it downstairs within the next fifteen minutes. I look outside the window and notice the sky is still dark outside causing me to groan with frustration and fling the comforter off of my body, shivering with the cold fall air.

Today is graduation day, with many of the wolves preparing to walk across the stage at noon. Chores will be delegated to the Omegas twenty years or older, meaning I will have most of the morning to myself after making breakfast. I can use this time to prepare to leave.

My talk with Lizaria last night opened my eyes to needing to leave, being free and allowing myself to fully accept the power a Beta wolf should have. I feel especially trapped and suffocated today of all days and the feeling of something bad about to happen sinks into me.

Another sigh escapes my lips while I take out a simple pair of leggings and green T-shirt from my dresser then head towards the shower, thinking about what I will need to leave this place and be on my own.

The lukewarm water falls harshly onto my body, leaving me shivering as soon as I finish washing off and wrap myself in a thin old towel. I only have to make it through today, and once everyone is too preoccupied from the graduation party tonight, I'll escape.

◆◆◆

The ringing in my left ear is persistent as I curl into a ball, my hands over my head protecting myself from any damage this beating will cause. I want nothing more than to look up and glare at Beta Bastian as he towers over me, rage radiating off of him in waves in my direction.

"You filthy bitch! I told you to have breakfast ready at exactly seven-thirty!" He screams at me, drops of what I can only assume to be spittle from his mouth landing on my exposed skin. Disgust creeps into me at his treatment, cementing my decision to leave tonight. A foot collides with my arms, his boot directing a blow to my head, making me thankful that I was quick enough to roll into a ball after the punch he threw my way moments ago that left me on the floor.

"Do you know what I saw instead when I came downstairs, you filthy excuse of an Omega?" He continues but I know better than to answer. Answering his rhetorical question will lead to a whipping with the silver-tipped whip. My silence must have pleased him as the kicks stopped, replaced by a hand grabbing my hair and pulling me up into a sitting position, making a whimper of pain escape my lips.

I notice a crowd forming in the dining hall. The food is already placed on the buffet table and ready to be devoured by the pack, but everyone here would rather watch this spectacle.

"I saw you placing the last dish at seven thirty-five!" Beta Bastian screams in reply to his own question, more spittle landing this time on my cheeks. I want to argue that I was actually refilling the bacon that had already been devoured by the pack members who arrived earlier, now sitting by the windows with a smug smile as they enjoyed the show, but they would call me a liar. This pack has little respect for anyone deemed an Omega since Bastian and Jasmine took over as temporary leaders. Its worse for me as I am the disowned daughter of the Betas. I am nothing but garbage in their eyes, so my treatment is worse than what the others get.

My body is flung backwards, and the back of my head collides with the wall behind me, bringing me from my thoughts. Stars shoot across my vision before the all-to-familiar feeling of a boot colliding with my stomach has me curling into a ball of pain once more. I can hear a few snickers and comments about how pathetic I am, these words fueling my rage that I have no other choice but to restrain.

"Geminie, get out of my sight and go make yourself useful to the pack." A final kick is thrown my way after Beta Bastian dismisses me. When I hear his footsteps fade away, I push myself off the ground and use the wall as support to stand. Even through the overwhelming pain, I can feel everyone watching me either openly with a mocking smile or subtly, waiting for another show. I finally realize why Lizaria always mentioned that I should leave as I stare at each and every wolf in the room.

Only a few cared about me in this pack, and the hope of one day becoming a Beta again has long been crushed. I have no other reason to stay here with Hidden Claws.

With a slight limp, I walk out of the dining room, refusing to show weakness and refusing to cry anymore. My mind is now made up. Making my way outside into the garden, I sit and take a deep breath of the crisp fall air. The trees surrounding the pack lands are starting to turn red and yellow with the changing seasons, and a slight chill is on the wind, breathing a fire inside me I thought I had given up.

Since I could not shift into a wolf, my next step would be leading a life as a human, maybe in a large city like Toronto, Ottawa or Mississauga. Perhaps even a smaller town like Bolton or Barrie would be comfortable. I'd love to be anywhere but here, along the Hudson Bay.

"Gems?" A small smile curls the edges of my lips and I turn to see Alex holding a plate piled with food in one hand and a gift bag in the other. A look of concern plays on my brother's face as he takes a seat across from me at the stone picnic table. Setting the plate before me, I eye the bag in his hands as my own automatically reaches out so I can devour the pancakes before me.

"What's that?" I ask, nodding towards the bag he sets on the floor just before he steals the fork from my hand and takes a bite of pancake.

"Food," My brother chuckles, handing the fork back to me and leaning back in the chair as I stab at another piece of fluffy goodness covered in maple syrup.

"Thank you, Captain Obvious, I am well aware there is a plate of food in front of me," I roll my eyes at his smirk, taking another bite of the food before waving towards the gift bag on the floor.

"What I meant is, what's with the bag?" His smirk turns into a bright smile before he motions me to finish eating. I know my brother well, and he always made sure that I ate before we talk since his parents rarely left me with enough food. Rolling my eyes and complying, I rush to finish off the plate of pancakes, finding a stash of bacon and sausages hidden underneath the pile which too get devoured. Finally, I push the now empty plate to the side while Alex places the bag in front of me with a grin.

"Happy birthday, Gemie." His deep voice brings small tears to my eyes as I gingerly remove the tissue paper obstructing the items inside. My eyes widen at a turquoise purse, a simple stylish bag that I have been eyeing from Michael Kors for weeks.

Lifting the bag, I feel something rattling inside as the weight of the bag is heavier than the display at the mall. I open the purse to discover a matching wallet holding important documents, from my birth certificate to my health card and even my brand new G2 class licence that I got a month ago. I thought I would have to report these stolen when I leave.

"I had to wait for Bastian and Jasmine to leave on a trip last week to gather your documents." Alex answers knowingly, smiling at me. Tears well in my eyes as I look down at the purse, trying to keep my mind from the despair of leaving my brother here when I leave Hidden Claws for good. Tucking the wallet away, my hand brushes against another small item in the purse. Curiously, I remove the object to find a small white box. I swiftly open it to discover a set of brand new keys—car keys, to be exact.

"Why?" I whisper, holding the keys in my hands. I never thought that I would be able to own a car until much later, especially knowing that I will be penniless when I leave. The inheritance left to me by my grandparents was given to Alex since Bastian and Jasmine would never give me any part of it. But with a car, I can live inside it until I save up enough for an apartment. With a car, this winter will be much more bearable on my own.

"I've been watching you sneak out for the last few months and... I've been following you." Alex admits sheepishly. Fear takes hold in my heart as I think about Lizaria and the Unicorns she protects. If Alex saw me, who else did?

"Don't worry, Gemie, no one else knows." Alex quickly reassures me, pulling me into a hug as he sighs.

"I know about that valley you go to and that Elf. I've watched you train with her, and she even confronted me one night. After promising that scary Elf-mom of yours that I wasn't going to harm you or the valley and explaining to her that I'm your big brother, she reluctantly agreed to let me keep watching over you at night." The fear and worry I felt are replaced with guilt, guilt at keeping this secret from my brother and for always running towards Lizaria when I needed to hide away from the Beta couple. I feel so guilty for making Alex worry about me.

"I'm sorry, Alex, but if they knew about Liz and the Unicorns, something bad would have happened." The apology leaves my lips before I know it and I am met with a chuckle.

"I know. Why do you think I asked to be on night patrol? Bastian is a power-hungry, lazy bastard. You would think as his only son and heir, he would go easy on me, but after what our so-called father did to you as a child and over the years, I don't expect much. That lazy bastard was more than happy to let me do the night shift," The sarcastic tone in his voice shocks me and I pull away from his hug to stare at my brother. Hatred and rage simmer in his eyes, and I understand in that moment that life for Alex hasn't been easy either. It was for sure easier than my own life in this pack, but I can see the struggles he has faced with Bastian and Jasmine as his parents as well just by looking at the dark circles permanently etched into his face. My brother looks exhausted, more than I ever realized before.

"Anyway, when I took your documents, I also took your inheritance documents from our grandparents and a copy of their will for you to use as well. It's all in the car. I need to get some sleep, but that Elf of yours came up with the idea of getting you a car and putting together what our parents are holding hostage for you. She told me last night that when you leave, she will follow us as soon as the two of us find a place for the unicorns." I nod slowly, surprised at everything I am learning today from my brother. Lizaria had already planned for me to leave Hidden Claws by the sounds of it, and she had enlisted Alex's help. I couldn't have been any luckier than I am today with an amazing brother and a thoughtful friend. After putting my gifts away in the gift bag, Alex walks me back into the pack house. As I start to climb the stairs and head to the attic after bidding him a good sleep, he calls out to me.

"The car is in that rundown shed by the edge of the pack territory. Get your stuff packed, and while everyone is at grad, I'll sneak it into your car. My stuff is already packed. Just let me know when it's time to leave." Without waiting for my reply, Alex yawns and heads into his room, a room he requested to live in after turning eighteen.

Smiling, I continue my walk towards the attic and my room, where I promptly lock the door. I have three hours to pack before needing to be ready for graduation, just three hours to decide what I can take and what to leave behind.

Today will be my final day as part of Hidden Claws, and the excitement of being free fuels my desire to take everything I own and not leave anything for this pack to hold hostage against me.

Chapter 9 - Graduation Blues

I quietly stand off to the side while wolves in their graduation gowns run around, chattering away with their friends. The well wishes and "I'll miss you" sound around the room. Left alone, I realize that although no one caused me trouble here at school, I was left with no friends and spent my "golden years" in high school as a literal lone wolf.

The halls behind the gymnasium where graduation will take place buzz with an excited and nervous energy.

"Geminie, are you ready?" Mrs. Horris asks. The wolf with graying hair looks around the halls and smiles. As our Principal, she has been the wolf who mentored and helped me through many things since entering grade nine. She understood me right away on the first day we met, when she watched me faint during my first day at school. As we sat in her office, my heart was racing, thinking that I would be in trouble. Mrs. Horris surprised me by handing me a warm meal from the cafeteria and a glass of orange juice. Her calm eyes carefully took in my thin body as she asked me one question: Are you an Omega?

I felt compelled to explain everything to her, from my life as an Omega and what led to that position being placed onto me, how this small chili and warm bread she placed before me was my first meal in four days, and how I never intended to faint and be late. It was this honesty that led to the Principal into helping me, and without her help, I would not have been able to graduate today. I would not be valedictorian or have the highest grades at the end of each and every class.

"I think I am." I answer, seeing Mrs. Horris nod as she fixes the golden sash placed across my body and gives me an encouraging smile. We make our way to the front of the graduation line, faculty nodding at me while the four other students with exceptional grades silently wave a greeting. The excited buzz in the halls slowly dies down as the music begins to play, and the doors to the gymnasium swing open.

The faculty begins their entrance first, taking slow, measured steps as they walk forward, barely paying any attention to the crowd. The rest of us follow behind as parents shout their children's names in praise of their success in graduation once they catch sight of them. Envy swells inside me, wishing I had their luck, that I had parents that loved me and were proud of my accomplishments. But wishing leaves an empty feeling and a bitter taste of resentment that I did not need. Tomorrow I will be far away from everyone and, with time, will find my own place in this life.

With the procession leading to the stage, I force a happy smile on my face and follow the few students with the honour of sitting amongst the faculty while the rest of the graduates file into the rows of seats below. As the last row takes their seat, the ceremony begins.

"Please welcome this year's valedictorian, Geminie Blake." After the introductory speech made by the principal congratulating us on a job well done in our success as graduates, as well as how much of an honour it has been teaching the future of each pack in the area, my name is called. I take a deep breath before standing, knowing my speech will be the last one before diplomas are handed out. I take careful steps towards the podium, shake hands with Mrs. Horris, and turn to face the crowd, waiting for the few cheers and wolf whistles thrown my way to quiet down, the crowd shocking me with their excitement for my speech.

"Good afternoon, faculty, parents and guardians, visiting Alphas and, lastly, my fellow graduates." I begin, taking a look around and spotting the Beta couple watching me. They were only here for appearances and nothing more, as representatives of the pack. Even though I hate the feeling, disappointment still washes over me. I hide it behind the smile I keep on my lips.

"Four years ago, we stepped into these doors as new students, eyes wide in curiosity at the building that would mould us for our future. I remember the first days of freshman year, and one thing that stuck with me was the quote, "Even if you take three steps forward, you'll find yourself being forced to take one step back; but keep moving because great things await." Those were the first words said to us by Mrs. Horris as she greeted us at our orientation, and to this day, those words ring true for each and every one of us." I continue, take a deep breath and try to imagine the future I will have after today, the obstacles I will face when I leave my pack. I think of the people and wolves I will one day meet and where I want life to take me.

A life I can call my own.

"As we move forward from these moments and friends we've made, we will face more challenges along the way, meet new people and learn new things. We will go through new experiences, from leading a pack, to protecting the ones we love, to even going on a journey to find ourselves. But today, know this." I pause again, the smile on my face morphing from fake to a genuine grin as the endless possibilities in front of me after today bring me peace of mind, my own words encouraging me to look towards my own future.

"We did it, we made it through high school, and we will make it through anything as long as we look forward to a new tomorrow and try our best to live our lives to the fullest." A cheer erupts after my words, and the staff thanks me for my speech as I take my seat once again. Just another few hours and today will end, and my freedom will begin. I could do this.

◆◆◆

"Geminie Blake. Honour student, valedictorian, Artistic Paw Award, Silver Literature Award, and the Golden Halo Award for most community hours served in the graduating class of 2019." I stand as my name is announced, walking up to the podium once again to shake hands with the faculty standing there; the heads of the English department, Arts department and the Vice-Principal each hold an award and envelope in their hands while I take my diploma from Mrs. Horris.

The trophies gleam in the light as I accept them, quickly hiding the envelopes with the monetary awards into the folder my diploma comes in while I thank each of these wolves for their teachings and guidance throughout my years in the school.

I take my seat again after pictures are taken for the school website, pictures I plan to save and print for when I find my own home and take the time other wolves are called to the stage to look at the halo in my hands, the paw covered in dripping paint and the "silver" quill on a silver book, each set on a wooden base.

These awards reminded me of how well I had done these last four years while living in hell within Hidden Claws, and that I will thrive wherever I go. My determination to leave is growing stronger once again.

As the list of graduates receive their diplomas and awards, and the ceremony ends, I make the trek back to the pack house alone, taking the time to enjoy the fall surroundings, reminding myself that my fate is in my own hands.

Chapter 10 – Rejection Feels Like Death

I sigh as I look at myself in the small mirror hanging from the wall. After the graduation ceremony, I made my way to my small attic room to see all the bags I had packed gone and a large gift box sitting on the bare mattress. The smile I had on my face had not left after noticing the pale pink dress inside and a note from Alex to enjoy the party—a party all Omegas had to help set up, from cooking all the food to placing all the decorations.

Now showered and dressed in the flowy, off-the-shoulder knee-length dress with a simple pair of black flats on my dainty feet, I sigh and look towards the open window behind me where the sounds of music drift in on the wind. The party is in full swing, and whether or not I want to go I know I could use the last night as a pack member to just enjoy some form of normalcy.

"Gemie?" A soft knock on the door catches my attention as Alex pops his head inside, giving me a soft smile and stepping into the small room.

"You look incredible." I blush at the compliment, my hand instinctively going to my stomach that sports a black, blue, and purple bruise from this morning. I know he means to spark some form in confidence in me, but the years of bruises and small scars left on my body are small reminders that although I am a werewolf, I will always be the weakest in the pack. Tomorrow, I will be with the humans, and no longer the weakest.

I hear a long sigh as Alex tugs me into a hug, his warmth reminding me that my brother will be by my side after tonight. That he will give up the pack he'd be second-in-command of as Beta for me. He'd do his best to live amongst humans or help us find a pack that will accept us for who we are eventually.

"I know what you're thinking, Geminie, so stop it. You do look amazing, and these idiots will regret their treatment of you one day." His arms tighten around me while his words give a small reassurance. Alex is right. One day these wolves will regret how they treated me, as the truth is always revealed eventually. A moment passes and I push away from my brother, sending him a small smile to show that I will be okay, and getting a relieved one in return from him.

"Let's head downstairs before I chicken out." I suggest with a nervous chuckle, running my fingers through my hair as Alex motions for me to take the lead. The walk down the stairs from the attic to the first floor is quiet, with older Omegas running around back and forth while the music from the party outside slowly gets louder and louder with each step.

Although this morning I promised myself to not look weak in front of everyone, I can't help but hesitate as we grow closer to the back door. The Betas made sure to spread the word that it was my fault the beloved Alpha and Luna were murdered. Many of the wolves outside, whether they were the younger generation, my generation or older, despised me. The thought of my last night being filled with hate-filled glares and whispers about why I'm at the party even though I'm a graduate myself makes me want to just turn around and leave without hesitation.

"I- I can't do this." I whisper meekly, pausing just inside the sliding doors to the patio as I catch a glimpse of wolves mingling with one another as some dance on the homemade dance floor. I could smell the bonfire on the wind, the smoky scent of pine logs burning giving the fall air a warm feeling.

"This is your day too, Gem. You deserve a night to just let loose." Alex encourages me and with those words, I feel hands on my shoulders as Alex pushes me out the door without hesitation. A squeal of surprise leaves my lips and once I catch my balance, I turn to glare at my brother only to notice him gone. As much as I love Alex, my brother could be such an asshole at times.

With a deep breath, I stand straight and turn to face the crowd of recent graduates from my pack. Some just nod at me while other ignore me, their focus more on the alcoholic drinks in their red solo cups. As expected, I am ignored, but the worry and anxiety I felt before being pushed outside slowly eased away.

And then I catch it, a strong scent that causes my heart to flutter.

[What's wrong?] Alex links me and I shrug, looking for the source of this scent.

[A scent. Something that is calling me towards it like a moth to a flame.] I answer, taking small steps towards the table full of food.

[Shit. Your mate is here.] I stop mid-step, shock filling me at realizing my mate is in this pack. This complicates the plan of leaving.

[Just enjoy your night, and if you meet him, you meet him. For now, focus on yourself, okay, Gemmy?] Alex advises before the link shuts off. Sighing, I take his advice and focus on enjoying my last night in this pack. Mate or not, I no longer want to be in Hidden Claws.

Spending the next hour either roasting marshmallows by the fire, keeping warm in the chilly fall night, and regretting that I didn't bring a jacket, I listen to the chatter of wolves who will become full-fledged Hunters and Trackers. These wolves will be taking over their parents' positions in the pack, and others will go off to college to learn professions needed in the pack, like doctors, teachers, and nurses. This makes me start to question where I want to go. I have money from scholarships now, so I could go to college and make a living amongst humans.

As I think about my future plans every so often the wind will carry a faint trace of this scent, one that causes my heart to skip a beat and make my thoughts muddled. I know my mate is walking around, but I ignore this feeling, turning my thoughts back to my future.

Now would be a suitable time to leave with everyone busy at the party and only Omegas running about the pack house and grounds, giving me a great way to sneak out unnoticed. I could figure out my future after Alex and I leave the pack.

"Attention please!" I stand, ready to leave when Beta Bastian's voice calls loud and clear above the music. The chatter dies down and someone turns off the music. I curse my luck, wanting nothing else but to leave unnoticed. Unfortunately for me, with the attention on the Beta and Mika standing next to him, no one can move without being punished.

"Our dear future Alpha, Mika, says he can smell the scent of his mate in this crowd." Beta Bastian continues. The chatter begins, this time the focus being on who in this pack might be the next Luna. My mind wanders back to the days Alpha Sorus used to tease Mika and me as being the next Alpha and Luna pair. Lace would jokingly say her and Luna Reena would plan my ceremony. Those memories feel like a lifetime ago, a life that was no longer mine.

"With this information, can we have all the unmated she-wolves line up in front of the bonfire? Today we will not only celebrate the graduates of the high school, but we will also welcome our future Luna." I roll my eyes at their excitement, knowing many will have their hopes dashed. Unfortunately for me, though, I will have to join the line as Beta Bastian will not let anyone walk away.

With a sigh, I watch the line grow longer and know that if I don't join soon, a beating will ensue quickly. With that thought in mind, I join at the very end. The line moves quicker than I thought, with girl after girl walking away dejectedly or escorted through tears by a friend once deemed not Mika's mate, while he stands there impatiently. Soon, only twenty girls out of the forty remain.

A scent is blown my way carried by the wind, one that has been taunting me all tonight.

"Not her." A deep masculine voice says, my mind focusing intently on the timber and pitch. A brunette in a slinky black dress walks out of the line, tears falling from her cheeks. I feel sympathy for this wolf, an Omega I have rarely talked to and only in passing while doing our chores. More girls are declined with a "Not her" or a "Next she-wolf."

I frown.

The line is growing closer and the wind brings the scent of mint and pine, reminding me of a fresh summer breath in the valley with nights spent laying beside Lizaria and the Unicorns.

Then it came.

The sparks snap me out of my daydream journeying from where a hand held my shoulder across my body and into my heart, kick-starting it into an unsteady rhythm while the delicious scent wraps around me once more.

"Mate." The word escapes my lips in a whisper while another hand slowly caresses my cheek. My closed eyes open to see Mika looking at me with a gentle gaze, the backyard so quiet that all you can hear is the crackling of the bonfire. It felt like eternity as the two of us gazed into each other's eyes and the plans I had focused on today begins to vanish from my mind. As the Luna, my life will change forever if I stay.

Then the unexpected happen.

The hand on my cheek is gone, replaced by a burning sting as Mika slaps me. I stumble back shocked that my mate would hit me, but that shock soon fades. This is Hidden Claws and no one likes me, as the blame of Alpha Sorus and Luna Reena's deaths hangs above me like a noose waiting to tighten around my neck.

"I refuse to be your mate." Mika seethes, anger radiating off of him in waves, causing lesser wolves to cower around us. I stay silent, unable to voice a reply. The Moon Goddess had cast her net of fate on us before either of us were even conceived. There was nothing he could do.

"You are the reason my parents are dead!" He continues, his fist shooting out to punch me, but I had enough of being beaten and dodge, using his momentum to throw him into the crowd behind me.

"You and I both know I never killed the Alpha and Luna!" I call out in rage, sick and tired of this accusation.

"I was seven, fucking seven years old when they were killed. You and Lace were there. You saw the same thing I did, those wolves demanding to know where the child of the Moon Goddess was!" I continued. I felt a wave of unease in the air, my eyes moving to where the Beta couple stood. Something felt off about them, but my focus right now is on my mate and his baseless accusation that spent eleven years weighing down on me.

"You could have done something!" Mika screams back and I growl, shocking not only myself but those around me.

"And what, dear mate, do you expect a seven-year-old to do? You were twelve and had more training than me at that time in combat." I counter, crossing my arms across my chest and glaring at him. I could see the hesitation in his eyes as he glares back. He knows I have a point and can't refute me. We were only pups and could do nothing but watch.

"You all have your heads up Bastian and Jasmine's asses that you can't even see what's right and wrong with this filthy pack." I continue, seeing Alex silently slink onto the porch and giving me a nod. He had everything ready if I wanted to leave now, considering how finding my mate is going. But this could be my chance to help Hidden Claws.

"Maybe it's a good thing I am your mate Mika, its about time this pack chan-"

"You are not my mate. I refuse to have someone as weak as you as Luna." He cuts me off, shocking me as I notice a look in his eyes. It's one I know too well and the feeling of helplessness slowly gathers in the pit of my stomach. I already knew what was coming and I couldn't stop it.

"I Mikael Alibaster and future Alpha of Hidden Claws reject you, Geminie Blake, as my mate and future Luna of this pack." A stabbing pain rips through my heart as if a million shards of glass tear it apart. I can feel my vision turn hazy from the pain as a whimper, causing another surprise reaction from the crowd, escapes my throat.

Whispers begin to float on the air at the turn of events as I force my body to stay standing. I felt like death is trying to tear me apart and bring me into it's silent slumber.

"Anything you want to say?" Mika asks, a smirk on his smug face as he slowly saunters towards me. He and I both know I have two options. Accept the rejection and have the pain ease for me or fight for the bond. I wanted to fight for this bond, one that I have been hoping for to change my life, one that I dreamt about each night, hoping for my mate to save me. I didn't want Mika and the cruel reality that came with him, but I wanted my mate, so I stay silent, glaring at the man while the pain pulsates through my body.

"Geminie, say it!" Bastian growls in warning, but for once in my life, I ignore his order. A fist is thrown my way at my insolence, and instinctively I catch it, glaring at Bastian whose face of anger turns into one of fear. The pleasure I feel knowing my so-called father fears me numbs the pain of the rejection initiation.

"Say. It. You. Bitch!" He growls through his teeth, his body shaking. I just chuckle and apply force to Bastian's wrist until the satisfying crunch beneath my hands rings in the silent yard, followed by a scream. With a small throw, I push Bastian aside and turn my attention back to my mate just in time to catch a slap across my left cheek that sends me sprawling onto the cold ground in burning pain.

Mika has once again slapped me.

A fist entangles into my hair, pulling me up from the ground while an angry Mika towers over me.

"Geminie Blake, you have two minutes to accept the rejection or I will kill you." I whimper with pain; his threat being processed through the ringing in my ears. He was serious, and I realize in this moment that I have no choice but to do as he says.

"I, Geminie Blake," I start off slowly, fighting to hold back my tears. If I continue this, I will feel the pain for three long years, but Mika will feel nothing. He will be able to go about his days as normal while I wallow in misery every time he sleeps with another she-wolf, the bond pining for it to be fixed with my soulmate.

I couldn't let that happen. He deserves the pain for not only this rejection but also the last eleven years of hell I faced.

With a silent prayer to the Moon Goddess and a sudden burst of strength, I reach up and clasp my hands around his hand, feeling multiple bones break with the precision of my movements as Mika releases me and screams.

Being harmed by your soulmate must have felt like a thousand burning knives slicing through him, just like how it's felt for me each time he slapped me tonight.

Now free from his grasp, I slowly stand, my breath ragged from the pain this process has brought. I know I only have a few minutes until I black out and have to do this next part fast.

"I, Geminie Blake, refuse your rejection. Instead, I reject you as my mate and your existence in my life." The air stills, and a wave of panic fills the yard as the crowd around us looks to Mika the moment he lets out a blood-curdling scream. Their future Alpha should be feeling a skull-crushing pain now that his existence has been rejected by me, and a marking of a blood-coloured ring slowly appears around his neck. He would have that mark displayed for the next three years if he could not repair the bond before it snaps. Once we no longer share a bond, the mark will vanish. He will definitely need to hide this mark for the next three years or be ridiculed by other Alphas. Mika will be considered weak, and so will this pack. If I'm being honest, I enjoy this thought.

The wolves forget about me as Mika falls to his knees, clutching at his neck and head and begging for the pain to stop. Now, no longer the focus of attention, I make my way toward the front of the house, leaning against the exterior as the pain coursing through my body blurs my vision. I focus on only one foot in front of the other, praying that I would be able to make it to safety before the pack hunts me down.

"Geminie!" Strong arms scoop me up, holding me close to a solid body as Alex's scent fills my nose. Relief washes over me as the pain begins to consume my body.

"I hooked up the portable tow in the back of my truck and have your car hooked up. I need you to stay awake, Geminie, to make it out of Hidden Claws." His words are muffled as if trying to reach me underwater, but the urgency is clear. I have to stay awake for us to make it out safely. My consciousness fades in and out of darkness, the pain increasing with the distance away from Mika while the bond urges me to go back, but I couldn't go back. Going back meant death. Only the cold air flowing over my body and the scent of pine keeps me grounded the farther away from the pack house Alex carries me until the next moment, I find myself laying on a seat with a wool blanket over me.

"Geminie, listen to me right now." Alex is yelling, it's clear he is mad. About what though?

"I already denounced myself from Hidden Claws. I need you to say the words. I can't cross the borders until you do." Ah, he is mad because of me. My mouth opens and closes, trying to fight the burning pain that constricts my throat to say the words. I can hear the howls of wolves and the revving of engines as the pack behind us slowly grows closer. But my body will not cooperate with the fire that threatens to consume me. A straw is placed in front of my mouth, and I greedily drink the ice-cold liquid that is offered, taking in the panicked look in Alex's eyes.

"Say the words, please, Gemie, before they reach us," He begs, the haze clearing slightly while I look at my brother. I take a deep breath and open my mouth.

"I, Geminie Blake, denounce myself as a member of Hidden Claws and enter the world as a Rogue." Relief radiates off of Alex, and the truck moves forwards. As we cross the border that hides the pack from humans and their technology, the bond fizzles away, and emptiness fills my mind as the pain of the rejection takes hold once again. Knowing that I'm safe, I allow the darkness to consume me while Alex drives us towards safety.

Chapter 11 - Truth

The days pass in a blurry haze as the slow rhythmic hum of the engine and light tunes from the radio soothe me in and out of sleep. Every now and then, when the burning in my body eases and I am conscious long enough to hear, I hear the radio host announce what day it is.

Sometimes my skin feels like it's rippling, like the waves on the lake with a soft summer breeze, sometimes it feels like stabbing sharp pains. Sometimes it feels like my bones would break with every bump Alex's truck hits, only to realign without warning. Sometimes I can smell the tang of blood in the air and wonder if it's from me or a poor animal hit on the side of the road. Sometimes a lullaby that is so familiar but hard to remember where I heard it from is sung to me, and in my moments of consciousness and asking Alex about it, I learn that no one in the pack has ever sung it to me.

I remember one night on the long drive, the sound of a dying animal howling filled my ears, but it wasn't until Alex pleaded for me to stay awake and bite down on a towel that I realized that animal was me.

"Hang on, Gem, I'm taking you to the temple of the Goddess. They should be able to help you." My brother assures me in as calm of a voice as he could muster. But even through the haze of pain and blackness surrounding me, I can hear the tremble of fear in his voice. I know he is trying his best to help me, but in the moment of alertness and lucidness, all I want is the sweet release of death to take over.

Time slips by once again while my mind has a tough time trying to decipher reality and my own pain-induced hallucinations before the world around me slows to a stop. Something cool kisses my burning skin when the animalistic cry sounds once more, and a sense of peace and tranquillity calms my racing mind until blackness seeps in once again.

I pray that this is death taking me away once and for all from the agony I have suffered.

◆◆◆

"Are you sure it's her?" A voice whispers, one I recognize as Alex. The sweet dream I was having is now forgotten as the conversation filled with hushed voices brings me back to consciousness.

"Yes, I am positive. Geminie has the mark on her right shoulder, and her name is even the same as the pup we have been looking for these last eighteen years." A woman replies, her voice light and musical like Lizaria's. I force myself to open my eyes, wanting to catch a glimpse of this woman, only to groan from the harsh light filtering in. Someone rushes from the other side of the room to where I presumably lay in a bed and places their hand on my forehead.

"You can open your eyes now. I've dimmed the lights for you." Alex coaxes me, his familiar scent giving me a sense of comfort and security. With his encouraging words, I try to open my eyes again, his face filled with relief greeting me once I succeed.

"Your fever is finally gone." He sighs, leaning back on the chair by my bedside as he runs his fingers through his already messy hair. He looks haggard, and guilt fills me knowing that my brother must have worried for my well-being while I had prayed for death.

"Anyway, how are you feeling, Gemie?" He asks, his smile growing after he yawns. I take a moment to stretch my body under the covers, feeling each and every muscle stretch with no pain and finding newfound muscles I had no clue I had. My body felt amazing, like all the beatings and fatigue from sleepless nights had never happened.

"For some reason, I feel incredible. No pain at all." I answer honestly, sending a questioning gaze to my brother. He sighs, handing me a glass of freezing cold water that I quickly down and motion for more. Alex obliges and fills the glass quickly using a jug that sits on the bedside table.

After two more glasses of water and one I now slowly sip from, Alex sighs once again and runs his fingers through his messy hair.

"The best explanation I can give you, Gem, is that when Mika rejected you, it kick-started the process of your shift," He begins, his face looking as if he had aged ten years within the last few days.

"You aren't really my sister, and you weren't supposed to shift for another two years." Alex continues, shoulders slumping in defeat as he looks to the ground at his feet. Confusion washes over me as this statement as I wait for my brother to continue.

"What Alex is trying to say is that you are not, in fact, a Blake." A musical voice continues after a long pause of silence reigns over the room for a moment too long. My head turns to see a woman standing by the door, her long, straight black hair and pale skin standing out against the beige wall behind her as she sends a smile my way.

"You are Geminie Starlight, Daughter of Maverick Starlight—Alpha of the Northern Snow—and Lisandra, our current Moon Goddess."

◆◆◆

"Let me get this straight." I start, running my fingers through my greasy hair and cringing at the feel of my locks. I am in desperate need of a shower, but with my mind racing with a million thoughts, I need to sort out the information I had just learnt first.

"Eighteen years ago, Alex's parents decided to kidnap me." I continue, seeing the look of guilt flash through my brother's eyes as he looks outside the window. I reach out, taking his hand and giving it a reassuring squeeze. He had no knowledge like me until today, and I could never hold a grudge against him.

"Yes. Their reasoning, from what we could gather, is that a week before you were born, the Blakes suffered a stillbirth. Their pup would have been a little girl like you. Their initial goal was to kill you, but clearly, something changed." Ira, the black-haired she-wolf, repeats this information to me once more, information that was still hard to grasp. Alex had explained that a month before his sister was supposed to be born, his parents sent him to summer camp. By the time the Blakes would have had their daughter settled into life at home, Alex would be just arriving back from camp to start his role as a big brother. Instead, he came home to me.

"I always felt something was off with you, especially when I returned home from camp and saw you crying in the crib, but no one cared about helping you." His voice brings me out of my thoughts as I turn to look at Alex, sadness deep in his eyes. Knowing we aren't related must be killing him, but knowing his parents kept the death of his baby sister from him must be destroying him even more. I carefully climb out of the bed, happy that before our discussion started, Ira had given me a long nightgown to put on While Alex went to find an Acolyte to bring us food. I close the gap between me and Alex, wrapping my arms around him and pulling him in for a hug.

"Alex, no matter what, you are my brother. You've been there for me since I was a baby. You protected me to the best of your abilities and gave me food and familial love. We are siblings no matter what happens." I whisper, feeling the tension in his body slowly release as he buries his face into my shoulder. His body starts shaking, and the feeling of a wet spot where his eyes rest clues me in that the strong wolf before me is sobbing silently. Reality is cruel and harsh, knowing that the day that Sorus and Reena were killed was because of the Blakes.

Alex never learned the truth of his biological sister because the Blakes wanted revenge on my mother for something that unfortunately happens in life and was out of her control. I was ripped away from my own birth parents and blamed for many things, all because I was the physical target for the Blakes' rage, not knowing nor able to prove my innocence.

Tears of my own begin to fall at the injustice that had been given to me for eighteen years and before I know it, I find myself clinging to my brother as we both grieve in our own way for the lives we have lived until now. With our emotions now spent and the flood of grief now open, I feel the weight on my shoulders that I've been carrying since being disowned by the Blakes finally fade away. My mind feels clearer and my body lighter by the time the tears run dry, and I am left taking deep breaths with Alex.

A box of tissues is placed in front of the two of us, causing Alex and I to look up at Ira with surprise and thanks as we each dry our tears away, and I find myself sitting back in bed. Today would mark the start of my life not as Geminie Blake, but as my true self, Geminie Starlight.

"Ira, what happens now? Where do Alex and I go, and what am I supposed to do?" I ask, giving this she-wolf a determined look. It was time for me to change my destiny and take my life back. I couldn't just sit there and do nothing and allow what the Blakes did to Alex and me to go without justice. But I need to grow stronger before I can take any revenge.

"You train, Geminie." She starts, giving me a smile as another member of the temple walks in with a cart full of what I assume are necessities for our stay.

"You, as well as Alex, will train here for a week. We will get you in contact with your father, and at the end of the week, you can decide whether you want to go to his pack and train there or create your own pack." With that, Ira bids us good night and leaves Alex and me to our thoughts.

Chapter 12 – A Shift in Life

Morning comes quicker than I thought as light streams in from the large window and into my eyes. After Ira's last words to us, Alex and I concluded that no matter what, we would create our own pack. I will accept my birth father when I meet him and build a relationship with him and any family from either side of my true mother and father. But the thought of joining another pack over being able to create my own brought a sense of unease. I know this unease comes from never wanting to be under someone else's power again.

Looking at Alex, who is still fast asleep beside me, I smile and silently creep out of bed before I tiptoe to the door and make my way out into the hallway. My goal is to shift for the first time consciously and figure out how to move in my wolf form.

The halls of the Temple of the Goddess twist and turn, making it hard for me to find any exit to the outside where I can shift without worry of accidentally destroying something. Every time I try a new hallway after retracing my steps from a dead end, I find myself at another dead end. Whoever built this temple is a genius at creating security features with the maze-like halls, but also an asshole since it's too easy to get lost in here.

Finally, a member of the Temple Acolyte notices my lost and confused self, taking the time to talk with me and guiding me to the nearest exit much to my relief. Fresh air surrounds me quickly as I take in the view of a clearing full of wildflowers mixed with moonflowers. Large trees surround the clearing, their fall colours indicating winter will be coming faster than expected, adding to the beauty surrounding the Temple.

Old Canadian maples, large birch, many species of straight pines and many sturdy oak trees in the forest before me that I could not wait to run through capture my attention the most. The scent of pure nature brings a comfort to me that no place other than the Hidden Valley has brought.

"If you need anything else, Miss Geminie, let a member of the Temple know." The she-wolf brings my attention back to her and away from the beauty of the forest. After thanking her, the Temple Acolyte walks back inside, leaving me alone to bask in the peaceful nature.

With a smile, I make my way closer to the forest, the sun warm against my skin and the cool soft grass tickling my feet. The carefree feeling I have never felt until now feels so liberating. I take a moment to sit in the clearing, the scent of wildflowers mixed with the scent of maple and pine surrounding me. I understand why the temple was set up here after the first Moon Goddess ascended her position, and why wolves use it as a sanctuary to escape a horrible pack. It brings a sense of security and calmness to one's mind and soul, a place to be closer to the Moon Goddess, to my mother.

This also makes the perfect setting to consciously shift for the first time.

I jump to my feet and stretch, a grin of excitement on my face thinking about finally being able to run in wolf form and what my wolf may look like. I take a deep breath, letting the calming scent of my surroundings wash over me as my mind is cleared of everything but the shift. My body will change from human to beast, paws hitting the forest floor and running past the trees, wind flowing through fur. And then the pain comes.

Falling onto my hands and knees, I feel my spine contort and bones snap as the pain causes me to open my mouth in a silent scream. Tears flow from my eyes, and fearing for my life, I fight against the shift. But fighting only makes the pain worse. My heart begins to beat faster as if my body is fighting death itself.

"Let it happen." A deep husky voice calls out, causing me to turn and face the owner of it. Leaning against the nearest oak tree is a tall male dressed in a navy V-neck shirt and dusty jeans. A pair of black hiking boots on his feet. His body screams of a powerful male, with sun-tanned skin that I know, even if he were to hide inside for a month, would never change in colour and long black hair pulled back into a bun on his head. Traces of tattoos peek from the collar of his shirt, and an easygoing grin graces his lips.

"If you keep fighting the shift, you'll kill yourself. You don't seem like the type to give up your life, so accept the shift. Accept the pain and take a deep breath." He continues, pushing off from the tree and slowly walking towards me. I feel no malice or threat in him towards me, only amusement and concern. I whimper from the pain but nod in understanding and close my eyes. I think about the shift, accepting it as the speed of my bones breaking moves from a slow torture that has me wishing for death to a breakneck speed, a speed that, although painful, is gone in a split second.

My body realigns itself with each break and shift in bones, my face elongates into that of a muzzle, and my hair retreats into my scalp while fur sprouts from my skin. Soon, I find myself panting, laying in the clearing with remnants of the nightgown I was wearing now, nothing but torn rags around me.

"Better, Little Wolf?" The mysterious man asks with a chuckle. I nod in response, letting out a sigh and rolling around on the grass happily. It felt liberating in fur form, more natural to me. The man chuckles at my pup-like actions, his dark, forest-green eyes never leaving my form even as I lay back quietly, my tail thumping against the earth.

"Why don't you try standing and testing out your legs?" He suggests, getting a yip of approval from me in response and another chuckle from him. A small pang shoots through my heart with his constant chuckling, thinking about the mate bond I had lost days ago due to the rejection. Although the mystery man is attractive and definitely the definition of a true man, my heart still yearned for the bond of my soulmate, even if my brain knows it will never happen. I guess my emotions must have shown on my wolfish face as I soon find fingers running through my fur in a comforting manner.

"What or whoever made you sad and seek sanctuary here, Little Wolf, they aren't worth it. You have a beautiful wolf form and a bright future ahead of you. I can feel it." His compliment and gentle words settle the pain in my heart. This stranger is right; Mika did not deserve me after the years of pain he put me through. I will do better than Hidden Claws.

"Now, about that standing thing." The subject changes, causing me to roll my eyes at this friendly stranger as he slowly backs away from me, giving me enough space to move but close enough that I feel like he will catch me if something happens. I knew from my rolling around earlier that I can move in some form, but standing would be another challenge to me.

Assessing each limb gingerly, stretching, and moving to see the strength I have, I slowly push my body off the ground. Some attempts leave me tumbling back to the soft grass, happy to be close to the ground already, until finally, on shaky, unsteady legs, I finally stand. Throughout my attempts to stand, which I assume took about thirty minutes, give or take, the man before me laughed every time I fell or my paw slipped out from under me, causing me to growl in frustration at his "moral support."

"I'm going to take a guess and say you are new at this, Little Wolf." He states with a deep chuckle. I roll my eyes at him and respond silently, Thank you for pointing that out, Captain Obvious. I think wishing I could link him this sarcastic retort but sadly cannot. The eye roll seems to elicit another chuckle from this friendly jerk, and I let out a small growl at him.

"Okay, okay. I get it, not amusing." He surrenders, hands up as he backs away with a grin.

"Why don't you try walking towards me now? See how your legs feel and if you can get used to the new coordination you'll have to perform in wolf form." Now, this was helpful, and I nod at his words. I slowly move my front left leg, testing my balance first while lifting it into the air and slowly putting it back down, repeating the same movement with each leg in turn. I'd be an idiot to start confidently walking right away, knowing I would fall flat on my snout and cause this man to burst into a laughing fit at my expense.

Of course, every now and then, I had to shake my head to move the long tuft of fur from my eyes so as not to impede my progress. That's when the stranger steps in and uses an extra hair tie to keep the hair out of my eyes and lets me resume testing my balance once more. Once confident enough with my balance, I take my first step. Then another, and another.

At first, I am wobbling like a newborn dear, feeling like at any moment, my legs will give out. But once muscle memory kicks in, my walking speed slowly increases, and I find myself less cautious of each step. Within another five steps, it feels like I've been walking in wolf form since the day I was born. As natural as breathing, I confidently trot towards the man, my tongue lolling out the left side of my mouth as happiness fills me. I watch as he slowly backs away from me, close enough to catch me if necessary, but always moving and making me move towards him until he stops, and I find myself standing in front of him, feeling triumphant at this accomplishment. His hands ruffle my fur, removing the hair tie from it as the long tuft falls in place once again.

"Good job, Little Wolf! Now smile." His word of praise fills my ears, and they quickly perk up, my tail thumping on the ground happily. A sudden flash and sound of a shutter follow quickly, making me jump and growl in surprise.

"Sorry, Little Wolf. I didn't mean to scare you, but I thought you would like to see what you look like." He apologizes while turning the latest Samsung screen towards me. My eyes widen as I take a look at the live photo, a pure white wolf clearly depicted. Her silver grey eyes hold a look of confidence and triumph in their depth. Her white fur is full and healthy, the gentle breeze flowing through it and causing the sun to reflect off of it like a prism. Hues of different colours constantly change direction in the live photo, where each ray of sun hits the wildflowers dancing around her. A tuft of long fur, almost like bangs, covers the left side of her face. The final touches are the small patches of silver fur with swirls and stars climbing up part of her paws.

She is beautiful!

No, I am beautiful.

"Have you had enough staring?" The man asks, and I nod, moving my eyes from the screen to him and watching as he puts his phone away and takes off his shirt and pants. Happy for the fur covering my face, I blush and turn to look away, hearing another of his deep chuckle at my reaction.

"How about we play, Little Wolf!" He exclaims playfully, the sounds of his own shift making me whip my head in his direction, where I now see a pure black wolf with a tuft of fur in the shape of a diamond in the center of his forehead. His forest-green eyes hold a hint of playfulness, and his teeth nip at my "bangs" before he takes off, me hot on his trail as the chase ensues.

Chapter 13 – Time to Train

"You know better then to run off!" Alex growls furiously, pacing the room in his anger. I just roll my eyes, focusing on drying my hair with the towel. After playing in the forest with the mysterious man, I returned to the temple covered in mud. I was lucky that a Temple Acolyte helped me to my room, where I was met with a frantic Alex trying to find me. His lecture began then, mud dripping onto the floor below me as he went on and on about me sneaking out in the morning without his knowledge until I managed to escape into the washroom where I promptly focused my energy on shifting into human form.

I knew he would be waiting for me to exit, so after showering, I took my sweet time running a bubble bath and enjoying hot water and endless time to myself for the first time ever.

"Alex, I don't get why you're mad. You needed sleep, and I just had to see what my wolf was like." I retort, causing my brother to stop dead in his track and send an incredulous look my way.

"Geminie, you are the future Moon Goddess for crying out loud!" He throws his hands in the air in frustration, as if scolding a pup.

"Gee, Captain Obvious, I had no clue!" I snap at him sarcastically, flinging the towel at him. "You don't get it, Gem, you need to be safe and guarded as our race's next Deity!" He argues back. This time I growl in frustration, snatching the pillow off the bed and aiming for his head.

"What I need, Alex, is a LIFE! I have been a slave and trapped for years, always watching what I do or how I act because I never knew when another beating would come." Rage washes over me as I reply to his statement. Seeing the guilt in Alex's eyes calms me down slightly, but I was no longer the same wolf I was a week ago. I want to live my life to the fullest now, find my birth parents and actually enjoy myself for once.

"Gem-"

"Save it, Alex. You know the life I have lived until now. You know I've been trained by Lizaria and can fight. I am safe here and because of this I plan to learn just who I am!" With that, I walk away from my brother, needing to cool off from his words. I understand his concerns and worry, but if his intention are to lock me away, then I won't allow it. I have already had my freedom taken from me because of Bastian and Jasmine, I refuse to lose anymore.

"Miss Geminie?" Walking along the corridors of the Temple, I soon find myself lost until a familiar voice calls out to me. I turn to see Ira coming towards me and sigh with relief. "Miss Ira," I greet politely, doing my best to suppress the anger still swirling inside me.

"You okay, Little One?" Her inquiring gaze reminds me of Lizaria, and without hesitation I explain to her the fight with Alex I have just had. I tell her my feelings on having to be guarded and protected like some damsel in distress and the thought of not being able to be free. I hate the thought of not being able to live my life now that I am free from Hidden Claws.

"Well, when you start training, I can guarantee the people who need to be protected will be your enemies. Most Goddesses possess powers beyond that of regular wolves and you definitely will have to find your own soon." Ira's words comfort my mind and being able to express my feelings helped to dissipate any anger I have left. The thought of training and becoming stronger excites me.

"When can I start training?" I blurt out without thinking, and the she-wolf before me chuckles.

"How about right now? I'll send an Acolyte to Alex to let him know you're with me, and he can go train with someone else." With her confirmation, Ira leads me down more twisting corridors. I hope that with her guidance, I will become strong enough to protect the life I want and those around me who I love.

◆◆◆

My body hits the ground hard, the wind knocked out of me as the she-wolf who Ira has me partnered with today growls in warning, heeding me not to stand. But I ignore her. With a grimace of pain, I stand on my paws, staying low to the ground.

"Remember, Geminie, you are not allowed to use your powers." Ira reminds me, as if I could forget. For the last few days she's been helping me connect with my powers while training my speed and stamina in wolf form.

Each day, she has me sit in a moon pool for hours on end, meditating and focusing on harnessing any sort of magic I could feel in the air. The elements were the ones that quickly came to me. I spent hours practicing controlling them until I could grasp onto them properly without the chance of harming another wolf unintentionally.

Once I was able to grasp the beginning of the powers I was gifted with, she would then take me to the arena to fight an Acolyte, either in human or wolf form. Within three days, I knew my wolf form lacks the endurance and training that my human form has achieved. I need to work on my speed and agility the most.

Speaking of training, the Acolyte before me lets out a threatening growl. Her fur stands up threateningly as I slowly circle her, watching for her next attack. She has a slight limp to the right hind leg where blood from my attack earlier still spills from. The Acolyte is in pain, and I can use this to my advantage. The she-wolf makes her move finally, letting out another ferocious growl before leaping into the air.

Instead of dodging, I run forwards, moving underneath the Acolyte while she is still air bound, and sink my teeth into the round calf on her hind leg. A howl of pain followed by whimpers is her response, so I use my momentum and throw her to the ground. Her body rolls once, twice, thrice, until hitting the wooden pole that is the barrier to the arena with a sickening thud.

Now is my chance.

I race towards her body and grasp her throat in my jaw, my hind paw on the wound I have inflicted. She whimpers beneath me and thrusts her throat toward me as best as possible, knowing her place in defeat. With the match now over, I release the she-wolf from my maw and give her wound a quick lick, helping to speed up the healing process. I have won; there is no need to continue.

"Yeah, Gem, that's my daughter!" Happy for the fur covering my body, I turn in the direction where Maverick Starlight stands with Alex, a proud grin on his face. Yesterday, my father arrived after news of me being found, and put the responsibility of his pack in the hands of my Uncle Stephen—his Beta. Rolling my eyes at his antics, I can't help but feel my heart swell at the parental praise he throws my way - the feeling of parental love something I feel like I can never get used to. Trotting away from my defeated opponent as Acolytes come to take her away to the infirmary, I head to Ira, who smiles at my approach.

"You are a fast learner, Little Wolf. I think it's time for you to make your own pack. We can talk about this after you've cleaned up." She praises me, surprising me with her honest opinion of my progress and the fact this Temple Priestess believes I am ready to be on my own. My tail thumps happily at the prospect of creating a place to call my home. As much as my father would love for me to join Northern Snow, I know that pack will become my little brother's when he comes of age. Although I am the eldest and therefore its rightful heir, I could not take away the title that he has been training for his whole life. I turn to look at Maverick, catching Connor gaze at me with the same silver-grey eyes inherited from our father, looking at me with awe.

[I'm going to go shift and bathe, I'll see you all in a moment.] I link to my family, seeing Alex nod and say something to Connor while my father turns to talk to Amberle. The spitfire of a she-wolf and her mate Dominic were in the middle of a peace treaty with my father when the news broke of my being found. She was curious about what kind of wolf I would be after being missing since the day I was born, and the two leaders of Blood Moon agreed to negotiate the terms of the treaty with my father while on the way to see me.

It was upon meeting her that we learned we are contærae, wolves whose spirits recognize each other with a spiritual bond. A contærae helps the Moon Goddess to grow, train, and follow the path of good. She soon agreed to be one of my training partners and teach me how to run a pack after I declined my father's offer to join Northern Snow and stated my intentions to create my own place to call home.

Amberle's mate, Dominic, is out hunting with the Temple Warriors and hence leaves his wife to her own devices, something I soon realize leads to some mischief from the fire-furred wolf.

With a grin and the vision of my future growing clearer each day, I trot towards the shower room so that the conversation Ira wants to have with me about creating a pack can happen a little quicker.

Chapter 14 – A Place to Call Home

I frown as my gaze focuses on the trees outside, staying close to the window and as far away from the others in the room. Alex sighs in frustration while my father sips his coffee awkwardly. Ira was called for an emergency after my shower, leaving an Acolyte to lead us to her office and wait for her return to discuss a good position for my own pack to be built. Amberle, to my amusement, decided to curl up on the sofa to take a nap. You would think a strong Alpha would be more energetic but seeing as only a few years ago she was in my position as a Rogue, I actually envy her ability to sleep whenever.

"Gem, I just don't understand why you do not want to go to your father's pack." Alex growls, running a hand through his hair in frustration after a moment of silence, causing me to close the book I was reading to glare at him.

"You would be safer there and not have to worry about pack duties. There will be protection for you and everything." My brother continues, causing my frustration to grow. I'm hearing the same argument all over again, just hours before choosing a pack location for myself.

"Enough, Alex!" A growl of warning follows my words. My blood is boiling in anger at my brother sounding like a broken record every day since meeting my father, a record that I was tempted to snap in half at this moment.

"I get it, you want the structure of an already established pack, but have you thought about my feelings? Everyone there is a stranger to me, and they will be questioning my every move either secretly or openly. With my little brother, they will be wondering if I will steal his position as the next Alpha." I start listing the problems I already know will arise with joining my father's pack and sigh. As happy as I am with getting to know my real family, I need my freedom, my own place to call home, and a chance at a proper life for myself. I'm tired of the gazes of others and the ridiculed and distrustful looks from those who don't know me and refuse to get to know me.

"You can either follow me and help me build a place where we can be ourselves and be free, or you can join my father's pack. But I need my freedom." I finish, ending this discussion and turning on my heels, intending to walk out the office and find someplace to calm down. Ira can come and find me later.

"Gem, where are you going?" Alex growls, his frustration radiating off of him.

"Away from here. When you are ready to get your head out of your ass, come find me!" I shout back over my shoulder, pushing the door open only to come face-to-face with a confused-looking Ira.

"Uh, is everything okay, Little Wolf?" Her voice calms my nerves slightly, her being one of few people who respects my wishes.

"Just the usual argument, Ira." My father's voice sounds behind me, his hand now on my shoulder as he gives it a reassuring squeeze.

"But we are ready to find Geminie a place for her pack." He adds, a look of pride in his eyes. Relief washes over me like a fresh, cooling rain on a scorching summer day and I smile, grateful for his understanding. It's not that I don't want to be in the same pack as my father, it's that I'm worried his pack will think I'm taking away what rightfully belongs to Connor. At least with creating my own pack, my family in Northern Snow can escape the northern climate of Canada and come relax far from pack duties.

"Well, if that's the case, I know I said I have many sights for you to see and decide on, but the emergency that I had to tend to had me to stumble across a map of a specific area that also includes the very thing you want." Ira continues, winking at me. My smile widens even more at the mention of my request, a place that would be safe for Ira and the Unicorns, with just as much - if not more - magic for them. Only Ira and I knew about this request, as the she-wolf had quickly gain my trust and respect in the short time we have known each other, letting me know my feelings were valid and my wants and needs were okay for me to have and work towards. I know Ira would always be on my side if I needed someone to talk to and confide in, and this she-wolf has not let me down yet.

One of these days, I will introduce her to Lizaria. A loud sigh is audible from the room, gaining a glare from Ira and an eye roll from me.

"Mister Alex, you are more than welcome to find another pack if you are unhappy with Geminie's decision." As if speaking to a misbehaving child, Ira scolds Alex on my behalf and I sent her a silent thank you. A moment of silence passes before she smiles, and I assume that Alex has given in.

"Good, glad to know you reluctantly will follow her lead. Now, I think it's time to go as the Warrior I sent to scout the area is waiting for us to create your new home!" With that, she takes my hand and begins leading me out of the winding maze of the temple. A bittersweet feeling rises inside me as I look around the building that provided me safety and security, a place where the truth was revealed and whose keepers helped me to finally regain my freedom and life.

"You can always come visit, Little Wolf." Ira states, the she-wolf most likely sensing my feelings about leaving the Temple. I nod, allowing her to guide me down an unfamiliar hallway and outside to an area I have not yet explored.

The first thing to greet me is Alex's truck, the tow still as dinged up as I remember, but I have a new found gratitude for the somewhat unreliable vehicle. With Alex at the wheel, this truck brought me to safety after one of the worst days I have experienced. Next to the truck is something I did not expect to see, as I take a step towards the 1970 Dodge Charger R/T in matte black, one I am itching to climb in and drive.

"I know it's been a few days, but Happy Birthday, Gem." Alex stands beside me, a bashful look on his face as I turn to look at my brother in shock, the anger from his overprotective nature fading away fast.

"Thank you!" I whisper, instinctively giving my brother a hug, which seems to shock him as our fights have been causing great tension between us.

"You know I would do anything for you, Gems." He whispers back and I nod, taking in his comforting scent. Even if we fight, Alex will always be there for me and I for him.

"Glad to see you two made up, but we need to hit the road. It's about a day's drive to where I want to take you!" Ira calls out and I smile. Alex pulls away from me to hand me a set of keys, nodding his head in the direction of my car. With a childish squeal, I rush to the driver's side, climbing in and adjusting the seat and mirrors before starting the car. the purr of the engine makes a childish grin spread across my face. Ira, the navigator of this trip, joins me in my car.

"Comfy." She states while buckling in and putting on a pair of sunglasses. I chuckle, putting the car into drive just as a dazed Amberle climbs into her own car and winks at me. Now, I start the journey to my new pack.

◆◆◆

The journey will take twenty-four hours to complete, as Ira had stated yesterday, so we stop at a motel as soon as the sky turns dark.

"Double Baconator, extra-large fries, and a large Coca-Cola for Gems." My father calls out as soon as he enters the room Ira and I share. Alex and Connor walk in with both arms full of takeout.

"I wanted the same!" Amberle calls out, coming over and sneaking a fry from my bag, making me roll my eyes and shove the fire-haired she-wolf away with a playful growl.

"Ooooh, feisty." She teases with a giggle, taking a bite of the stolen fry. Alex chuckles, handing her a bag and another to Ira before sighing and taking a seat on the floor.

"So, what's the plan when we get to this perfect pack place?" My brother asks before tearing into a burger of his own. Ira holds out a finger, her mouth full of food with a look of bliss on her face.

"One, I am so glad to be out with you and taking you to your new pack location. I haven't had a burger from any fast food joint since the 1970s." She says before taking a sip of her drink. My father starts to laugh in response.

"That's like fifty years ago!" Connor exclaims in shock, speaking through a mouth full of food.

"Connor, chew, swallow, speak!" Amberle scolds, and I high-five the feisty she-wolf as my father chuckles and Connor looks away embarrassed.

"Yep, and two—there is already a wolf who works for the temple there to ensure the area is cleared of Rogues and Soulless. We will meet up with him tomorrow." Ira continues, answering both of my brothers.

"Can we trust him?" My father asks and Ira smiles.

"All I can say is he had a rough past similar to Geminie here. Considering he is a Rogue himself; he may ask to join the pack." I smile at the prospect of my first packmate after Alex. I eat in silent, thinking of what this wolf may be like, hoping he has some form of training that can be used to help grow the pack in the next few weeks. I want to be stronger than Hidden Claws.

"If he is a good wolf, I'll let him join as a third member." I state, already seeing Alex poised to argue. He sends me a pointed look; one I ignore for the moment as we finish our Wendy's meals. Soon, my father announces we should get to bed for the long journey tomorrow and makes sure to drag Alex out behind him before he can start a fight.

"Your brother sure is overprotective." Amberle states and I groan, laying back onto my bed.

"That's a good thing. My brother was one of my tormenters growing up." She continues on and I sigh.

"He has always been there for me in Hidden Claws, helping and protecting me when I needed it. But now that we're away from the pack and I can finally shift, his overprotectiveness is suffocating. I'm no longer a wolfless Omega, I am an Alpha and the Future Moon Goddess. I need to be able to learn and grow." I explain, closing my eyes and releasing a deep sigh. Since becoming a Rogue and learning my true heritage, I've been able to experience life without the fear of a beating or being screamed at. I've been able to train both my human and wolf forms without worry, and finally been able to eat my fill of food without any worry or fear of consequences.

"Hopefully, he eases up after a few weeks of starting the new pack. Your brother loves you, even after learning you two aren't related." Ira chimes in.

"Hopefully. If not, I will have to kick his ass a few times." I agree, yawning as sleep creeps in and I drift off. Tomorrow, I will finally be able to see my new pack.

Chapter 15 – A New Pack

"See that trail just ahead of us?" Ira asks, pointing to a barely touched trail which I assume is for ATV use.

"Yes." I confirm, slowing down as I wait for her to continue.

"Good, turn left onto it and keep driving until we reach a clearing," She exclaims. I smile as I switch my left turn signal on and slowly turn onto the barely there dirt path. I cringe as the tires to my precious car bounce on the bumpy terrain, Ira clinging onto the handle above the passenger window. Only one vehicle can fit, with the bushes and grass brushing against the side of my car. Hopefully, there will be no scratches by the time we reach our destination.

[Remind me to get this godforsaken path cleared and properly paved.] Alex links and I chuckle.

[Trust me, this will be priority number one when the pack is established.] I agree instantly. The final stretch is slow, with the speed of our cars staying around twenty kilometres an hour so as to not drive into a tree or flip the car over if a tire hits a large root or rock.

Feeling like an eternity under the cover of trees, something that makes me itch and want to run in wolf form under, the "road" grows slightly bigger as the shadows blend into dazzling sunlight and we exit into a large clearing. Noticing a black Hummer parked just to the right, I steer in that direction and park beside it, the others following suit.

Climbing out of my car, I walk around to see the area better, a grin on my face at the sight before me. The clearing is huge, wildflowers covering most of the ground in the late fall weather, making me smile. We would have to dig up a few and make a couple of gardens to preserve these flowers.

Off to the west, just outside the forest, is a large, crystal-blue lake. I can picture a pack house here, one with a path leading to a small dock we could use for fishing on or docking small rowboats. On the north side and directly opposite of where we all stand are tall mountains that would provide great training terrain for future pack members, giving us an opportunity to train in higher altitude.

"There is an entrance in the mountains by a waterfall, with a river that flows into the lake. You can have your friend move there." Ira whispers low enough for only my ears to hear. I grin, excited to explore the new hidden valley for Lizaria and the Unicorns to move into, knowing the Elf will need to have the herd move away from Hidden Claws quickly before Mika becomes Alpha and the Blakes could find them.

"Hey Ira, what took you so long?" A deep voice calls out to our left and I turn to see the man I met the first time I shifted. Turning to face the black-haired, tattooed man who helped me through my first shift, I smile and take in his appearance once more. He stands there with no shirt or shoes on, a pair of jeans hang loosely around his hips. For once, I get a glimpse of his tattoos, noticing them all designed in black ink; the intricate lines, swirls and pattern running along his muscular torso.

"What took us so long was the fact we had to drive through the worst pathway ever, and I had to bring your new Alpha." Ira states with an eye roll and I chuckle. Putting two and two together, I deduct that this wolf who Ira mentioned last night will be the first member joining the pack as soon as it's established. The thought of it makes me excited as I have a feeling this wolf will make a great Theta or Head Warrior. He is a perfect addition if I do say so myself.

[He looks strong.] Alex links me and I nod, turning to look back at my brother, only to realize he is standing beside me.

[Theta?] I ask and he shrugs.

[Maybe. Or a second Beta.] I smile, turning to look back at the wolf who sizes everyone with his gaze, a flicker of approval in his deep forest-green eyes becoming ones I wanted to look at a little longer. His gaze returns to the trio consisting of Ira, Alex and I as he takes a few steps towards us, holding his hand out to Alex.

"It's nice to meet you, Sir, and thank you for accepting me." He states, Alex letting out an awkward chuckle as he takes the offered hand in a firm handshake as I try my best to hold in my laughter.

"It's nice to meet you too, but I am not the Alpha," Alex replies, causing a look of confusion to cross this wolf's face as he looks around. I couldn't hold in my laughter any longer as I bend over clutching my sides, hearing my father chuckle behind me as well.

"If you're not the Alpha, who is?" The man asks slowly, his eyes scanning the crowd while I compose myself, a few chuckles escaping every so often. His confusion soon fades to a look of astonishment as our eyes meet and I give a cheeky grin to the handsome man.

"A female Alpha, I would have never guessed!" He exclaims, stepping forward and holding out his hand. I take it expecting a handshake but am surprised when he bows and brings his lips to the back of my hand, planting a soft warm kiss.

"I am sorry for jumping to conclusions. I am Ariven Cross and look forward to serving you Alpha..." Ariven trails off, Alex letting out a low growl of warning as the wolf before me releases my hand, rolling his eyes at Alex's childishness before retuning his attention to me.

"Geminie Starlight but call me Gem." I answer his unspoken question.

"And I am Alex Blake." Alex cuts in rudely, eyeing Ariven. I sigh, smacking my brother on the back of the head at his rude behaviour.

"I see. Guessing this is your mate, then Gem." Ariven concludes, a perfectly sculpted eyebrow raised above his eye. I fake gag, the thought of my brother being my mate disgusting me.

"Gross, no! Alex is my brother. My mate-" I start to correct him, my explanation stopping short as a piercing pain runs through me, causing me to gasp in pain and clutch my stomach as the ground slowly comes closer to my face. Strong arms catch me before I collapse, Ariven's familiar scent that I remember from our first meeting surrounding me as he holds me gently against his body.

"Mika, that bastard. First he rejected you, and now he is fucking some whore." Alex growls in anger, my brother pacing as his eyes hold frustrations in them.

"Gem was rejected?" Ariven asks, scooping me up bridal style into his arms as I let out a scream, the pain in my abdomen feeling like my insides are being clawed out by a silver knife.

"Yes, by her mate Mikael Alibaster." Amberle answers, a towel with her scent on it wiping away the sweat forming on my brow from the pain.

"Why would anyone do that to her?" Ariven asks, his concern evident in the way he holds me gently but tight enough so that I don't jostle much as he moves.

"Because she is weak! She should be safe and secured in a pack, not creating one!" Alex states with a growl, one that is met with my own furious growl before a whimper replaces it, the stabbing pain bringing tears to my eyes.

"That is no way to talk to your Alpha! Sister or not, Geminie deserves respect!" Ariven growls in warning at Alex, causing my brother to stop pacing at the realization of what he just said.

"Gem, I... I didn't-" Alex stutters with a look of panic on his face.

"Go for a run, Alex." I cut him off, the power of my blood making it a command. I catch my brother stiffen before giving a short nod, slowly walking away from me until he reaches the treeline, where he shifts into his brown wolf and runs off. He needs to cool off, and I need to speak to him after the pain subsides.

"Gem, take this and sleep. You will feel better in a few hours." Ira's warm voice fills my ears as a pill is pushed against my lips. I accept it and soon darkness seeps in and the pain fades away.

◆◆◆

"How is she?" A concerned voice calls out softly as someone else sighs in reply.

"I think she will be fine, and maybe wake up soon." Someone answers, hands softly running through my hair. I smile contently, the pain from earlier now gone. I just want to sleep in the warm embrace that holds me tight.

"I know you're awake, Alpha Geminie." A deep voice chuckles and I peek slightly from under my eyelashes to see Ariven looking down at me, the warm embrace most likely being his.

"Sshh. Beauty sleep now." I mumble, yawning as my relaxed body beckons me to sleep more.

"You are beautiful. Why not get up and work on your pack house?" Ariven persuades me, making me sigh and roll my eyes.

"Party pooper." I grumble in response, getting another deep chuckle from the man holding me.

"I assume you are ready to establish your pack and pack house." Ira's voice sounds from above me. Ariven helps me to sit up on the grass in front of him as Ira takes a seat beside me, holding out a sketchbook and a case of pencils.

"What do I do with that?" I ask, accepting the art supplies and opening the book to a blank page.

"Well, as you know, many packs had to be built from the ground up the hard way. But, with you being the next Moon Goddess, all you have to do it is draw any design you want, and then we will place the book on the spot where the pack house will be under the light of the moon, and voilà, a pack is formed." Ira explains, the theory behind creating a pack of the Moon Goddess making me smile.

"So, sort of like a witch's spell?" Comes my follow-up question.

"Similar to it, but purer." Ira continues with a smile, tapping on the book in my lap. I smile and take a moment to look at the land before me, the lake, the clearing as a whole and begin to draw.

I start with the pack house, deciding on a building big enough to house offices, a large pack dining room and kitchen, a lounge as well as a few entertainment rooms. I add rooms where pups can go into and play, rooms wolves coming from patrol duty can come watch a game on the TV and relax with a warm meal before returning home for some needed rest.

With the basement being designed as one of many training areas I plan to have, I move on to a separate area just behind the kitchen where a laundry room will be. I hated the basement laundry room, the dingy, dark, moist air and the lack of sunlight of a place I never wanted to be in again.

This pack will be different, with a state-of-the-art laundry room, windows to allow both sunlight and fresh air in, and multiple clotheslines to be used in the summer heat to air dry the clean laundry. The finishing touches end on the third floor, with guest rooms.

"How far away is the mountain base?" I ask out of curiosity.

"About an hour run in wolf form away." Ariven answers and I smile, deciding where I want my own home to be. I start right away on my house, deciding on a modest three-bedroom cottage with a large garden and an even larger pond. I smile as I design the quaint area, the pathway leading from the forest to my house, the large bay windows where I can sit in and read, a kitchen where I can cook food and never feel hunger again.

Of course, there will be a well, one that allows the moonlight to shine inside and down into a moon pool, a place to meditate, like the one in the Temple of the Goddess on the Full Moon and be able to see my Mother.

My hands move on their own after that, my mind focused on my own pack, the school I will have built, the training center, the supply room for storing food, goods and everything else that will be needed for the pack, and then a pack infirmary for our sick and wounded. Keeping in mind other needs of a pack, needs that were never met at Hidden Claws, I design a dorm meant for new wolves as well as for those wanting their own space once coming of age. No one will be homeless in my pack.

Finally, I add small cottages dotting the pack scape, some around the lake, some in the forest and some just before the mountains, each with varying size to fit my future pack members needs.

"I think I am done." I state, putting my pencil down and flipping through the designs, smiling at the work I have created, knowing that soon this will be a reality.

"Good. The next step is to place the book where your pack house will be and say what comes to mind. The magic will work right away, and your pack will be established." Ira instructs me, giving me a smile. I stand, stretching my stiff body for a moment before making my way towards the place I want my pack house to be. I know it will take a few years to establish a pack, as I take in the lush land under the moonlight and the scent of the lake on the wind. Reaching what will be the centre of the pack house, I turn to look back at everyone waiting where I left them, a look of anticipation on their faces. Then Alex appears out of the forest behind our group giving me a smile.

[Go on, Gemmy, you'll make a great Alpha.] My brother links me and I smile, turning back to the spot in front of me where I promptly place the sketchbook on top of. Taking a few steps back, I look up to the Full Moon now directly above me and take a deep breath.

Mother give me strength. I pray, taking a moment to allow the right words to flow.

"I, Geminie Starlight, declare these lands as the Alpha of Silver Crystal Crescent Pack. Those who oppose me are my enemies and those who seek a family shall become part of mine." I state, power radiating from my voice and body as the light of the moon illuminates the land that will be mine.

The sketchbook on the ground glows brightly, the earth moving causing me to back away as walls begin to grow out of the ground in various places, the earth turning to stone as pathways and driveways are created. I soon find myself beside the group once more as we all stare in awe at the display of magic.

Houses are formed within minutes, the training facility erected and ready to be used right away, and the dirt trail we took to enter the pack grounds now paved in an even road, leading into the forest and hopefully towards the main road.

Finally, the clearing becomes quiet, and a fully formed pack stands before us, the pack house a welcoming cream-coloured building with both a vegetable and flower garden, a driveway big enough to house multiple cars, and large windows to allow as much sunlight as possible.

I smile, a sense of belonging and home filling me. A shimmering light directly above me halts my steps, my body tense in anticipation for anything amiss. But the shimmering light soon forms multiple papers, hovering just above my head.

“Take it. Those are the deeds to the land and the paperwork for utilities. It’s yours, Geminie.” Ira declares, encouraging me with a smile to reach for the papers, which I gladly do. I watch as the blank sheets slowly fill with words, my name bright and bold at the very end, and pride swells inside me.

"Welcome home, Alpha." I shiver at Ariven's voice, his lips behind my ear and I smile up at him.

"Let's go home."

Chapter 16 – Mother

"Alpha, are you in here?" A voice calls out, the sound distorted and dreamlike as I float in the moon pool. The silver water shimmers with the light of the Full Moon above me. It has been over two years since my rejection, two years since founding Silver Crystal Crescent Pack, and two years since meeting my mother Lisandra for training in the dreamscape.

"Quiet, she is going to the dreamscape to train with her mother." Ariven warns in as low a voice possible while my eyes close and I let the magic surround me.

My eyes open and I find myself gazing down at earth, the sky alight with stars as the galaxy shines above me. I am in the dreamscape, a lush garden of moonflowers growing from moonstones surrounding me with the trickle of a small stream sounding from my left.

"Gem, you're late." The melodic voice of my mother reaches me, and I smile as I rush to her arms and hold her tight. For the past two years, I have gotten to know her, and came to realize the death of the Alpha and Luna from my old pack was caused by my kidnapping. My mother had learned I was hidden in Hidden Claws and told my father such where he promptly ordered my retrieval. Their death was caused by some of his pack members defying orders and seeking their own revenge by killing the Alpha pair. It was a tragic event that should have never happened, and the wolves involved were punished with the death penalty as well.

"Sorry, Mother. I had some unexpected events in the pack happen that had to be taken care of." I answer, enjoying the warmth of her embrace as if I was a pup again. Our hug ends too soon as she links her arm with mine and leads me to a gazebo where a tea set and snacks wait for us.

Once seated, our lesson begins, and Mother continues the history lesson from last week, starting with the rule of the fourth Moon Goddess, Alexandra the Dark. The rule led to the bubonic plague that spread throughout Europe, killing both humans and Wolves alike from the disease and starving vampires to death, nearly causing their extinction from lack of food. I listen attentively, taking notes in the book given to me by my Mother and jotting down my own thoughts of what not to do. If wolves and humans were to go extinct, so will other races.

"Since the plague only lasted five years, did that mean Alexandra was replaced as the next Moon Goddess?" I ask, getting a smile from my mother.

"That's right, her twin sister Goddess Mirabella with the help of the Goddess of Destiny Morai and a few light witches replaced her right away. Mirabella then helped to suppress the plague and help wolves heal." My mother answers and I smile thinking of my ancestor.

"You said something interesting before, that the second Moon Goddess is actually a twin." I continue, my mother letting out a sigh as she looks towards a bright star.

"Yes. The First King, King Spirit, and his Queen, the first Moon Goddess Luna, had three children. They had a son and twin daughters. They soon realized their son would not make a great ruler, and planned to hand the throne to their Princess, one with hair as pure as snow named Crystalline. But she went missing and, as such, the Prince took the throne when he came of age and the second Moon Goddess, our ancestor, became the Moon Goddess." My mother answers, taking out a white box and handing it to me. Inside is a moonstone of the purest white carved into a snowflake, the magic inside flowing through my body as soon as I touch it.

"This necklace will react to a moonstone that was given to the lost Princess. Her necklace is a moonstone that looks identical to a Full Moon, and under the moonlight, it shimmers like our hair. It is our duty to find and train the lost Princess or her descendant and restore her to the throne one day." Mother continues. I go to hand the necklace back to her, but she refuses and instead helps to secure the necklace around my neck.

"Your twenty-first birthday is in a few months, consider this an early gift. You are ready to wear it and take responsibility for the task handed down to each new Goddess, of finding the lost daughter to the Alpha King Spirit." She explains, the pride of her placing such an important task on me making me smile happily.

"I can't wait for that day so I can come down and visit everyone for a week, including your father." She chuckles and I cringe, already knowing that this might lead to another sibling. Connor will be taking over as Alpha soon, meaning my father will have more time to visit my mother. If that happens, Connor and I will get to be older siblings to a new brother or sister in no time.

"Speaking of Father, Connor and he say hi and that they miss you." I change the topic quickly, getting a chuckle from my mother in response.

"I miss them too. I wish I could have raised you pups, but I had already been instated as the next Moon Goddess before meeting your father." My mother sighs sadly. I stand, walking to her side and giving my mother a tight hug. I can feel her sadness, one that I empathize with, wishing that I had been raised by my true family. But I would have never had Alex as my brother and would not have created a pack as open and accepting as my own.

"When did you know dad was your mate?" I ask quietly, feeling her arms wrap around me as well.

"It was on the day of his birth actually. A Full Moon was shining on his mother who was in the middle of the forest as their pack was being attacked about four hundred years ago. The moment he was born and let out his first cry, I knew instantly. I couldn't abandon my responsibilities but kept track of him over the years. When he became Alpha, he grew his pack. For one hundred years, he stayed celibate, waiting for his mate, for me." I watch my mother's face soften as she explains how she knew father and here were meant to be, how he grew Northern Snow to where it is today.

"Then, while visiting another pack, he was ambushed and nearly killed. That's when I was finally able to break through the barrier and save him just in time. After the initial shock, I was ready to return to the Moon when my mother said she would step in and give us some time to get to know each other. A few months later, we were married and mated." I smile, listening to my mother fondly retell the past as I return to my seat and sip on the hot tea. I sigh, thinking about my rejection with Mika and if I will ever gain a second-chance mate like other wolves when the time is right, or if I will be alone for hundreds of years.

Our talk returns to the history lesson and then onto what my mother calls "deity training," as she teaches me how to pair mates with a list the Goddess of Destiny hands to her every couple of years.

"You see, every wolf has a person who is their perfect match at conception. Of course, their perfect match does change and, as such, the list also includes wolves who are compatible but not yet perfect for their souls to resonate with." She begins, pointing at a name. The name of a newly conceive wolf shimmers before the list changes to where only her name and the list of her soulmate and potential mates appear.

"This is where the second-chance mate comes into play as within three years, their souls resonate with one another once the rejected party goes through changes of their own to grow and become stronger." Mother continues explaining, handing me a list of a she-wolf that is only a few minutes old. I smile, reading the names of her perfect mate and her compatible ones, wondering how her life will play out.

"Sometimes within the three years, their first mate and the rejected party make up and they are able to complete the mating bond. Other times they end up with completely different wolves." She finishes, and I think of Amberle and Dominic. Those two are perfect for each other, even though Amberle was rejected by her first mate and Dominic had to kill his first mate for trying to destroy his pack and murdering his mother. Life may be planned out on a map by the Goddess of Destiny, but she has written out multiple paths, twists, and turns.

Sometimes life veers into the alternate paths, sometimes they create their own. But all paths are intertwined. We spend what feels like hours talking about mates and pairings until I yawn, the magic that keeps me in the dreamscape weakening.

"I have to go soon." I yawn, rubbing my tired eyes.

"I know, darling. The Full Moon lasts for three days, so we have two more days to train." My mother concedes, pulling me in for one last tight hug and planting a kiss on my forehead.

"I will see you tomorrow then, mom." I whisper, closing my eyes as her embrace slips away.

◆◆◆

A finger poking my cheek has me stirring, the warm water making me want to fall asleep and rest after the training I have had. I need time to process all the information given to me today.

"Geeeeem." Someone calls out gently, this someone most likely the owner of the finger that is repeatedly poking my cheek. I count the rhythm of the poking and time it just right that when the person disturbing me goes to poke my cheek again, I turn my face slightly and bite their finger gently. Hearing a familiar chuckle, I open my eyes to see Ariven staring down at me warmly.

“How is mom doing?” He asks, not fazed by me biting his finger as his free hand twirls a wet strand of my hair around his index finger.

“Gwood. She sways hi.” I mumble, biting slightly harder on the offending finger in my mouth before releasing it.

“That’s good, darling. Nice necklace, a gift from your mother?” I lift my hand to the place where Ariven points, finding a familiar feeling necklace around my neck. I smile, feeling the magic flow inside me again and close my eyes, thanking my mother for the gift and trusting me with the responsibility of finding the lost Princess, my Great-something Aunt.

“Anything happen since being in the dreamscape?” I ask quietly, turning to look at Ariven who sighs.

“Yes. A pack has been declining lately since their Alpha took over and they requested help, asking if we can be there in a few days.” Ariven answers as he scoops me into his arms and out of the moon pool. I sigh, since making an Alliance with Amberle and Dominic and becoming a strong pack, Silver Crystal Crescent has been receiving many requests to help with training.

“Did they request specific ranks?” I ask, needing more details as we exit the basement up the stairs and pass the living area of my house before heading to the next floor.

“Yes, the Alpha, Theta and a few of our top Warriors and Trackers.” The answer doesn’t surprise me, and I frown. To request this many people means the situation is serious.

“Tell Alex he is in charge as of tomorrow and have everything ready to leave by one in the afternoon.”

“Already done, Gem.” He whispers as he crawls into my bed with me in his lap. I was exhausted.

"Riv?"

"Yes, Gem?"

"Will you ask Lizaria to keep an eye on this pack for me as well? I trust her to keep an eye on the pack with Alex." I yawn and snuggle into him, feeling his arms tighten around me.

"Of course." I smile at his response. The sound of the TV being turned on fills the comfortable silence and the sweet bliss of sleep. Visiting Mother Is always mentally exhausting and requires a lot of sleep to recover.

Chapter 17 – Leaving to Help

"How long will you be gone?" I sigh as Alex helps me pack my luggage into my car, my brother giving me a smile. Since creating my pack and making Alex my Beta, my brother has mellowed out on his overprotective attitude towards me. It helps that he found his mate in the form of a Rogue wolf seeking a pack after being thrown out by her Alpha for refusing to sleep with him and fighting back.

"I have no idea. At most week or two. Did Riv tell you where we are going? I've asked him but he always changes the subject." I answer, asking my own question as Lizaria walks to us with a very pregnant Missy beside her, the Beta Female glowing with her pregnancy.

"No he did not, but I can always come with you." Alex answers and I role my eyes.

"No, you have a pregnant wife who will be bursting any day now." I retort as Missy reaches us and chuckles.

"That and I'd kick your ass for missing the birth of your pup." The small spitfire of a wolf confirms and I send a smile her way. I love my sister-in-law; the she-wolf quickly becoming a good friend when she stumbled onto my pack grounds, watching her frustrate and annoy my brother when the two realized they were mates and kicking his ass time and time again when he tried to protect her like a porcelain doll. But Missy Blake is anything but breakable.

Every time my brother would argue with her to not go on a training mission or help track down the groups of Soulless, she would drag him to the training ground and promptly beat my brother to the point of needing to be bedridden for a few days. I respected my Beta Female and slightly feared her as well.

"Besides, with Gem and Ariven gone, I need your help protecting the Unicorns from Soulless. I've noticed that when they devour a unicorn, their strength increases." Lizaria states towards Alex as the Elf leans against my car, her hair glowing in the afternoon sun.

"Fine, I can't win against you three combined, and Missy is right. I would feel extremely guilty missing the birth of my pup." Alex concedes, wrapping his arm around his mate and pulling her close to him. My heart twists in pain and I hold back the envy I feel, wanting nothing more than to be in the arms of my own mate, but I will have to wait a few more months for that. I refuse to go back to Mika and want to have a second-chance mate.

Alex and Missy stay to chat for a few minutes, making me promise to call and give an update on the pack we are going to as well as to let me know if changes happen in our own pack before the five-foot she-wolf drags my six-foot-five brother to the pack house in search for chocolate ice-cream. I couldn't help but laugh at the duo, happy to have someone keep my brother on his toes.

"Did Ariven tell you where you are going?" Lizaria asks once we are alone.

"No. He changes the subject or just says it's a pack I know." I answer, a frown on my face. Ariven knows I hate going into a situation blind but he has promised me multiple times today that we will be fine and that once I get to the pack in need of aid I will understand. I just hope that nothing on this trip goes wrong.

"Hopefully its an allied pack or a new small one looking for advice to grow and get stronger." Lizaria reasons and I agree, but something tells me that this trip is not so simple.

"Ready to go, Gem?" Ariven's voice cuts the conversation short between Lizaria and I, the Elf giving me a have fun before she saunters off in the direction of the pack house, most likely going to help Missy annoy Alex. Ariven slips his luggage into my car before shutting the trunk and turning to me with a bright smile.

"Yes, I am. Do you want to drive or should I?" I ask, holding out the keys.

"I'll drive, darling. You can rest or finally start writing that book you've been thinking about." Ariven answers, taking the keys from my hand and ruffling my hair. I blush, heading to the trunk and taking out my laptop deciding that his idea of starting on that book is a great way to pass the time before climbing into the passenger seat.

"Do you know who requested our help?" I ask as the car is put into gear and we drive away from the pack house.

"Yes, the Beta of the pack. She is actually the sister of the Alpha." His answer confuses me since normally a request for help or allyship is done by the Alpha of the pack. Betas normally stand back and support the Alpha, not go behind their back.

"Do you think this will be a mutiny and take over situation?" This is the most likely scenario running through my mind as I think of how many times a Beta related to the Alpha of the pack would cause a mutiny in order to help the pack grow and prevent the further decline.

"No. She seems to genuinely care about this pack. Her worry is that the people who took care of her and her brother are clouding the Alpha's judgement, which is why he refused to reach out for help." I can tell Ariven is being vague on his answers, refusing to look in my direction for this conversation, when normally he would sneak a few glances my way even if he was driving. I frown but decide to trust my friend.

"How long will it take for us to get to get to this pack?"

"About five days, Gem. I already found a few hotels along the way for our group to sleep overnight." I nod to his answer, opening my laptop and bringing up the document with ideas for a fantasy novel I've been wanting to write.

With a few days of not needing to worry about Alpha duties, I now have some free time to try something I've always wanted to do.

Chapter 18 – Meeting the Past

The drive to the pack in need of aid is as smooth as can be, the only delay being at our third hotel when the searing pain of my so-called mate fucking some she-wolf caused me to be immobile for a day. My body felt like knives leaving tiny slivers on my skin as the torture of this feeling had Ariven drugging me and making me sleep for a day and night, only to be awoken by the sound of wolves chattering and moving around.

"Where are we?" I mumble drowsily, burying my face in the pillow below me as Ariven's scent wraps around me. A deep chuckle shakes the pillow I am snuggling into, and I quickly realize that it's actually Ariven's body.

"Am I comfortable, darling?" Ariven asks, his hand running gently through my hair.

"Yes." I answer, hiding my hot face from his view. Another deep chuckle and gentle hands playing with my hair slowly lull me back to sleep.

"We are in the guest house at the pack in aid. One of their members, the previous Beta Female if I am not mistaken, came in screaming about us being a day late and how disrespectful you are for not immediately coming to greet the Alpha. The twins quickly put her in her place, reminding the she-wolf that we came as per requested and can leave just as easily." Ariven's words are quiet, his warm embrace and soft words adding to the calmness that begs me to fall asleep again.

"She sounds like a bitch." I mumble, gaining another chuckle.

"That she is, and you have an hour to get ready and deal with said bitch, her mate, the Alpha, and the Beta."

"Can't they wait another day?" I groan, turning my head to look at Ariven.

"No. You and I need to study their defenses and training."

"Is that all?"

"Nope. There is also us having to investigate the Soulless. Amberle and Ira called while you were out cold. The Soulless attacks here mimic the ones that destroyed Forest Paw a few years ago." I sit up, intrigued that Fire Foot would request something of me while helping another pack. But as this also includes the Leader from the Temple of the Goddess, I must accept. The thought of Soulless banding together, murdering innocent wolves, and destroying packs causes my blood to boil. Those foul-smelling wolves with blood as black as tar are the bane of our existence.

No one knows how they are made, all we can speculate is the lack of pack and mate causes their humanity to shatter and their animal instincts take over until they become sick to the point of near death, living just to kill and maim. I should bring this up with the Alpha of this pack to gain intel for Amberle and Ira.

"You said I have an hour until we meet this pack's higher up?" I ask Ariven, climbing off the bed and gathering an already prepared garment bag from my luggage with a pair of black heels.

"Yes." Ariven answers and I smile.

"Give me twenty minutes. We can eavesdrop on them and see where the problem lies." With that, I make my way to the bathroom, a sense of déjà-vu running through me. I sigh, deciding to put the nagging feeling aside and place my garment bag on the hook beside the door before starting the shower and undressing.

The warm spray helps to ease the remaining tension the pain from Mika's infidelity to the bond caused. I hate when he would fool around with some pack whore, the pain being so unbearable as the Moon Goddess that only medication can help. Sometimes I envy regular she-wolves who feel this pain, as all they need is a Tylenol or Advil to alleviate their pain. If Alpha Sorus and Luna Reena knew how their son behaved, they would be furious, and his punishment would result in Mika being bed-bound for weeks to repent for harming his mate in any way.

As I shower, I think about the end of the mate bond, wondering who my mother has paired me with as my second-chance mate and if the next bond will also end in a rejection. I know the Goddess of Destiny has given a few matches to my mother, but she forbade me from looking into my own book when in the dreamscape to protect the future for myself and the pack I have created.

Maybe I can convince her to pair Ariven and I together. I have feelings for him, something I came to realize last year. He treats me like I am his world and I feel safe when with him. He is the one I want. Within twenty minutes, I am showered, dried, and dressed, my curly prism-coloured hair put into a messy bun with small strands framing my face. A slight touch of makeup to finish the look and slipping on the black heels, and I am ready to meet this pack's Alpha and his elite. Hopefully, this meeting goes well.

Exiting the bathroom, I walk into the bedroom to see Ariven dressed in a pair of fitted black slacks and a navy blue dress shirt, the sleeves rolled to his elbows, displaying the recent tattoos in all their glory. His long, black hair is tied in a high pony and I roll my eyes at the casual yet businesslike attire of the man usually in jeans, a T-shirt, and boots.

"Ready?" He asks, holding a three-ringed binder out to me that I gladly take. It is information on the pack, information I have yet to read as I became focused on writing and then withered in pain at the end of the journey here. I will have to skim the information during the meeting.

Exiting the bedroom, I walk with Ariven down familiar halls and a familiar staircase, the sense of déjà-vu growing once more.

"Are we heading to their pack house to meet?" I ask as I step off the last step, intending to walk towards the door.

"No, I asked the Alpha and his packmates to join us in the meeting room here." Ariven answers, leading me down the right corridor. As each step brings me closer to the meeting room, familiar scents reach my nose.

Suspicious, I stop just before the door and turn to Ariven a raised brow as I clue in to what pack we may be at.

[I want to listen to their reactions, Ariven, so you go in first.] I link my Theta, motioning to the door and stepping aside so the wolves inside cannot see or hear me. If my hunch is correct, Ariven kept very important information from me. My friend sighs, an apologetic look on his face before he squares his shoulders and pushes open the door.

"Sorry we are late. The journey here was long and one of our wolves had to rest due to a mate bond issue." Ariven states, his voice loud and clear. The smell that assaults me confirms my hunch, anger and hatred bubbling inside me.

"I understand. I am also sorry for interrupting you and your pack. My Beta had no right to call for aid behind my back, but after going through the reports, I soon realized she is right." A voice that I wish to never hear again calls out. His words piercing my heart like jagged blade of glass. I clench my fists, feeling my nails dig into the palm of my hand and taking dep breaths to ground myself—the scent of my tormentors do not help in the slightest. I lean against the wall, trying to get my bearings and calm my raging emotions to no avail. Then the Full Moon reveals itself from behind large clouds, its light shining down on me and calming me as if my mother is beside me giving me a hug and protecting me in her warm embrace.

Finally able to calm down, I remind myself that I am an Alpha and the Future Moon Goddess. My kidnappers and my abusers do not control me anymore. I am in charge of my future and destiny.

"I am Mikael Alibaster, Alpha of Hidden Claws." Mika introduces himself. I can feel the power of an Alpha radiating off of him. But it is weak. I realize that years of being under Bastian and Jasmine's control left the wolf who rejected me less than what his parents were.

"Ariven Cross of Silver Crystal Crescent." Ariven's deep voice answers and I smile. Its showtime. I stand from my spot leaning on the door, take another look at the Full Moon and square my shoulders as I walk into the room. "

Well Alpha Cross, I am thankful for your pack coming to help mine." Mika states, his tone friendly and warm. I grin, already knowing the chaos that is about to unfold.

"Actually Mika, Ariven is my Theta, my third-in-command and the commander of my Head Tracker and Head Hunter. I am the Alpha of Silver Crystal Crescent." I state confidently as I walkthrough the door, allowing the power of my blood to radiate through me and intimidate the wolves in the room. I watch as Bastian and Jasmine visibly shrink into their chairs, eyes wide with fear and astonishment while Mika does his best to stand before me, but I can see his body wanting to submit. Out of the two of us, I am the strongest and more powerful.

"I would say it's nice to see you all again, but if my Theta hadn't tricked me to accept your aid like your Beta tricked you into requesting said aid, I would have rather watched this place burn to the ground." I state with disgust dripping in my tone, watching the wolves bristle at my disrespect.

"Unfortunately, being an Alpha, I have to be a responsible adult and help those that request it." I continue, taking the available seat at the head of the table and sitting down, motioning for Ariven and Mika to do the same. Lace has been quiet this whole time, her head facing her lap as she does her best to be unnoticed. I commend her internally for this.

[You owe me an explanation, Ariven Lucas Cross.] I growl through the link, feeling his unease as my friend takes the seat next to me.

[I understand, Geminie.] His voice is quiet, submissive, and I understand that he is ready to take responsibility for tricking me. Good.

"Now, Mika, care to explain why you have caused the decline of Hidden Claws after the hard work Alpha Sorus and Luna Reena had put in?"

Chapter 19 – Confronting the Past

"What the hell are you doing here, Geminie?!" Mika growls, refusing to sit as his anger radiates across the room. I roll my eyes at his outburst, flipping through the binder prepared for today and taking out a contract signed by him.

"That, my dear EX-mate, is a good question. As I stated, being an Alpha with a request I already approved of as well as the Future Moon Goddess, I have obligations I must fulfill." I state matter-of-factly, throwing the contract towards Mika and leaning back on the chair.

"Besides, the Head Priestess would give me an earful for neglecting my duties as the Daughter of the Moon Goddess." I add at the end, my eyes glowing silver as I try my best to hide my rising emotions. Lace gasps in shock, her head snapping in my direction as she sizes me up.

"What do you mean?" The she-wolf questions, once again causing me to roll my eyes.

"It is as I stated. I am Geminie Starlight, daughter of Maverick and Lisandra Starlight and Future Moon Goddess." I answer, watching the reaction of Bastian and Jasmine as their body continues to shrink in their chair. Their time is limited, and the three of us knew it.

"That's impossible! Everyone knows that Goddess Lisandra's daughter was kidnapped from her crib the day she was born!" Mika shouts, slamming the table and causing a crack to appear. I smile, my eyes turning to slits as I keep my eyes on my kidnappers, Ariven inching closer to my seat.

"Why don't you ask the Blakes? They can explain why I was taken from my mother, and why my father sent the Elites to look for me. They can answer for the death of your parents. It is their fault your parents, my Alpha and Luna were killed." I state, standing from my chair and slowly walking towards the ex-Beta couple.

"I have no idea what this bitch is talking about!" Bastian shouts, standing to his feet as the chair behind him crashes to the ground.

"Watch your tongue, criminal. This is an Alpha and the Future Goddess." Ariven warns, but I hold my hand out to stop him. This is my battle.

"Really? So you didn't take me from the Forest of the Goddess minutes after I was born? You didn't plan to kill me because of the death of your real daughter?" I ask, tilting my head to the side and tapping my left index finger against my chin in thought.

"Is this true, Mr. Blake?" Mika asks, stepping up to stand beside me with clenched fists.

"This... This is a trick! A-a lie!" I watch as my male kidnapper has the audacity to lie, stuttering as he slowly backs away and looks around, most likely for an exit.

"If this is a lie, then why are you backing away from the table?" I ask, taking another step forward.

"Or better yet, was the death of your Alpha and Luna also a trick because of your crime?" I continue, my ears twitching from the muffled sobs of Lace as the realization that the couple that mentored and raised them were also the cause of their parents' deaths.

"Did you really have a daughter or was that just an excuse to obtain power over this pack?" I add, edging the two wolves into a corner.

"Shut up, you filthy whore!" Jasmine screams, standing from her chair and taking a few steps. I am surprised by her speed, as the familiar hand of hers connects with my left cheek, my head turning to the side from her slap.

"We should have killed you the moment your mother gave birth to a bitch like you!" The she-wolf continues and I growl, my barely held together emotions reaching their boiling point. The sky outside the window turns dark, the light in the ceiling hanging above the table barely able to illuminate everything.

"Geminie." Ariven warns, but I cut him off with a feral growl, my instincts demanding blood. Jasmine freezes, a look of regret on her face after realizing what she had just done. I allow the bitch to slowly back away, my body shaking as I take a deep breath, inhaling her fear before taking a few steps towards her. I watch as she goes to turn, most likely to run into the arms of her mate, but it is too late.

My hand shoots forwards and I grab the she-wolf by the neck, letting the anger inside me release through my fingertips like the power of lightning. I feel Jasmine's body begin to twitch while I let her have a taste of the abuse her and her husband put me through for eighteen years of my life, a life stolen from me by these two, a life that should have been spent with my real mother and father.

Outside, the dark clouds release their own lightning strikes, the loud sounds of trees splitting and wind howling caused by the storm created by my unhinged emotions, emotions I kept bottled up for years.

"Stop her, please! She is killing my mate!" Bastian pleads, his voice filled with agony. Mika and Lace try to move closer to me, but I growl, causing the two lesser Alphas to fall to their knees. No one would take this revenge away from me. I already have permission from my mother to kill this bitch and her husband.

"Darling." Strong arms wrap around me, Ariven's calming scent washing over my body as his lips kiss the back of my neck just between my shoulder blades. The storm raging outside subsides, but the black clouds remain as the power I release into Jasmine retreats into me.

"That's enough, Geminie. I know how you want to kill her, but your father also deserves his revenge too. Besides, there are innocents in this pack who will be harmed the longer you let your emotions control you." Ariven is right, as his lips continue to rest on the spot he kissed, his thumb rubbing small circles over my stomach and calming me down.

I take a deep breath, my grip on Jasmine's neck loosening until the she-wolf falls into a heap on the floor, gasping for breath and clutching her now-bruised and charred skin. There will be a scar of my hand there from now on, a reminder that her life is now in my hands.

Deciding to ignore the two wolves, I turn into Ariven's embrace, wrapping my arms around him while burying my face into his chest and inhaling his scent in deep breaths. I need to calm myself in order not to lose control and kill innocents.

"Theta Cross." A female voice cuts in and I peek out to see Maddie and her brother Matt standing in the doorway.

"Take these wolves to the dungeon and hold them until Alpha Maverick arrives with his pack to transfer them to Northern Snow." Ariven orders. The twins get to work, placing leather-lined silver cuffs on my kidnappers' wrists and dragging the two wolves towards the door.

"Hold it! I think I have the right to punish these wolves as they not only attacked a visiting Alpha, but also the future Luna of Hidden Claws!" Mika shouts, standing to his feet now that he is no longer oppressed by my raging power. I bristle at his words, pulling away from Ariven to growl at the foolish ex-mate of mine and send him a glare.

"You lost the right to call me your Luna. You lost any right to have me in your life as nothing more than an aid!" I snarl, Ariven keeping his arms wrapped around me to prevent another emotional outburst. He stays quiet, allowing me to voice the words I have needed to say for the last few years.

"You rejected me! You abused me because the Blakes said to when you knew the truth. You put me through two and a half years of torment every time you fucked some pack whore. I felt like I was dying every time. You even fucking did it a few nights ago!" I continue, seeing the guilt and hurt on Mika's face as tears begin to stream down my own.

"I am only here for two reasons: to help this pack as agreed upon and to find intel on the Soulless army. That's it." With that, I take Ariven's hand and walk out of the room, leaving a protesting Mika who is stopped by his sister and two hostile packmates of mine wanting to rip into the leaders of Hidden Claw. But I could care less, I need a run.

Chapter 20 – Following my Paws

I run as fast as my four legs can carry me, my fur ruffling in the wind as I jump over ditches, fallen trees, and streams. I need to release the remainder of the pent-up anger before I can return to helping Hidden Claws. I can't allow my emotions to get the better of me while here. My paws carry me to a familiar path, wading through a stream that quickly turns into a river leading to a familiar waterfall that I have not visited in years. With ease, I slip behind the vines and continue down the tunnel until the secret valley, where Lizaria and the unicorns used to live.

This is my old safe haven away from Hidden Claws. Trotting to the familiar willow tree, I curl into a ball underneath and open the link that can reach through time and space thanks to my mother.

[Liz.] I call out, a whimper to my voice.

[Yes, Little Wolf?] Her voice calms me and I give a small smile, happy to know the Elf can hear me.

[The pack, it's Hidden Claws.] I answer. I then retell the events of meeting the Alpha, of how my kidnappers tried to deny their wrong doings, how I let my anger and emotions control me, and how I wanted to give in and kill Jasmine. I had to get everything off my chest, including confronting Mika, and there are one of two people I can trust to just listen.

[Little Wolf, I know you resent Ariven right now for tricking you to agreeing.]

[Of course I do-]

[***But*** this is what you need, Geminie. Ariven may have tricked you, and that was wrong, but going there and confronting the past will help you become a better Moon Goddess.] Lizaria continues, not allowing me to protest her statement, as we both know the Elf has a point. Confronting the three wolves felt amazing, like a weight lifted off my shoulders knowing that Bastian and Jasmine will receive their punishment, and that Mika learns just how badly he fucked up.

[So, what do I do now?] I ask, watching the rippling of the pink water in the breeze.

[You do what you agreed to do and then come back home, Little Wolf.] Lizaria answers and I smile, wishing to hug my surrogate mother. I ask if there is anything she wants from the Hidden Valley before I leave, and she gives me a list of herbs to find. After that, I say goodbye and disconnect the link as I enjoy the silence of the valley, the wildflowers still in full bloom. All that is missing are the unicorns running around.

With the moon high in the sky illuminating the lonely valley, I lay my head on my paws and decide to sleep here for the night, away from everyone, as I just need some time in a place I feel safe.

◆◆◆

A pecking on my forehead has me waking up with a start, a flock of birds taking flight in fright. Taking a deep breath, I look around and remember falling asleep in the valley last night after an emotional meeting.

[Geminie, are you okay?] Ariven's voice calls out through the link as I take one last look at the valley and turn towards the exit.

[Fine. I just needed some time alone.] I reply, feeling relief through the link from Ariven. Guilt swells inside me at worrying my pack and leaving them to clean up the mess of a meeting last night. Hopefully, the twins had taken the Blakes away to wait for my father's men as ordered.

[Alex called. I broke the news about his parents, and all he had to say was good riddance.] I walk along the stream towards the vines as Ariven fills me in on what I missed last night. Lace had to drag Mika away to their pack house as she feared I would kill my ex if I saw him in my lodgings. Her fear isn't wrong, though, as I did think briefly about using my power on him when I was on the verge of killing Jasmine.

He then goes on to explain the meeting being postponed until today at noon, with a luncheon buffet will be prepared in the pack house. Lace has already prepared the reports on training as well as the financial records of the pack. One thing is for sure is if this pack still treats Omegas as in the past, their treatment will be the first thing to change.

[So, where did you go?] After the briefing of what happened last night after I left to what is expected of today, Ariven asks the one question I know he has been itching to ask. Our friendship over the last two years has grown to something more romantic, and I know he worries about my wellbeing especially after losing control of myself.

[I went to the only place I felt safe.] I answer honestly, retracing my steps through the forest and heading towards the direction of the guest house.

[The valley?]

[Yes.] Our link is cut after that, with Ariven understanding the need to be alone and process everything after reminding me the meeting will be in four hours. I walk slowly through the calm, quiet forest of the morning, spotting wolves from Hidden Claws on patrol and following behind to watch how the few I have seen do their job.

Sadly, the wolves miss many areas that would be blind spots to the pack, spots that can be used by Soulless for an attack on this pack. I make a mental note of the general area of each blind spot and watch the lazy wolves who during mid-patrol decide to hunt down a deer and take a quick lunch break, leaving half the carcass to rot. This deer could have been used to feed the pack, but these two wolves were greedy.

[Ariven?] I call out as I continue to follow these Hidden Claws wolves, always staying down wind but close enough that these wolves should have spotted me.

[Yes.]

[Ask Mika who is on patrol on the northwest side of the pack.] I command, the link going silent for a few moments as I continue to follow the wolves.

[Mika says Sebastian and Samule Bright. Why?] Ariven returns three minutes later and I frown. Sebastian and Samule were horrible wolves, their parents are best friends with the Blakes. Because of this closeness, the twins became my main bullies, always causing a scene or sabotaging my chores in order to get me punished. I now understand why these wolves are lazy doing their job.

[Add Mika to our Link.] I order, feeling a presence in my mind soon pop in like a connection rushing in. I want to fight this instinct telling me not to trust this new connection, but with a few deep breaths I accept the link and the connection merges smoothly into my mind.

[Mika here.] His voice flows into my mind and I shiver with disgust, not liking Mika in my space more than usual. Pushing personal feelings aside, I share memories of what the Bright twins have been doing, feeling anger and annoyance from both men inside the link, as Ariven and Mika each let out a growl in frustration.

[Damnit! How could these two be so incompetent?!] Mika questions and I chuckle.

[Considering their Alpha was someone's bitch for years, makes sense to me.] I retort without thinking, hearing Ariven chuckle. I have a feeling this is not what Mika wants to hear as I feel his annoyance directed to me. I shrug it off, ignoring my ex-mate, and decide to trot back to the guest house.

[You need to learn which wolves are with you as Alpha, and which are with the Blakes. I have a powder that can help that made by a local witch to my pack. We use it on Rogues we question when joining our pack to get their honesty.] I continue, hearing a sigh from Mika as my response.

[I can get some portioned out and bring it to the meeting.] Ariven volunteers and I thank my friend. With this issue brought to light, I remind the two I will be at the meeting and that Mika is to have a list of all wolves, their pack rank, and the list of jobs each wolf does. This pack needs restructuring after nearly fourteen years of the Blakes' influence. After Mika agrees, I push him out of the link and sigh, my mind becoming peaceful once more with him gone from it.

[Can we talk?] Ariven asks and I growl.

[Later. I am still mad at you.] I answer, shutting off the link and focusing on returning to the guest house so I can prepare for this meeting, now that I know what to expect.

Chapter 21 – Restructuring

I sigh as Mika and Lace continue to argue over the pack's finances, with Lace wondering why six-thousand dollars were spent on alcohol monthly as Mika tries to move the conversation into a different direction. I have a hunch on why the money was spent that way, one that causes me immense pain every time Mika decides to throw a she-wolf into bed with him. But I will let Lace figure it out on her own.

"Mika, please tell me you did not spend six-thousand on she-wolves?" Lace asks, rubbing the bridge of her nose.

"It was Bastian's idea. He said I needed a mate and would throw lavish parties for me to meet she-wolves!" Mika finally shouts out and I roll my eyes. Of course it would be that bastard's idea, knowing what happens to a she-wolf when her mate screws around with another she-wolf is something every werewolf learns in sex-ed.

"No wonder Geminie hates you! I hate you!" Lace shouts, the room going silent as I look at a fuming Lace who glares at her brother. If looks could kill, Mika would be dead.

"What do you mean?" Mika asks quietly, hurt evident on his face as he stares in disbelief.

"I was one of the few wolves who never harmed Geminie after she was disowned. I watched you and your friends hurt her, watched as you beat her. She wasn't the reason our parents were killed, the Blakes were. Fuck, you were there that night and watched our mother get be-headed." Lace continues, eyes full of tears as she clenches her fists. I can feel the power of an Alpha radiate off of her, something I have yet to feel from Mika, and surprise fills me. Maybe Mika isn't fit to be an Alpha. But Lace sure is.

"You allowed them to make our pack weak, even after becoming Alpha. You stopped allowing Omegas to train, and so I had to secretly train them in order to keep up their basic combat skills. I had to run the pack, something an Alpha should do, since you and Bastian went out to party every month.

I had to organize patrols and hunting parties so that we didn't starve. You did nothing, Mika!" She is screaming by the time she ends her rant, tears of anger and frustration running down her cheeks. I instinctually rush to Lace's side and pull her into a hug, the blonde she-wolf instantly subbing into my shoulder the moment she feels my comfort.

"You ruined our pack, a pack our parents and ancestors worked hard on. You're not fit to be an Alpha." She whimpers making me sigh. Lace is right, Mika is not fit to be an Alpha if the paperwork is any indication. Every last sheet - except the finances - has her signature on it, some even with her own handwriting, as I notice rescheduling on some. Even the list of Omegas she kept separate for the secret training was brought and scrutinized.

"I am the oldest, that's why I am Alpha!" Mika exclaims. I frown, glaring at the wolf across the table from Lace and I.

"Oldest doesn't necessarily means best fit." I point out, seeing a look of defeat on his face. I sigh, motioning for us to take a break. Without hesitation, Mika rushes out of the room, and Lace collapses into her chair. Ariven smiles as he hands the two of us bottles of water before exiting the room as well.

[I'll follow Mika and leave you ladies to talk.] He links me and I thank him, taking the chair beside Lace as we sit in awkward silence.

"I never blamed you, Gem." Lace cuts the silence and I turn to look at the deflated she-wolf, who is now fidgeting with the cap of her water bottle.

"I knew that the death of my parents was caused by someone in the pack doing a bad deed. I even looked into the situation and had a witch help me bring up my memories. They were from your father's pack, weren't they?" She continues and I sigh, something I find myself doing a lot lately since coming here, before running a hand through my hair as I stare out the window.

"Yeah, they were." I admit, remembering the interrogation that happened just before the Luna was killed.

"Technically, it is my fault the Alpha and Luna were killed."

"But you were kidnapped and believed you were a Blake." Lace cuts in, taking my hand and staring at me. I give a small smile as tears fill my eyes. It's been years since she and I had a conversation, and the emotions welling inside me are bittersweet.

"I know that now. But had I not been kidnapped, Alpha Sorus and Luna Reena - your parents - would still be here." I rebut.

"It's the Blakes' fault. After they took over, the pack changed. Omegas were treated as nothing but slaves during their rule. Favoured wolves rarely trained, while those who were not close to the pair were trained mercilessly. I watched as pack members left one by one and the power declined. When you rejected my brother, it got worse. I wanted to leave with you and Alex, but I couldn't let my family's pack break down." My heart breaks as Lace explains the things she had to do short of selling her body to keep this pack together, how she had to make money through creating herbal medicines and cosmetics that soon became the business Lacey Face with how popular the products became.

I listen as the she-wolf I once considered a sister releases her pent-up worries and resentment one by one, sometimes chiming in with my own memories of an event or handing her a tissue when she cries. By the time our talk ends, an hour has passed.

"You should be Alpha, Lace." I state, feeling the love for her pack radiating off of Lace in waves and her Alpha power slowly growing. I have a feeling that Jasmine tried to suppress her in order to make Mika their puppet, but this she-wolf persevered and came out stronger instead.

"I don't know if I can do it though." Lace voices and I smile, pulling her in for a hug as our bond slowly rebuilds itself.

"You can. You've done it for years already and just need a little more training." A voice cuts in before I can say anything, causing Lace and I to turn to the doorway, where Mika and Ariven stand. Mika walks towards us, coming to stand before his sister as he lets out a deep sigh.

"You held this pack together, while Bastian and I nearly destroyed it. You made a business through high school, and instead of going to college, grew that business to support the pack needs. You are a better Alpha than I am." Mika admits, shocking both Lace and me. The room is left in silence as I watch Lace's eyes glaze over then Mika's, the two having a conversation through their link—a conversation I wished to be apart of.

[You think he will give up being Alpha?] Ariven asks and I smile, turning to look at him as he saunters over to me to play with my hair. I swat his hand away, still upset with Ariven for tricking me. He lets out a sigh and takes a seat opposite me. I am not ready to deal with Ariven as I still feel betrayed.

[Yes. He will do what's right for his pack. But Lace would make him her Beta. She won't give up on the only family she has left.] I answer. We wait patiently for the siblings to talk until Mika lets out a sigh and walks to his seat.

"We will announce to the pack that I am stepping down for Lace to become Alpha. Then, we can start training the wolves the right way." Mika exclaims and I smile at him, the first friendly smile I have given my ex-mate in years.

"You're doing the right thing, Mika." I state before we continue the meeting. Lace's Alpha power radiates off of her as a new found confidence shines in her eyes. Hidden Claws will grow again, and maybe an alliance with this pack will be beneficial for my own.

◆◆◆

"When will you announce stepping down as Alpha?" I ask Mika as the four of us end our meeting. With the plan for Lace to become Alpha in a week, there is a lot to do with Hidden Claws, Starting with mass training today in three hours.

"Tonight, during the welcome banquet for your pack. It's only fair." Mika answers, sighing as he runs a hand through his hair.

"I had no idea the amount of damage to this pack caused between the Blakes and I. They all deserve better." I hum in agreement, my own torment in the pack coming to mind at how horrible this pack became during the reign of the Blakes. With the way the twins from Hidden Claws behaved on their patrol, this pack needs a large restructuring.

"Both of you will be at training, correct?" I ask as I stand from my chair and stretch, catching Mika staring a little too long at me.

"Of course, Gemie, and thank you for coming to help. Your wolves agreed to patrol for us, right?" Lace answers, giving me a bright smile that I return with my own.

"Yes, they did." I answer then take my leave with Ariven hot on my heels, intending to use the next three hours to prepare for the training session and prep the four wolves for their patrol.

Chapter 22 – Sharpening the Hidden Claws

As I stand on the side of the familiar outdoors training ground, I watch as wolves pile in, some whispering about my wolves stationed at equal intervals around the grounds, some questioning why I'm here when I left the pack three years ago. I just keep a stoic smile on my face, Ariven chuckling as he watches the wolves stretch, each breaking into their own cliques.

I spy the Hunters that used to make my life a living nightmare, wolves I am itching to destroy in a fight.

Then I see the trackers that ignored my existence, their excuse always being their job is more important than a "Lowly Omega". I am neutral towards them as they neither joined in my abuse nor stepped into help me.

My eyes wander to the Omegas, their malnourished bodies still a sight to see, one which I know will change under Lace's rule with time. Seeing Misbah and Lilly again, their skinny bodies still the same as usual but the two hold their heads high with pride.

"See those two wolves over there?" I ask Ariven, pointing out my two friends whom I missed these last few years.

"Yes, why?" He asks and I smile.

"I plan to take them and their families back to Silver Crystal Crescent with us. They helped me when I became an Omega, and I have a feeling they would agree to moving." I answer happily, already planning the two empty cabins that the ladies would adore. Ariven chuckles as Mika and Lace finally appears on the training ground, making their way towards us with apologetic looks.

"Sorry, Mika was placing all the pack assets into my name and we lost track of time." Lace explains as soon as she reaches my side. I understand and just motion for her to stand beside me as I turn my attention to Mika.

"For now, you are still the Alpha. This means today, you lead the training. I want to see where every wolf is at and how they are trained to be able to restructure your training procedures." I state, watching as he bristles at my command. I take a deep breath, waiting for Mika to argue back with me as Lace walks away towards the Omegas to what I hopefully assume is explain the training today.

"Oy, Mika, what's with this bitch Geminie being back at the pack?" Sebastian Bright calls out, a shit-eating grin on his face. Trailing behind him is his brother Samule and a group of Hunters. I frown as they come to stand before the three of us, seeing Lace and the Omegas look on with worry.

[Lace, up to making a bet?] I ask, linking the she-wolf as I smirk.

[What do you have in mind?] She asks, a familiar mischievous glint in her eyes that I haven't seen in years.

[If I can beat these six punks in a fight, Misbah, Lilly and their families can relocate with me.] I state, watching Lace roll her eyes.

[Cocky, are we?]

[Very. I may have seemed weak to the pack, but I had an ancient Elf training me for years to fight.] I retort, watching her eye widen in shock.

"Look at me when I'm speaking to you!" Samule shouts, Ariven stepping in front of me protectively.

"Oh, I'm sorry, were you speaking to me Sammy boy?" I ask with mock concern, leaning against a tree and twirling a strand of hair between my fingers.

"You damn well know I was, bitch!" He curses, anger radiating off of this ignorant wolf in waves. Mika and Ariven let out a growl of warning, but I stop them, a smirk on my face as I look at the Warriors before me.

"Sorry, but I was dealing with Alpha things, you wouldn't understand. I missed whatever you were saying completely." My answer infuriates the group further and a ripple of whispers break out between the wolves watching. My packmates chuckle, guessing where this is headed.

[Ten minutes. Beat them in ten and you win the bet. If not, I want to meet this Elf and have her train me for a month!] Lace replies, and it is the motivation I need to continue taunting these all-brawn-no-brain men.

Pushing off from the tree, I slowly walk towards the group of Hunters, taking in their appearance and stance, looking for any weak spot.

"You're not an Alpha." A tanned boy calls out and I recognize him as Amir. I chuckle, taking in his cocky stance as he favours the left side.

"Want to bet?" I ask, coming to stand beside Ariven who just looks at me with a raised brow.

"I bet fucking tall, dark and broody here is the Alpha and you're just his whore but you are no Alpha Geminie." Sebastian calls out. Mika lets out a feral growl at his insubordinate packmate. I roll my eyes at his possessive attitude and send him a warning growl of my own, happy when Mika begrudgingly backs down. These pups are mine to deal with.

"And I bet I can beat the six of you in a fight at once." I egg him on, taking another step forward. This catches everyone's attention as the six males weigh their options. If my hunch is correct, they must assume that I am still the same old weak Geminie who is unable to defend herself and won't want to fight a weakling because they will be considered heartless and cruel. That's fine with me.

After a few minutes of the group using their singular brain cell to answer, I push past them, bumping my shoulder into Sebastian and watching the Hunter stumble to the right, his anger reaching new limits.

"That's it. You're on you bitch! Just don't go crying when you're near death!" Sebastian screams as his arm swings in my direction.

[Start the timer.] I link Lace as I drop down into a crouch narrowly missing a fist to the face. Pushing back up, I use my momentum to throw my own punch, catching Sebastian in the chin and hearing a satisfying crunch as blood seeps out of his mouth. Sebastian falls backwards, eyes rolling to the back of his head comically as he passes out.

`"Someone roll him onto his side so he doesn't choke on his own blood. His jaw and teeth may be broken." I state in a monotone voice and turn around just in time to dodge Samule's kick.

"You bitch, that's my brother you just injured!" He seethes, spit flying from his lips. I roll my eyes, instinct telling me to crouch just in time to miss another fist being thrown my way by Amir.

[Eight minutes, thirty seconds left.] Lace links me, and I wink in her direction before swinging my leg out to trip Amir sending him tumbling into a blond haired blue eyed Hunter named Jordan who looked ready to kick me as well. The two fall to the ground, leaving Samule and two wolves facing me for a moment. I had about thirty seconds before Amir and Jordan untangle their limbs from each other to defeat one of the three.

A black-haired wolf I finally recognize as Alex's ex-friend James takes the first swing, his rage clouding his judgement as I roll my eyes at him stupidly screaming. What are we, an anime? With a sigh, I dodge his attempt at a punch, turning my body behind him where I send a swift kick to the back of his femur, hearing a loud crack. This time his scream of anger turns into a blood-curdling scream of pain and I wince, my ears sore from this banshee like wolf.

Amir and Jordan are up on their feet, the blond ready to fight but Amir slowly backs away with his hands held up in the air.

"I was wrong to fight against you, Geminie. I'm sorry." The tanned man states as he limps away to join the rest of the pack in watching the fight. I taste the air for any hint of trickery, but all I taste is truth. Amir is smart, knowing when to back down and submit.

[Does that count as a defeat?] I ask Lace, dodging Samule and Jordan, then wincing as their fists connect with the other's nose in a crunch. Blood flows down their face as their shocked looks stare at one another, causing me to chuckle. These Hunters are not the brightest.

[Yes. Amir submitted, so you beat him.] I smile at Lace's reluctant response but frown at her next words.

[Six minutes. Time is ticking away, and you have three more to deal with.] Her reminder dampens the fun I am having and fuels the need to win this bet. Now is the time to get serious.

A red-headed wolf I have never seen before today comes rushing at me, his fist inches from connecting with my face. Just as he is about to hit me, I grab his wrist, using the wolf's momentum to throw him face first onto the ground and making him gather a mouth full of dirt. With a stomp of my foot and a twist of my wrist, his right arm and left leg snap. This wolf is down for the count.

Jordan and Samule are next, both recovering from the shock of breaking each other's noses and focusing their anger in my direction. I want to leave Samuel for last. Without hesitation, I grab the blond by his ankle as he aims a kick in my direction. With a chuckle, I watch fear enter his eyes as I snap the ankle under my grasp, pulling the blond closer to me by the broken limb and sending a fist to his face. His body goes limp and the wolf is out cold.

Slowly lowering his limp body to the ground, I feel a fist connect to the right side of my face and am sent sprawling to the ground. Surprised, I roll to my feet and turn to glare at Samule who has a smug look on his bloody face.

"Why so happy?" I ask chuckling, ignoring the sting on my cheek.

"I've already beaten everyone else. You're just left for last," His smug look falls from my taunting and the laughter from my wolves, his anger growing at the humiliation. Samule says nothing as he rushes to me and I to him. Then the unthinkable happens.

Samule leaps into the air shifting into a grey and brown wolf. He knows the rules to a fight. Unless told to shift by the Alpha watching on, you fight in human form. Samule just broke this cardinal rule. I drop to my knees just in time to slide under his huge body, the ground rough on my skin. In moments though I am up on my feet and twirl around just in time to send a roundhouse kick to Samule's face, the wolf whimpering as he is sent sprawling to the ground. I waste no time in rushing to his body and grabbing him by the scruff of his neck, where I hold him down and send punch after punch to any part of his body that I can. Samule flails in my grasp, his claws leaving shallow cuts in my leg that I ignore as I continue to send punches into his body.

"Submit!" I order, allowing my Alpha blood to surface and bring power into my command. He fights it, sending me a growl, to which I answer with a swift fist to his snout.

"I said, submit!" My command is a growl as I fight the urge to shift and tear into this disrespectful wolf with claws and teeth. I wait for a moment as Samule has an inner battle until finally, his body goes limp, and he shows his neck as much as possible. He has submitted to me.

"Lace, time?" I call out for all to hear and the she-wolf chuckles as I drop Samule none to gently onto the ground and walk away.

"Thirty seconds left. You won the bet." The Alpha she-wolf calls out, and I cheer triumphantly. I see the confusion in everyone else's eyes for a moment as Ariven walks over and hands me a much needed bottle of water that I chug immediately.

"Mika, is Geminie here for you two to reconcile and mate?" A confused wolf asks, causing me to nearly choke on the water and send a glare in this wolf's direction.

"No, I am not and never will be Mika's mate. He lost that the day he rejected me on my birthday!" I answer cutting off whatever Mika was going to say. A hushed whisper crawls through the crowd of Hidden Claws wolves that I ignore, motioning for ten of my own wolves to come forward.

"Get these five to the infirmary ASAP. They won't be able to train for the next few days." I order. I allow silence to settle over the training field while my pack mates carry the injured wolves away, Mika standing under a tree as he stares at me. Annoyed, I walk over to where my ex-mate stands and glare at him, hands on my hips.

"What is your problem?" I ask in a low voice.

"Why did you deny us being mates?" He fires back, and I chuckle.

"Because we aren't. You and I rejected each other, remember?" He looks away after my statement, sighing and running a hand through his messy hair. I scoff, turning around, ready to ignore Mika and begin walking away toward Lace.

"We could be mates again." He calls out quietly, halting my steps for a moment. The wind ruffles the leaves in the tree behind me as my gaze stares straight ahead, a sense of melancholy washing over me. I could never look back, the past hurt too deeply for me to even consider taking Mika back as a mate. He never deserved me.

"No, we can't." I answer, closing my eyes and taking a deep breath. When I open them again, I see Ariven standing beside Lace and looking at me, his forest-green eyes locking onto mine instinctively, and I smile. I may be mad at him, but Ariven is home to me.

Chapter 23 - A Bond Breaking

"Riv, please go away." I groan, throwing a pillow at the man's head as I bury myself in the warm blankets, seeking the cover of darkness and more sleep. It's been a week since arriving at Hidden Claws, the experience still bitter with the horrid memories from my childhood making fulfilling this request for aid hard. The second request sent by Amberle and Ira of looking for Soulless added stress to my already stressful job and for the last few nights I spent running around no-mans land outside pack territory to look for evidence of the Soulless caravan and their possible leader. Last night I had a lead that I had to chase down and in the end it left me coming to the guest house at four in the morning and exhausted with the need for sleep.

"Come on, Gem. You've been distant from me after the last few days. I just want to come cuddle with you and talk." Ariven's husky voice pleads, his hand finding my hair that he promptly plays with. I want to melt into his touch, allow him to explain his thinking of tricking me to accept Lace's request. But right now I want sleep and to be alone.

"Ariven, leave me alone. I got in at four in the morning, and you wake me just to talk. Go find someone else to preach to or annoy." I growl in warning, flicking my wrist in his direction and sending a blast of air at his body. His weight on the bed is gone as I hear him crash to the floor—packmates will wonder what is happening, but I don't care. I just want to sleep.

"Fine, I understand you need your space. I'll be back by eleven to wake you up for training." He concedes as I snuggle closer under the covers, sleep taking hold of my body once more. His footsteps grow faint, and the door to the room is lightly shut just as I let sleep take its hold over me.

♦♦♦

I jolt awake as the dream I was having ends abruptly, with the harsh feeling of ice-cold water drenching my body. I begin shivering, my bed completely soaking wet, with ice cubes littered around me.

"Hey Matt, Ariven was right about using a bucket of ice water to wake up the Alpha." I turn immediately to the sound of the voice and catch Maddie and Matt leaning against the wall, fist-bumping each other and laughing.

"I guess so, Madds." Matt answers laughing. I am going to kill these two for ruining my bed and sleep.

"One." I growl, flicking my fingers as the water evaporates and the chill in my body fades away. The twins freeze, fear creeping into their eyes the moment they realize my anger is directed their way.

"Two." I continue, Maddie dropping the bucket and running out the room screaming as if a murderer is chasing her, Matt hot on her heels.

"Three!" I shout, bounding out of bed in pursuit of my prey - the twins. Doors open with pack mates poking their heads out only to spy me chasing after the twins, furious that they would ruin my sleep by dumping ice water onto me.

Their screams ring clear through the halls of the guest house, some of my pack mates coming out to watch the show knowing that although Maddie and Matt Bridge are amazing Hunters, they are pranksters always causing a headache for me. Once the two run outside, I take the time to trip them by shifting the earth under their feet. Their tumble to the ground gives me enough of a start that as the two manage to climb to their feet once more, they are met with my fingers grabbing them by the ears.

"Who the hell told you two to wake me up the way you did?!" I demand, watching the twins wince as their eyes shift around. No one will help them though as they got themselves into this mess.

"I did, darling. You were supposed to be up an hour ago as we have a meeting with Lace and Mika before the Alpha Ceremony tonight." Ariven calls out, causing me to release the twins now that I know who the mastermind behind today's rude awakening is.

My anger is directed at Ariven now, my Theta slowly walking towards me with hands up in surrender. I growl as he comes too close, the betrayal of him hiding that Hidden Claws was the pack to request help, tricking me into accepting said request and now having me being woken up rudely knowing I am exhausted being the breaking point.

"Ariven Lucas Cross, you have crossed a line." I growl, walking over and, without thinking, slapping the wolf before me across the face in rage.

"First, you accepted a request from the pack that abused me, hiding this fact until it was too late and tricking me into coming!" I shout, my body shaking as I allow the hurt and betrayal to finally have their space.

"Then you go on thinking that this betrayal is fine and that I am okay with being here when I am not. I hate being here, even if the trip is going smoothly. You try to act like everything is normal between us when it's not! I trusted you, and you used it to trick me!" I continue, anger fading as tears start to flow from my eyes. I wrap my arms around myself, trying my best not to become a sobbing mess as the hurt takes control, the hurt from my friend, the hurt from facing my old pack, the hurt from facing the mate who rejected me, the mate I grew up with who betrayed me.

"And finally, you allow Matt and Maddie to wake me up knowing how exhausted I am from dealing with being around my old pack and old abusers, as well as trying to get intel on the Soulless to send to Ira and Amberle." I finish, my voice weak. I want to go home to my pack Silver Crystal Crescent. I no longer want to stay in Hidden Claws. Ariven can take over training; I am just too mentally and physically exhausted to continue pretending that everything is fine between the wolves of Hidden Claws and me, that things are fine between Ariven and me when they aren't.

"I'm sorry, darling. I never wanted to hurt or betray you." Strong arms pull me into a body I always find comfort in for the last three years, Ariven's scent wrapping around me as one hand combs through my hair gently. Allowing myself to feel weak, my hands clutch his shirt, and I sob. The hurt, pain and betrayal from the years of abuse in Hidden Claws, from Ariven's trickery, and the fact Mika has spent every waking hour since arriving back here trying to rekindle the mate bond are too much to bear.

"I know you never wanted to come back here, even refused to talk about the past to me when you would wake from a nightmare. I couldn't keep watching you go on like that and knew you had to face your demons, darling. I did it to help you." His words are gentle, guilt blending in with his own pain as he tightens his hold on me, allowing me to just cry.

"You needed this to become a strong Alpha, a strong Goddess. Mika is your weakness, the bond still strong enough to cause you pain, to cause your heart to hurt and the pain of him with another wolf to nearly kill you. I couldn't watch you go through that for another month." Ariven finishes, kissing my forehead and tucking me under his chin. His steady heartbeat and the truth of his words help me to calm myself, my sobbing being the outlet to release all the pain until nothing but numbness remains.

"I'm sorry I slapped you." Comes my quiet whisper. Ariven just chuckles for a moment as he pulls away, his eyes staring into my own as he wipes away my tears.

"I deserved it, Geminie, so don't apologize." He smiles at me before surprising me and planting a gentle kiss on my lips.

Surprised at first, I find myself closing my eyes and leaning into his touch, my heart fluttering and mind going blank with nothing but Ariven as my focus. The kiss is cut short as a loud feral growl causes the two of us to separate and Ariven pushes me away just in time as a blur tackles him to the ground.

"Stay the fuck away from my mate!" Mika's angry voice calls out, the scent of Ariven's blood filling the air as my ex's nails turn to claws and Ariven's skin is cut deeply. My mind snaps: watching the man I consider my home being injured angers m e to no end and the grip on my power slips. Mika falls off of Ariven, clutching at his throat as I slowly draw the air from his lungs.

"For the last time, Mika, I am not your mate and will never be your mate!" I state, allowing my Alpha blood to radiate the power inside. I see the panic in Mika's eyes, his face slowly losing all colour, and the thought of strangling him is tempting.

"Geminie, stop. You'll kill him." Ariven is by my side once more, his strong arms wrapping around me and pulling me flush against him once again. I consider his words, looking into his worried-filled eyes, and decide that Mika has learned his lesson. As soon as I pull my power back and hear Mika take a deep breath, something inside me pops and fizzles out, a peace of mind I have not felt in two years fills me, making my body go limp. If Ariven wasn't holding onto me I would have collapsed onto the ground.

"No! No! No!" Mika exclaims, a crazed look in his eyes as he stares at me, clutching his head. He crawls towards me, taking my hand as tears fill his eyes, a pained expression on his face. I feel nothing at his contact. No sparks, no heat, nothing. It's then I realize that the bond has finally broken. We are free from each other, and now I can gain a proper mate, a mate who will love me for who I am.

"Like I said, Mika, I am not your mate." Reiterating my statement, I look at Ariven who gets the hint and scoops me into his arms, carrying my tired body into the guest house and leaving Mika to mourn the broken bond by himself.

Chapter 24 – Alpha Lace

"Thank you for making me accept this request." I whisper to Ariven as we cuddle in bed, the television playing some gaming channel on YouTube that Ariven watches while I doze on his chest, his hands gently rubbing circles on my back. An hour has gone by since the bond broke between Mika and I, pack mates coming to inform me that he is still outside waiting for me to come and talk, for him to apologize for the years of hurt he has given me. I just tell them to make sure that his pack stays away for the wolf to grieve and that no one attacks him. It's the least I can do for Mika, considering our history and the lack of animosity he has shown on this trip.

"You don't have to thank me. I tricked and betrayed your trust to get you here." Ariven answers, and I smile, planting a kiss over his heart and snuggling closer to the man below me. This reaction gives me a deep chuckle in response, his own light kiss being placed on my forehead before he continues to draw circles on my back, and I contently doze in and out of sleep.

"Gem, John said I could find you in here." Lace's voice calls out before she enters my room, a look of surprise on her face when she spots Ariven and I cuddling. I sigh, already knowing where this conversation is going, as I climb off of Ariven and walk toward the soon-to-be Alpha.

"Before you ask, yes the bond broke. No, I do not care for your brother. No, I will not mate with him now or ever. Yes, we can build a friendship." I state before the blonde can fire her questions at me. Lace chuckles, leaning against the wall as she rolls her eyes for a moment.

"Honestly, you deserve better. I was just coming to ask if you could come help me get dressed for the ceremony. Mika is already at our house since the idiot finally regrets what he has done to you." My friend retorts, waving at Ariven who smiles and waves back, the smiling causing the cuts from early to pull making him wince. I check on the injuries, relieved to see they should be healed before the ceremony before Lace impatiently takes my hand in hers and drags me out the door.

"Have fun, darling!" Ariven calls out instead of coming to save me from Lace's clutches.

◆◆◆

"I told you this dress would look amazing on you, Gem!" Lace exclaims, pushing me towards the floor-length mirror with our reflections staring back at us. My eyes widen at the floor-length, silver fit-and-flare gown adorning my body, the simple sweetheart neckline and long sleeves giving me an ethereal glow as my prismatic hair flows around me in loose curls. Lace has done an amazing job on me, her skilled hands placing just enough makeup to highlight my features and making me look like the Goddess I am meant to be.

"You look amazing too! I always said gold was your colour." I compliment, moving aside so the blonde she-wolf can see her reflection as well. A strapless A-line gold dress hangs from her body, with minimal jewellery and makeup on as the power in her blood radiates off of her. She holds herself in a graceful way that demands the attention of the room, as a true Alpha should, and I can't be any prouder to be called her friend.

The sky is dark as night settles in, and the half-moon is high in the sky as the ceremony is waiting to begin. I turn to study Lace, seeing in her Alpha Sorus' determination and the grace of Luna Reena. They would have been proud to see their daughter being the Alpha this pack needs. A knock on the door alerts our attention to someone coming in, and Ariven's scent wafts through as soon as it is opened the cuts caused by Mika finally healed leaving no scare at all thankfully.

"Sorry to intrude, but the ceremony starts in ten minutes, and I came to gather Geminie." He states, coming to stand beside me and holding out his hand. I happily take it, watching as he bows and places a kiss on top before gently pulling me to his side.

[If he isn't your second-chance mate, I want to meet your mother and yell at her myself!] Lace links me, causing me to blush and glare at the soon-to-be Alpha. She just smirks, waving her hand in a "shoo-shoo" gesture that has Ariven chuckling. We wish her luck before exiting the room and making our way down the stairs of the familiar pack house.

"My room used to be in the attic." I reminisce quietly, stopping mid-step and turning to look back in the direction of the attic entrance. I wonder what happened to my oasis away from the Blakes and the pack, where I would go and nurse my wounds from a rough day of punishment.

Did they find the stash of food I had hidden? Was it demolished and turned into something new? I want to know these answers but also want to keep the past in the past. I no longer felt hatred and fear towards this place, towards the pack. Dwelling on the past is something I decide I no longer want to do as I take one last look up the stairs and turn back to continue our descent.

Only a few Omegas are working the celebration today, volunteering to perform the jobs as cooks and servers while the rest of the pack witness Lace taking power over Hidden Claws. It is definitely a step up from how Omegas were treated a little over a week ago, with some of the Omegas able to openly train with the rest of the pack and having gained weight from proper nutrition. It's a step in the right direction with a new reign if you ask me. Ariven and I continue to chat about training that will take place tomorrow and which wolves will be too drunk to focus.

"Have you told them about a specific fiery tempered wolf and her husband coming to help with training?" Ariven asks as we enter the large backyard and make our way to our seats.

"Nope. I plan to leave it until last minute. Amberle wants to have some fun with this pack and see where the defenses fall short." I answer chuckling, already picturing the chaos my friend will cause. Since becoming a mother, Amberle has had a rough time getting away from her two children and focusing more on being an Alpha and mother instead of helping to train allied packs. With Blue - her adoptive father- agreeing to take over to watch the pack and his grand-pups, Amberle jumped at the chance when I called last night before my recon mission on the Soulless to join me in training Hidden Claws.

I have a feeling the she-wolf just wants to make Mika's life miserable for a few days and I am fine with it. Ariven chuckles as he helps me to take a seat in front of the stage, a stage set up under the ancient maple tree that has been standing on Hidden Claw's territory since the creation of the pack, its roots buried and slinking throughout the pack lands. Mika is already sitting in his designated spot, his eyes scanning my body. I ignore him and instead turn my focus to the man beside me and happily straighten the tie he is wearing that has shifted out of place.

"I cannot wait to get out of this suit." Ariven states with an exasperated sigh. I roll my eyes at his pouting and snuggling close to his side, waiting for midnight, when the moon is high in the sky and the ceremony will begin. We don't wait long as the unlit torches suddenly ignite, the flames a golden hue instead of the regular red, orange, and yellow, and Lace's scent drifts in on the wind.

Those seated rise, turning to face the new Alpha as Lace, with her blonde hair piled atop her head and flowing dress, walks down the golden carpet. She exudes grace and power with each step, her head held high and shoulders back—a true Alpha. I look to the moon for a brief moment, sending a silent prayer for her rule to be strong and her parents to watch over her, before my attention is turned back to Lace who pauses to smile at me, a smile that I return with my own encouraging one as she continues to the stage where she bows to her brother. As the current Alpha, it is Mika's job to pass down the title.

"Guests, you may be seated." Mika calls out, the crowd quickly taking their seats. Mika turns to his sister, a podium with a crescent moon-shaped bowl made of gold between them filled with pink water from the lake we played in as children. Its magic is the core of Hidden Claws and is rooted deep in the maple tree.

"Today, Lace Alibaster will be transferred the title of Alpha to Hidden Claws." Mika begins, staring at his sister with proud eyes as he takes a cup of water and hands it to her.

"Do you, Lace, promise to uphold the law of the pack and that of werewolf kind to protect and serve those we call family in Hidden Claws?" He continues. Lace smiles, looking over the crowd and to the maple tree behind her before turning back to Mika.

"I do." She answers without hesitation, determination in her pale green eyes.

"Please, take this cup and drink the water of the Crescent Moon Lake to show the unity of the pack and the magic that sustains it." Mika returns, lace gingerly taking the small cup and drinking the contents inside in one quick gulp. A shimmer of rose gold surrounds her, surprising me as the magic helps to solidify and grow the power of her blood. She is strong, stronger than Mika, and with some training, would make an incredible Alpha.

"Do you, Lace, accept the responsibilities that come with caring for a pack and the land the pack owns, to abide by the natural law set by the Moon Goddess and deities themselves?" Mika asks as he takes the cup from her hand and sets it down on the podium.

"I do." Her voice radiates her growing power. The wolves in the crowd shiver, ready to submit to the Alpha Female at a moment's notice, and pride swells inside me.

"Then, please, slice your hand and drip your blood into the bowl with mine." Mika states, handing a clean knife to Lace before taking his own. The siblings each hold their right hands up, taking the sharp golden blades and slicing along the inside of their palms. The iron scent of blood fills the air, one more powerful than the other, and instantly you can tell who is meant to be Alpha and who is not.

The siblings, with their cut palms facing each other, grasp one another's hands, their grip releasing their mixed blood with gentle drops into the pink water, dying it a darker pink. My mind flashes to the night of their parents' deaths, fear taking over as I relive the Luna and her crying, but something else catches my attention, - a pair of ice-blue eyes hidden in the shadows. A pair of ice-blue eyes I know all too well.

[Gem!] Ariven shouts into the link, dragging me from my memories and back to the present, where Mika hands Lace a gold towel to wipe her hand, the knife wound now gone and healed.

[You okay?] He asks, and I turn to look at a pair of concerned forest-green eyes. I nod, leaning closer and breathing in his scent, thinking for a moment that those eyes could not be a coincidence. Where they are, trouble is bound to follow.

[I need to call my father later.] I answer before closing the link and focusing on the ceremony before me.

"I declare Lace Alibaster the new Alpha of Hidden Claws. May her reign be strong!" Mika calls out, the wolves of Hidden Claws taking a knee as a resounding

"May her reign be strong" echoes around us. Mika steps back as he too bends a knee in submission to his sister, while Lace finishes the ceremony by taking the golden bowl and walking toward the roots of the maple tree. First, the nails on her right hand become claws, and she leaves her marks at the base, the fresh marks a contrast to all the ones left by Alphas before her. Then she takes the water from the golden cup and slowly pours it onto the fresh claw marks.

She is now the Alpha; one I could not be prouder of.

Tomorrow, we will sign an alliance treaty and continue training both the pack wolves and her as the Alpha.

"I just want to thank you all. Thank you for believing in me, for trusting me long enough to stay in our declining pack and for helping me train those in unfortunate circumstances due to the previous Betas of this pack." Lace begins, returning the bowl to the podium and facing her pack.

"Today marks a new beginning, one where Geminie, the Future Moon Goddess, and I are friends and allies. One where Omegas have just as many rights and opportunities as the rest of the pack. One in which Hidden Claws will be on par with Blood Moon and Silver Crystal Crescent." She pauses, taking a deep breath as she looks to the moon with a sad smile on her face that I have seen one too many times on the anniversary of her parents' deaths.

"I will make my parents and ancestors proud and the pack so strong that no Soulless will dare to attack us." She finishes, a look of determination on her face.

Then we hear it.

A long slow howl rings through the night and the crowd freezes. We are under attack.

Chapter 25 – First Attack

The familiar howl ends as multiple pairs of red eyes appear from the forest, the stench of death and decay reaching the ceremony grounds. Days of being in hiding while I searched for these Soulless bands and nothing turned up. Only now do they decide to show up on a day meant for celebrating.

"Lace, link the Omegas and have them and all the children and those too weak to fight hide in the safe rooms. Mika, call the Warriors on duty and make sure they get those out to safety." I order, rushing to my feet and kicking off the strappy heels that Lace forced me to wear. At least the stilettos will make a great weapon.

I watch the Soulless stumbling in as if their limbs are being controlled like marionettes, waiting for an opening to attack and I see it, the first wolf in the middle is leading the pack, his blood red eyes tinted with black. He is the leader. Taking aim, I throw the first stiletto, happy as the sharp thin heel imbeds itself into the right eye of this wolf and smiling when he howls in agony, blood seeping out from the wound I inflicted.

"Everyone, shift!" I shout, the sounds of clothes tearing and bones breaking with both Hidden Claws and Silver Crystal Crescent wolves allowing their fur forms to come forward while I focus on slowing down the Soulless.

Deciding to stay back until absolutely necessary, I close my eyes and breathe, allowing the light of the moon to seep into me while I feel for the weaker of the Soulless with my powers. If I can take them out, the rest can focus on attacking in pairs.

Pinpointing the weaklings, I open my eyes that are now glowing silver, and suck the air from their lungs, giving each wolf a quick death and praying for their souls to find peace. The Goddess of Reincarnation will have a field day tonight with the souls we will be sending her way. With the weaklings gone, I feel the earth beneath my bare feet, feeling for the Soulless movements as a battle commences before me.

Wolves from both Lace's and my pack work together as a team, each taking turns and tag-teaming the Soulless. Some have problems as these somewhat intelligent Soulless group together, fighting back and injuring our wolves. Quickly, I make walls, separating the two-on-one fights, making it easier for the pack wolves to take down the Soulless one at a time, but soon my power becomes nearly spent as I reach my limit.

"Are your wolves safe?" I ask Lace, seeing the Alpha nod.

"Many are in the pack house. The rest are in their own safe rooms." She answers, giving me all the information I need before destroying the walls around the Soulless and focusing on creating a barrier around the pack house. No one deserves to die at the hands of these feral wolves.

[Geminie, behind you!] Ariven links frantically just in time for me to dodge as black dirty fur crashes in the spot I just vacated, the stench of death strong as black blood drips from the wolf with a wounded eye.

Recognizing the wolf I injured earlier, I shift without hesitation, rushing the wolf as he climbs to his paws just in time to swipe my paw across his face, claws tearing into his flesh and tearing out his other eye. Now blinded and bleeding and his face covered in the tar colour blood, the Alpha wolf before me howls in anger and pain, rushing around trying to find me. I stay a few feet away, waiting for the right time to strike. The wolf trips on a chair from the ceremony, tumbling to the ground with his neck exposed and I take the opportunity to pounce, my fangs tearing into the soft flesh and ripping his jugular open.

My white fur is now stained with the stench of Soulless blood, forcing me to fight back the vomit that wants to spew forth. I still have more wolves to kill. A searing pain in my right side alerts me to a small Soulless that injured me and who is quick to back away, their movements silent and precise, making me question if this wolf used to be a Tracker, and a high-ranking one at that. Ready to chase this wolf, I take one step and realize the searing pain has multiplied as if hundreds of knives have been inserted into my skin, with little, tiny cuts. I hold back a howl of my own; I've been poisoned, and I am pissed. Fires erupts from my wound, neutralizing the poison, and the pain dulls within seconds, my body regaining movement.

Fear radiates off the small wolf who had snuck up on me as it turns towards the fighting, intent on running away. Unfortunately for them, they pissed off the wrong wolf. Each step I take leaves a singed paw print in the grass until I am close enough to engulf the small wolf in flames emanating from my body, the wolf turning to ash with instant death.

Now in survival mode, I attack any wolf who smells like death and decay, watching bodies drop and turn to ash until that familiar, long, slow howl resounds through the night. As if by magic, the remaining Soulless retreat from the pack house grounds, with wolves in pursuit, but I stand still, fear taking over. He is back. The source of many nightmares and fear has returned. And if I am correct, he is the leader of the Soulless.

"Geminie, the Soulless are gone. You can put out your flames." A voice calls out. I growl in warning, ears flattening against my head as I watch a hand be burned by my flames, and a scream is heard. The owner of the hand rushes to where a small pond waits.

"What the hell is wrong with her?!" Comes the shout of the angry person who has been burned. I growl again, slinking low to the ground. I have to protect myself.

"Something spooked her. She is protecting herself with her flames. I have only seen this once when someone tried to rape her while drunk." A deeper voice answers as a blurry silhouette appears in front of me.

"I am her mate; there is no need to protect herself from me!" The first voice retorts. Something inside me want to burn him some more, but the second voice chimes in.

"Some mate. Everyone abused her for years because your Beta decided to get revenge on the Moon Goddess and got your parents killed for their stupidity." This man is angry on my behalf, and instinct tells me to trust him. My flames dampen slightly, the thought of hurting this person bringing me a bit of pain as I whimper slightly.

"Hi, darling, you're safe now." His voice is low as the person before me takes a seat on the grass, his posture non-threatening. I growl, though, not wanting to remove my protection from my body.

"No need to be afraid. I am here to protect you, Geminie." Ariven's voice registers in my mind, my animalistic side calming down, and the flames open a small passageway. A hand enters, palm up in surrender as it nears me, until the tips of his fingers caress my fur. His familiar and calming scent surrounds my body, the flames going out as if blowing out a candle, and I soon find myself curled in his lap, my body shifting from wolf to human, and I cling onto his arm.

"You okay, darling?" Ariven asks, holding me tightly to him as he plants a kiss on my temple.

"No." Is my whispered reply, my eyes tightly shut while I focus on breathing and calming down.

"Want to talk about it?" His hand is drawing soothing circles on my back, and the tension in my body melts away.

"Not yet." He sighs, one of worry and not exasperation, and lifts me bridal style into his arms. I feel his steady heartbeat and listen to his breathing as he walks away from the mess in front of the pack house and towards the guest house when Mika calls out suddenly.

"Gem, that was Him, wasn't it?" He asks, causing me to look my ex in the eye and nod slowly. A look of worry crosses Mika's face as a member of my pack helps to put ointment onto his burned skin. He looks at the moon for a moment, Ariven looking between us with a questioning brow.

"Make sure Ariven is with you at all times. If he's back, something bad is about to happen." I just nod after Mika finishes saying his piece, and Ariven continues his walk to the guest house. I needed to feel safer than I currently am, needed to hide away from view for a moment and just feel like a weak, young adult. I need my home again.

Chapter 26 – Memories

"Geminie, are you okay in there?" Ariven's voice calls out but I stay silent. Sitting on the floor in the bathtub, I allow the warm water to fall onto my shivering body from the shower above. I feel cold, not from the warm air but from the fear still coursing through me. All I can think about is my fourteenth birthday, a day that killed the innocence inside me.

The water stops and strong arms lift me from my siting position, wrapping me in a large soft and fluffy towel as Ariven's scent fills me.

"It's okay, darling. No one can hurt you." He whispers, his hands slowly rubbing my back. We sit on the bathroom floor, my body shaking while clinging to his now damp shirt and fighting back the tears threatening to spill. Ice-blue eyes hunt me in my mind, eyes that held pleasure and greed inside them.

"No one can hurt you Geminie, not with me here." Ariven reassures, tucking my head under his chin not caring for my dripping wet hair. Finally, the tears spill and I sob into his shoulder, Ariven holding me tighter and humming a lullaby while the fear inside me runs it's course.

"Talk to me, baby. I can't help if you stay silent, love." He pleads, the worry and hurt evident in his voice. I couldn't hold it in any longer, the secret that only five people know about.

"I'm not pure." I choke out, more tears flowing from my eyes.

"Bastian set me up, and... and I was raped." This comes out as a whisper. Ariven's body goes stiff before he pulls me tighter to him, his arms keeping me in a protective cocoon while I delve into what happened.

♦♦♦

"Excuse me, Beta, but where are we going?" I ask, turning from looking at the trees passing by us to look at the man beside me. I thought that today would be just like usual: wake up, get dressed, do chores, and go to bed.

Instead, I was surprised when I opened my bedroom door in the attic to see Beta Bastian in front of me, the father who disowned me, holding a pink gift bag in hand as he gives me a small smile.

Hope of being his daughter and a Beta once more fills me when he handed me the bag and tells me to change into the gift inside. After agreeing and opening the bag, I found a beautiful, baby blue sundress that fit me perfectly, my slowly maturing body accentuated by the soft cotton and lace. From there, I left with the Beta and have been driving to the "surprise" he mentioned earlier this morning.

The car turns down a side road, slowing down as trees become sparse and a field of wild flowers come into view. Worry creeps into me, this being neutral territory and Rogues are around meaning an attack is possible. But the view of the flowers reassure me that no one else is here. So what were we doing here?

"Geminie." Beta Bastian calls out putting the car in park and giving me a smile, one that sends shivers down my spine. "You are here to pay off a debt I owe to a Rogue." My seat belt is unbuckled as he talks, the uneasy feeling creeping inside me once more.

"He asked for a plaything, a female plaything. All you have to do is make it to the pack house. If you make it there before he catches you, the debt is paid. If he catches you, the debt is still paid but he can spend the rest of the day doing whatever he wants with you." Realization hits me at what Bastian has done. He is using me to satisfy some depraved Rogue's desires in order to escape a debt owed to said Rogue. I am just a means to an end.

"Oh, and happy birthday, bitch." Beta Bastian finishes, the door being opened and my body being pushed out of the Jeep and sprawled onto the floor. I don't even have time to get up and beg to be let back in before Beta Bastian shifts into gear and rushes off, the tires leaving a deep groove in the wildflower field.

"Yeah, happy birthday to me." I mutter sarcastically, standing and dusting off the dress I'm wearing. It all makes sense why I would receive a brand new dress, when normally Omegas receive hand-me-downs of clothes donated to charity from the human churches. None of us had received anything new since the Blakes took control as they wait for Mika to become of age. Deciding not to dwell on the negative and stay in the same spot, I retrieve my phone from the only pocket of the dress, grateful that Alex pays in secret for the bill, and google search the general direction of the pack house. With a groan, I learn I have a four-hour walk ahead of me.

"Better get to walking." I grumble, heading west toward the direction of the pack. The forest is filled with the chitter of birds and rustling of leaves, the noise calming me down as I try not to think of the possibility of Rogues and Soulless in the area, waiting to ambush easy prey. I am happy that I had worn a pair of white sneakers and not heels as the trek is rough with many roots above the ground.

Every so often, I check my phone, making sure I am heading in the right direction and seeing just how much time has passed. By now, I am tired and thirsty, in need of an ice-cold glass of water. With only one and a half hours to go, I power through, intending to make it to the safety of the pack lines before I rest.

Snap.

The sound of twigs breaking behind me stops me mid-step. The forest is silent as I had not registered the change, being too focused with returning to Hidden Claws. The wind blows from behind me, carrying the stench of a wolf mixed with decay. A Rogue that has yet to turn into a Soulless.

"Hello, little prey." A voice calls out from the trees, echoing around me, making it hard to pinpoint where the Rogue is.

"Beta Bastian says you are to pay the debt owed to me anyway I see fit if I can catch you." He chuckles maniacally. Fear wraps a tight grip around me, knowing now that what the Beta said was the truth. He owed a debt, and I would be the payment one way or another. I shudder, trying not to think about what can happen to me if I am caught.

Without hesitation, I bolt, running towards the direction of the pack lines weaving through trees and running through streams, in the hope of losing the wolf behind me. I try every trick Alex taught me on how to mask my scent, even running through a patch of flowers and rubbing the petals on my skin in order to do my best to run away undetected.

A hum of energy calls to me after time has passed, my legs sore from the exertion, and my body weak from lack of food and water. I am close to my so-called home. Only a few feet left, and I will be safe.

A shadow jumps into my path, forcing me to stop, with a large grey wolf with ice-blue eyes staring back at me. The wolf soon shifts and a naked man that looks to be in his twenties sends me a repulsive smile, his eyes roving over my body. Licking his lips, the man slowly stalks towards me, his blood humming with power, indicating he is or was an Alpha.

"Thanks for the chase, lovely prey, but now I am ready to get what is owed to me." His voice is full of charm, but all I feel is fear. My tired, sore legs refuse to move, but even if I can run, I realize that this wolf has been watching me since Beta Bastian dropped me off. I never once lost him. Before I know it, I am thrown to the ground, the naked wolf above me ripping my new dress to shreds while his lips kiss every inch of my skin. As promised by the Beta, I paid a debt that day and had so much stolen from me by the Rogue wolf.

◆◆◆

"Mika found me that night curled in a ball sobbing. He was on patrol that day and smelt the Rogue, his scent everywhere, including on and inside me." I mumble, exhaustion taking over my body. Soft kisses are placed on my temple, and I register the fact that I am curled in bed with Ariven wrapped around me, a soft blanket covering us.

"I'm sorry you had to go through that, Geminie." My friend whispers, wiping away stray tears from my face. The fear has faded, finally able to talk to someone I trust about this night and why I hate my birthday so much.

"He carried me to the pack doctor, getting a rape test done and my statement about what happened. It was the first time I saw him furious with Bastian." I add, thinking back to the nights I spent in the hospitals. The times a nurse would wake me from a nightmare and hold me while I sobbed and the pain I felt for days on end. I never want to go through that pain again.

"I hate to ask this, but do you think that this Rogue has anything to do with the Soulless?" He asks quietly. I pause to think about Ariven's question, but the answer is obvious, so obvious that I'm mad I did not think about it myself.

"If Lupus is here, then it is safe to say he is the Leader of the Soulless and the enemy we have to worry about."

Chapter 27 – Acceptance

"Darling. It's time to wake up." I groan, the warmth of the bed too tempting to get up as I snuggle deeper under the blanket with an amused, deep chuckle coming from behind me. Strong arms wrap around my waist, pulling me closer to a familiar body.

"Come on Gem, we promised Lace to train the wolves of Hidden Claws today." Ariven's voice registers in my mind. I sigh, turning in his arms to snuggle closer to him, my mind still a sleep-filled haze. Last night was exhausting between the attack from the Soulless, to the memories of being raped by Lupus surfacing, and crying as I explain my past to Ariven. Fingers run through my hair, lulling me in and out of sleep as my face is buried into the crook of his neck.

"Geminie, you're naked." I bolt awake with the statement, making sure to cover myself for a moment with Ariven clutching his stomach, laughing so hard at my brief moment of panic.

"C'mon, Gem; it's not the first time you've been naked in my arms." He teases, sitting up and tucking a strand of hair behind my ear.

"I get that, but usually I wear my shorts and tank top. Why am I naked?" My question comes out in confusion, wondering what happened after the talk with Ariven.

"You cried yourself to sleep as we talked, and every time I tried to set you down, you wouldn't let go. So I couldn't help you dress." Ariven answers calmly, moving closer and pulling me into his lap. His eyes stare into mine, the forest-green that I adore so much reflecting my image back as he leans closer to me.

Eyes searching for permission, Ariven stops moving, our lips inches away from one another. I nod my head slightly, my breath hitching and heart beating in anticipation until, finally, he connects our lips together. The kiss is slow but not so gentle. I can feel him claiming me in a way that makes me blush and my stomach flutter. I want him.

The kiss is ended prematurely with the door to our room being swung opened, Maddie and Matt strolling in with easy going grins. These twins are going to be the bane of my existence.

"Hey—" Maddie begins, trailing off as she notices the glare I send her and her brother.

"Were we, uh, interrupting something?" Matt asks, just as clueless as his sister. I growl in frustration, not liking being interrupted and couldn't wait to be back home in my own cabin with locks and wards created by Lizaria. I need to remind her to make one specifically for keeping the twins out.

"Every time with you two!" I growl, Ariven chuckling as he pulls me tighter to him.

"Don't you two ever know how to mind link?!" I ask with another growl.

[We do—] Maddie starts.

[—But we like to annoy you.] Matt finishes. Without hesitation, I send the twins out with a gust of wind, making sure they slam into the wall across the room not so gently and that the door is slammed shut and locked. This won't keep them out, but it will definitely give them a scare and me some peace of mind for the time being.

"Why did we let them into the pack two years ago?" I ask, leaning into Ariven and letting out an annoyed sigh.

"Because you are soft-hearted and wanted to protect them from the Rogue pack that was hunting them down." Ariven retorts, slipping a finger under my chin and moving closer to my lips. "Now, where were we?" His voice is husky, his lips returning to mine as my hands snake into his long hair. His strong arms hold me tight, protective, and possessive all in one. I shiver when he nips at my bottom lips, his tongue sliding in without hesitation until I let out a small moan. A moment passes and he pulls away, the kiss leaving both of us breathless.

"I think I need a cold shower." He groans, pressing his forehead to mine. A swift kiss is planted on my forehead and I am gently removed from his lap and placed on the bed. As Ariven gets up, keeping the front of his body turned away from me. I reach for his hand and stop him from walking away.

"Riv," I call out quietly, looking down at the floor.

"Could... Could we go on a-"

"Yes, darling, we can go on a date." He answers before I can finish asking. Once again, my head is lifted as a chaste kiss is planted on my lips, my face feeling hot, and I just know I'm as red as a tomato.

"Now, I'm going to shower. You get changed and be ready to go for training." He mock orders me. I nod, not trusting myself to speak, while Ariven walks into the bathroom, the door closing then followed by the spray of water. I sigh, deciding that Ariven is right and that I need to get up and ready myself for the day. I did promise Lace to train her wolves and get them up to par with the Soulless pack that is constantly growing.

Leaving the warmth of the bed, I walk to the closet and take out a black sports bra and leggings, changing into them before searching for my sneakers. The door to the bathroom opens behind me, a cloud of steam rushing out.

"Hey, have you seen my sneake-" I start asking, pausing as I turn towards Ariven walking out with a towel hung loosely around his hips, drops of water snaking down his well-toned body.

"I think I saw them downstairs." He answers, chuckling as he catches my expression.

"See something you like, darling?" His voice is a seductive purr that has me blushing and looking away quickly.

"I'll see you downstairs." I mumble, ignoring his playful demeanour and rushing out the bedroom door with his laughter echoing behind me.

◆◆◆

Waiting for everyone to arrive to the training grounds, Lace and I decide to talk about the alliance treaty I plan to sign before leaving. Both of us promise to be there for each other not only as allies, but also as friends.

"I'm happy you came back, Gem, even if it was to help make Hidden Claws strong again." Lace whispers, and I smile.

"To be honest, if Ariven had told me we were coming here, I would have denied any help and let this pack rot. He was right that coming here would help me heal." I state honestly, seeing the understanding look that Lace shoots my way. I know she would not have blamed me for not helping, and I am grateful for that. I might have even offered her a place in my pack had I not helped, and she came looking for me, apologizing and explaining her side.

"Looks like everyone is here." I change the subject so that we can focus on training as Mika arrives last.

"What took you so long?" Lace asks, and Mika just sighs.

"Long story short, Gem's dad scares me." Mika answers, and I chuckle. My father linked me as soon as he arrived at Hidden Claws, finally free from pack duties, to make his way down here with some Warriors to take care of the Blakes this morning. I had a feeling he would be speaking to Mika before I see any signs of him.

"What did he do?" I ask out of curiosity, watching Mika shiver with fear for a moment.

"I don't want to talk about it." He mumbles and looks away. I guess Mika had a front-row seat of just the type of torture tactics my father can perform on wolves, considering the Blakes are traitors to the Goddess and the Crown. Deciding to drop the subject, I lead the siblings towards the group of wolves going through the warm-up stretch Ariven is leading and motion for them to stop.

"Okay, wolves, the last few days of me being here has been spent analyzing how you all train and to be honest, you all could use some work." I call out, waiting for everyone to stand to attention before I continue, watching a few eager faces brighten up at the prospect of being properly trained.

"Many of you might remember, I was once a member of this pack. As such, I remember the days Alpha Sorus and Luna Reena had everyone run twenty miles." I see the look of dread on their faces and internally groan.

"I also know that when the Blakes took over, they stopped this. This means the majority of you are out of shape." A look of guilt washes across the group in front of me, and I know my words are true. Great, I have even more work ahead of me.

"So, I am going to go easy on all of you. Since the youngest of this group is sixteen and just starting to really focus on training, you all will run ten miles, and after a quick break, we will go into hand-to-hand practice. Lace and I will be looking to see whom we can trust to train the pups ages ten to fifteen, so work hard and know a promotion is up for grabs." I continue, seeing a look of relief and confusion on the Hidden Claws pack faces. A she-wolf with curly red hair tied into a bun raises her hand.

"Yes?" I ask, allowing her to speak.

"Why do we have to train the pups?" She asks. I motion for Lace to answer.

"Because we want every wolf to know basic defense. With the Soulless population on the rise, knowing defense can turn the tide in any fight and give the pups enough time until help can arrive." Hushed conversations arise after the answer is given, some agreeing to pups training, some thinking they are too young. I roll my eyes, ready to cut in and get training going, but Ariven beats me to it.

"The reason why Silver Crystal Crescent was able to grow so fast is because everyone is trained from the age of five. We make games for the pups to enjoy that help to improve their small bodies. It is beneficial to their health overall and makes transitioning to regular training easier." His statement cuts the conversations short, and I smile, ready to start the training for the day.

"So, just a few rules before we start the run. One, no shifting into wolf form. We want to train your human side to be just as strong as your wolf. Two, anyone who shifts will have to perform one-hundred suicides after being injected with a small dose of Wolfsbane." A collective groan goes through the crowd, and I chuckle. Suicides suck. Suicides while weak with Wolfsbane suck even worse.

"Geminie will be in wolf form as we expect your human form to be able to keep up with a wolf. Of course, she won't be going too fast, but will be running and trying to keep the pace similar to a Soulless on the verge of death." Lace cuts in making me I smile before I run behind a large tree while Lace continues to explain everything included in todays training to her pack. I quickly remove my clothes, folding and storing them in a water proof bin then shift into my wolf form. As usual, the tuft of fur keeps falling into my face and I growl in frustration as I trot from my hiding spot toward Ariven.

The crowd gasps in surprise as the sun reflects off of my fur, the prism-colour caused by sunlight shimmering with the silver stars on my body. Ignoring the awestruck stares, especially the one from Mika, I paw at Ariven's pocket and shake my head, indicating the fur blocking my eyes is annoying me. He chuckles and reaches into his pocket, revealing two hair clips when he pulls his hand back out.

Bending down, he helps to pin my fur back, and I am able to see properly without fur in my face.

"Come on, guys, we all saw her wolf last night during the fight." Mika growls, stopping his pack from continuing to talk about me. I roll my eyes, deciding now is a good time to start the run and trot off down a route that will be challenging for a ten-mile run.

"And that's our cue to run!" Ariven calls out, the sound of the group running being heard behind me makes me run faster to really test theses wolves' limits.

Chapter 28 – Unexpected Hot Training

"I think you're trying to kill us!" A she-wolf calls out. Looking over my shoulder, I spy a petite brunette trying her best to keep up with me, her face flushed with exhaustion. I search through my memories and finally place her as Lena, a she-wolf whose mother was the second-in-command to the Trackers in the pack. I remembered the days she would push me into lockers downstairs and ruin my homework. She caused many headaches and is the reason I had to make duplicates of my work.

I huff out a breath, wanting to get a bit of petty revenge and pretend to ignore her, picking up speed and making sure she stayed just far enough behind.

"I... I'm s... sorry Gem... inie..." She huffs, the strain evident in her voice. She manages to keep up with me, my indifference falling as my ears point in her direction. Slowing down my pace, I allow the she-wolf to catch her breath while my packmates call out through the link that some of the Hidden Claws wolves have passed out.

"I was... A bitch to you. You didn't deserve it." Lena continues. I nod, agreeing to her statement and noticing her breath evening out. She is definitely a strong wolf and a good candidate to train the pups. I slow down a little more while we continue the rest of the run in silence, my hostile pettiness gone now.

Finally, the starting point comes into view and a sigh of relief is heard from the she-wolf beside me. We turn to look at each other in union, a grin on her face as we nod, a silent agreement to race to the end. Wolf against human, the two of us push ourselves to the limit, each pulling ahead of the other every so often. The wind rushing through my fur makes me feel like I'm flying, and I relish in the challenge that Lena provides. Her human form is strong, not surprising, as her mother most likely trained her to be a top-notch Tracker.

The run soon ends with Lena and I crossing the boundary into the training field at the same time, the race between us a draw. I watch Lena fall to the ground, gasping for breath, her face red and sweat dripping down her skin. Chuckling as best a wolf can, I trot to where my clothes are stored and shift, putting my clothes on swiftly and walking towards Lena, stopping once to grab a few water bottles from the cooler.

"Apology accepted, Lena." I call out, the she-wolf sitting up at the sound of my voice, just in time to catch a bottle of water I throw her way.

"Really?" Shocked and confused, Lena takes a moment to look at me with scepticism. I chuckle, coming to sit beside her and taking a sip of cool water.

"Yeah, really. You gave me a sincere apology and you are a strong wolf. Lace needs that in her pack." I answer, watching her take greedy gulps of her own water and accepting the second one I hand her way once she finishes the first.

"You're stronger than I realized." She admits, and I smile, thinking back to the nights Lizaria would train me.

"Thanks. I had some help training as a pup, to be honest." I see her questioning gaze but choose to ignore it, deciding to stretch and wait for the wolves to trickle in from the run. Lace is the first wolf I see, her body flushed and dripping in sweat as she runs over to Lena and me, accepting a water bottle.

"Goddess, I need to run more!" She groans, flopping to the ground, and I laugh at her dramatic action.

"If it makes you feel better, you're just behind Lena here." I state, Lace looking to Lena with hopeful eyes.

"Care to jog with me every night so I can get better?" The Alpha Female asks to which Lena smiles back.

"Of course. I could use a running friend since my mother retired."

"Speaking of which, the position of Head Tracker is yours if you want it." Lace proposes, and Lena happily accepts without hesitation. The three of us stretch, waiting for more wolves to join.

Every so often, groups of three to five will come, barely walking in, their bodies slumped over and covered in sweat as both males and females collapse to the ground, some catching their breath and some passing out. I sigh, realizing just how much work needs to be done for these wolves to be able to keep up with my own pack. Finally, Mika comes trailing in with Ariven behind him giving me a hopeless look.

He'll need extra training to be a top Alpha again.

"New rule." I call out after twenty minutes of resting.

"We will have two training shifts, at ten in the morning and six in the afternoon." The crowd groans at my words, their bodies slumping at the thought of more running. I chuckle, looking to Lace in amusement as she growls at her wolves, happy to see her keep them in check.

"You will all be split into two groups. Group A will run in the morning while group B patrols and protects the pack, then Group A will patrol in the night while Group B runs. Each run will be ten miles, and as your stamina and strength improve, we will increase the intensity by two miles. The first group to run twenty miles will receive one thousand dollars per group member." I continue, seeing excitement run through the exhausted wolves at the prospect of a challenge and a real prize at the end. I have a feeling this will encourage them all.

"Mika will be the leader of Group A, and Lace will be the leader of Group B. You are allowed to run and train on your own time if you so choose, but no one will be allowed to do that in wolf form. Leaders, choose your teams." I motion for Lace and Mika to take control as they pick their team members one by one, with Lace on the left and Mika on the right. I had to train both the Alpha pups and make sure Lace and Mika can get along with the change in leadership and Lace being the new Alpha. I know she wants to make her brother her Beta, as Mika had made her his, but with his strength, he barely even qualified as a Hunter or Warrior. His running wouldn't even allow him to be a Tracker. With the teams chosen, I am not surprised to see Lena beside Lace, the she-wolf a good fit for the team. Mika chose many strong wolves and Lace chose the weaker ones, which interested me. I know Lace see potential in these wolves while I have a feeling Mika just wants to win. Unfortunately for him, the strong wolves will need the most help in stamina while Lace's wolves will need help in strength training.

"Okay, so to keep things even, we will be working in teams. This challenge will be to see just how strong each team can become within a short amount of time." I begin to explain, noticing at how evenly split the teams are and surprised Mika did not choose all the wolves he was once friendly with. I can see he is thinking with his brain for once.

"So, within your teams, partner up and we will go through a few exercises for you all to try. One will be an attacker and one a defender." I continue, motioning for Maddie and Matt to demonstrate the hand-to-hand combat we will be working on. Once the demonstrations were done, with Matt sporting a new black eye, I allow the wolves of Hidden Claws to break into their groups of two as they work hard.

Lace and Lena each separate and pair with two weaker wolves, allowing the wolves to practice on them first while Mika pairs with a strong Warrior on his team. I can't help but smile. The Hidden Claws wolves showing me respect as a fellow wolf while accepting my help in growing strong once again is something I never thought possible.

"What's with the smile, darling?" Ariven's voice comes from behind, his hands massaging my stiff shoulders. Tingles crawl along my skin, and I chalk it up to goosebumps from the contact after a long run.

"I'm happy. Our wolves are getting along with Hidden Claws, we have a new ally, and I can put the past behind me." I answer, leaning into his chest as Ariven chuckles and wraps his arms around me. I watch Leery, one of my Trackers, walk up to a wolf in Mika's team. She helps correct his defensive stance and waits to see the results as the wolf's partner attacks. In the end, the wolf she helps throws his partner to the ground and gives a triumphant cheer.

"Thank you for making me accept this job, Riv." My smile widens as a kiss is placed on top of my head, the two of us silently watching the wolves before us train.

Slowly, my body begins to heat up, so I suggest we go stand under the tree where we can observe the group and see where we can improve training but nothing helps. After downing my tenth ice-cold water bottle, realization strikes me like a bolt of lightning as to why my body is heating up. Mother had reassured me that until I met my second-chance mate, I would not go into heat. I could be free of the pain that not being around your mate can cause while in heat and looked forward to not having it for a while. Right now, though, the signs were as clear as day. I can feel the one spot between my legs throb, my body heating up as I start to pant.

"Ariven." I call out meekly, clinging to the tree, waiting for my Theta to return with more water.

"Gem, are you okay?" A moment later, I hear the sweetest voice that chills my body slightly, and I sigh. I feel my body slide along the tree as my knees grow weak. Loud thumps on the ground are followed by strong arms scooping me up and close to a solid chest, the contact forcing my hot body to cool once more, and I sigh in relief.

"Gem— Fuck!" A deep breath takes in my scent followed by a possessive growl. I turn to see male wolves slowly walking near me, their eyes glazed over from the pheromones secreting off of me. The scent of lust is in the air and I groan, my heat flaring up one again.

"Training is over, now!" Ariven growls out, forcing the unmated wolves to cower and back away from his possessive growl as his hold on me tightens.

"We'll hold them back, get our Alpha to safety." Matt calls out somewhere in the crowd. Ariven takes off, him mumbling where to go and I open the link.

[Go straight.] I state, my mind turning hazy. I share the pathway to the Hidden Valley, having Ariven run through the streams and river to hide our scent and dunk me in the cold fall water every so often to ease the pain of the heat. Soon, I hear the rushing of the waterfall, Ariven taking the tunnel until the scent of the familiar Hidden Valley hits me. My body is placed on a soft bed of grass, Ariven laying on top of me with a very noticeable erection pressed to my thigh as his lips crash onto mine in a passionate and possessive kiss.

"Mine." He growls before his tongue delves into my mouth and battles mine in a dominant dance of passion.

Chapter 29 – Claiming a Second Chance

I think back to the time Ariven and I got drunk as his lips continue to move against mine and small moans escape us. We were having a heart-to-heart talk as I explained my rejection, how I couldn't wait for the bond with Mika and I to break to find my second chance.

For Ariven, his mate was taken from him just after the two found out they were expecting their first pup. A jealous packmate shot her with a silver bullet, wanting Ariven for herself. He went mad, destroying that she-wolf in seconds before the devastating grief took hold of him. He ended up a Rogue and leaving to the Temple of The Goddess without any consequences for killing the she-wolf that murdered his mate and unborn pup in cold blood.

"Your mind is straying, my darling." He whispers in my ear, bringing me from my thoughts with his husky lust-filled voice. I blush, his hand grasping my curly hair and tugging on the strands gently to expose my neck, where he takes a deep breath inhaling my scent and lightly licks from my collarbone to my ear.

A moan leaves my lips, and I wrap my legs around his waist, grinding into him and gaining the sweet sound of his own long groan of pleasure. Our hands work fast until both of us are lying in the tall grass naked, skin to skin as we kiss and explore every inch of each other. His lips return to mine, one hand holding my head as his tongue is once again claiming my mouth while the other slowly runs along my skin causing the heat to burst into a ball of flames instead of cooling. I couldn't take the teasing much long.

"Geminie?" He asks, gasping for breath after our kiss ends, leaving small pecks along my neck and jawline.

"Mate me, please. I can't take it anymore." I beg, grinding into his hard cock and feeling his tip at the entrance of my soaking wet pussy. His free hand is placed on my abdomen, stopping me from moving and making me whimper with the loss of friction.

"Are you sure, darling?" He asks, his hot breath caressing my collarbone where he gently nips my skin.

"Yes, Ariven." My answer is followed by a moan as I feel his hand slide down my skin, and a finger is gently inserted into me, moving slowly around my soaking wet pussy.

"Please! Mate me, mark me. Just make me yours!" I pant, grinding into his hand as his lips kiss me once more.

"Just remember, once you're mine, I am never letting go!" He states, and I nod in understanding, wanting nothing more than him, my best friend, my trusted pack member, and now my Mate.

Ariven smirks, kissing me one more time before his lips trail down to my breast, taking his time to suck and bite on my nipples while he inserts another finger inside me stretching me. I cry out his name, my body shivering wanting more than just his touch while he leaves a trail of kisses and bite marks. With a pop, his fingers leave my insides, but before I can miss the feeling of being filled, his mouth is at my entrance, tongue lapping up my cum and massaging my pussy.

With hands on my hips, Ariven keeps me from moving, from grinding into his face as he takes his time savouring me. My body heats up, mind going blank with nothing but pleasure and the need to mate until I feel my lower half clench and I scream out Ariven's name once more.

Coming down from my high of pleasure, I notice Ariven positioned above me, my legs around his waist with the tip of his cock pressed to my entrance, a smirk on that face of his.

"It's time to make you mine, darling Geminie." He whispers, lowering his face to mine where I smell myself on his breath. I gasp as he enters me, the feeling of his cock against my walls making me shiver. My arms reach around his neck and I cling to him. Our lips find one another, tasting the sweetness of my cum on his tongue as moans and the sounds of him thrusting in and out of me fill the air. I can feel the tightening of my abdomen once more, feeling myself getting to the verge of release while I grind in rhythm to Ariven's thrusts until his lips leave mine and trail along my neck and collarbone.

His canines graze my sensitive, heated skin. I know he is in search of placing his mark.

"I can feel your body getting ready, baby girl." He moans, his thrusts getting hard and faster. My answer is a long moan while tilting my head to the side, giving him easier access to my neck, his lips finding a spot just at the base of my neck just before my collar bone where he nips the skin gently. A gasp of pleasure is forced from my mouth. The feeling of relief is ready to spill over and I cling to my mate, our bodies heated and sweaty.

"Come for me, Geminie, and let me make you mine." He moans out an order, his teeth nipping where my mark will be. My mind goes blank, my legs tightening around his waist as my pussy squeezes his cock. I come as ordered, his teeth grazing my skin, and as he sinks them into me, I feel him stiffen above me, and his cock throbs inside, releasing himself inside me just as my body goes limp and I fall asleep.

Chapter 30 – Hot Spring Catch-Up

The sensation of fingers drawing soft circles on my skin wakes me from my deep sleep. My naked body is pressed against another, their scent wrapping around me, making me feel safe and secure. I sigh happily, snuggling closer to Ariven as he chuckles, placing a soft kiss on my forehead.

"Good morning, darling." He whispers, his hand moving from drawing circles on my skin to running through my hair. "Good morning, handsome." I reply with a yawn, opening my eyes to find my mate staring back at me. The early morning breeze brings the scent of wildflowers to me, reminding me that we spent the last week hidden away from my wolves and Hidden Claws, lost in the pleasure the heat brought.

My body is sore, my neck slightly throbbing from being teased and bitten where my mark is, as Ariven and I claimed each other day after day. The hunger the heat brought felt stronger than ones experienced in the past, and the only theory I have is because my mate is beside me this time, able to help quench the fire running through my veins.

"How are you feeling today?" I yawn again as Ariven asks his question, seeing his easy-going smile as his fingers trail to his mark on my neck, making me shiver slightly.

"Sore and tired. I'm not sure I can walk to the guest house." I answer, turning onto my back and stretching to see which spots on my body were the worst.

"I saw a hot spring nearby that we can soak in if you'd like." I smile at the idea, agreeing instantly to this idea and asking Ariven to carry me there. I have a feeling that if I try to stand my knees will buckle and I will fall to the ground like a newborn deer trying to walk for the first time.

As I'm happily snuggled in his arms, Ariven informs me that during the last seven days when I was in my heat-filled haze he would hold me while I slept and link with Lace, Mika, Maddie, and Matt. The twins supervised training making sure everyone abided by the rules, and Lace's team managed to increase their strength and stamina the fastest, but Mika and his team also were able to run the ten miles without passing out now.

Pride swells inside me at the leadership the siblings have been able to prove, knowing that Lace is prioritizing her team's time with training and working on their weak spots while Mika focuses on his team's stamina and endurance. I can see these two returning Hidden Claws to its former glory in no time.

"Alex also linked me last night. His and Missy's pup was born, and Amberle came to visit them to see how they were doing handling the pack with a newborn." I smile, thinking of the new member of my family and deciding to stop on our return trip to buy a few things for the pup and Missy, knowing the she-wolf will need her coffee addiction fed and some feminine products to help get her through a few weeks.

I can't wait to go home and see my brother being so haggard with sleepless nights caused by a newborn and running a pack at the same time.

"Your dad asked to see you before he left. Maddie told him about your heat, and instead he linked me. I told him we were a little busy finishing the mate bond. I have a feeling I have an ass whooping coming my way when we go to visit him." Ariven informs me as we cuddle in the hot spring. I chuckle, knowing that my mate is correct in my father giving his new son-in-law a good ass beating when the chance arrives, and I will be front row and centre, recording it all to share with the pack and to embarrass my mate for many years to come.

"Were there any Soulless attacks on Hidden Claws while we were unreachable?" I ask, the heat from the water easing my sore muscles and making me drowsy.

"Yes, two small attacks, but they did not last long. As Lace put it, it was as if they were looking for something or someone." I frown, thinking about what the Soulless would look for, but then I freeze, jolting away from Ariven and staring at him as panic rises inside me.

"Me." I state, running a hand through my wet hair. It all makes sense why his Soulless pack would perform small attacks on Hidden Claws.

"What do you mean, you, Gem?" Ariven pulls me back to his lap, holding me tightly while I take deep breaths of his scent, his lips placing gentle kisses on my mark that help to calm me down.

"Their leader sent them to find me."

Chapter 31 – An impromptu Meeting

After realizing that Lupus is after me, Ariven and I quickly rush back to the guest house while I link for Lace, Mika, and Lena to join us in the meeting room there. After changing into clothes quickly, thanks to Maddie and Matt waiting for us just inside the building with said clothes, the four of us joined the Hidden Claws wolves right away.

"What's with the impromptu meeting?" Mika asks as soon as I enter the room, grabbing a blueberry scone on my way to take a seat.

"I'll explain later, but first, I need some details on the two small attacks while I was indisposed." My reply is straight to the point, and I look to Lena, the she-wolf looking between Mika and Ariven as my former mate gives my new mate a death glare.

"There were five wolves each time. At first, there were no signs, no scent of them. It wasn't until Lena and I were nearly on top of the first group during the end of our patrol that we noticed them outside the pack house." Lace answers after a moment of silence. I take a bite of my scone and think for a moment. The first group being near the pack house meant they were looking and scouting. Their lack of scent-

"They have a witch. Whether she is a part of the team or abducted by Lupus, the witch is helping them." I state, running a hand through my hair. This added to the complexity of the Soulless problem. Instinct tells me there is a war brewing.

"What about the second group?" Ariven asks as he hands me a mug of peppermint tea and another scone before taking a seat beside me.

"They were by the guest house. I was coming over to see how you were when I walked into the group in the forest just outside." Mika answers, looking me in the eye. I can see the hurt and pain of losing me as his mate. Honestly, it's his own fault and his own problem to deal with. He rejected me, abused me, and made my life hell. He's just lucky that he's changed, and we can build somewhat of a friendship.

"At any point in these attacks, did you see a wolf with ice-blue eyes?" I ask, looking at the three wolves in front of me. "Lace and I never saw anyone like that." Lena answers, looking at Mika.

"I did, but he took off as soon as he realized backup was coming to kill his Soulless." Mika says, and I frown.

"You saw Lupus. Every Soulless has bright red or black eyes. Ice-blue is the only rare colour I have seen in the Soulless world." I close my eyes, realizing the problem is bigger than expected, too much for just our two packs to handle. I'll have to call in some help from one of the strongest wolves I know.

"Double the patrol and look for moonstones. They will counteract the witch's magic so your pack can sense the Soulless like usual." I order, standing from my chair and making my way to the door.

"Where are you going?" Mika asks, taking a few steps forward, only to be stopped by his sister, who shakes her head in warning as Ariven steps closer to me, wary of my ex-mate.

"I am going to be calling in some backup. Trust me when I say we are going to need her with this war brewing." With my answer given, I leave the room with my thoughts in a mess. It will take her another week to join us, and hopefully, she can bring a few strong wolves with her.

Chapter 32 – A Fiery Introduction

"You are sure she is coming?" Lace asks as she, Mika, Ariven, and I relax on the steps to the pack house. I roll my eyes, leaning into Ariven and yawning. Since realizing that Lupus wants me for some unknown reason, the nightmares have been plaguing me.

"Amberle is nothing if not punctually late. She also keeps her promises and promised me she would be here today." My response is lazy, not caring to explain how Amberle operates, considering she is one wolf that scares me some days. Being a trained Tracker and Alpha as well, Amberle has been my best friend and confidant when I needed some advice. As well as being a fellow rejected, she understood the pain I went through for the last three years. Ariven's arms tighten around me, pulling me closer to him as his lips place a gentle kiss on top of my head. I smile, the sparks from our mate bond tingling along my skin.

"How will we know she is here?" Mika grinds out, his voice holding a hint of anger. I open my eyes slightly to see him glaring at Ariven, and I sigh internally. There is no use in Mika being jealous, considering he had his chance and ruined it.

"You'll know. She has this... Way of introducing herself." Ariven answers cryptically, playing with my loose curls. I can see the jealousy in Mika's eyes and the way he looks at Ariven's hands whenever my mate holds me. I can't help but egg him on even more, relishing in the touch of my mate while pissing off my ex being the perfect petty behaviour to amuse and entertain me these last eight days while training Lace's pack. Sounds of howls resound from the middle of the forest surrounding Hidden Claws, Mika's and Lace's eyes glazing over and I chuckle.

"Damnit. First Soulless, now a Rogue at our borders!" Lace curses, rushing from her seat on the steps and taking a few steps away from us.

"Where are you going?" I call out, keeping my senses open as shouts and whimpers are heard. I chuckle, imagining the chaos happening and what response I will soon be receiving from her.

"To help my pack!" Lace shouts over her shoulder as Mika stares at Ariven and I incredulously.

"Why are you so calm?" He asks anger in his voice as his body tenses and fists clench.

"Because there's no threat." Ariven retorts with a snort, his eyes keeping track of Mika's movements, ready to protect me at a moment's notice. Again, I roll my eyes and wait for the inevitable.

[Someone looks comfortable.] Amberle links me, and I smile.

[Very. Having fun?] I ask, hearing her chuckle as my confirmation. She is close, I can sense it. More screams and howls ring through the air, Mika scoffing at us as he turns to join his sister who also sends a glare our way. I get their point of wanting to protect their pack, but there is no danger as there is no Rogue loose in their pack.

"Mika, watch out!" Lace shouts just as a red, orange, and yellow blur rushes out of the trees and tackles Mika to the ground. I smile, the wind blowing through the fiery wolf's fur as Amberle holds my ex mate down, her lips pulled back in a snarl as she waits to see if the Alpha wolf below her will try anything. She is fierce and beautiful as always.

"Fire, be nice." A deep voice chides her as if a parent talking to their child, and I burst into laughter as Dominic comes out and leans against a tree. Amberle turns her head to face her mate, eyes rolling in annoyance as she looks between Mika and me.

"I don't care who he is. You still have to be nice." A rumble of disapproval is heard from my friend as she glares at her mate, another pause of silence.

"I get it, you're worried about someone you see like a baby sister, but does Gem look like she is hurting?" Dominic points to me just as instantly as Amberle turns to stare at Ariven, who is looking on in amusement, and I still in a laughing fit at this interaction. She stares for a moment, growling and snapping her attention back to Mika when he tries to move, snapping with teeth close to his face. I can sense the fear from him with Amberle keeping him held captive.

"Come on Ams, there are clothes in the bathroom, first door to the right." I manage to sputter out while my laughing fit comes to an end. She stares at Mika for a moment before slowly stepping away from him and trotting to where Ariven and I sat. Nuzzling my face, she looks between Ariven and I, then to our marks with a wolfish grin before trotting inside.

[About damn time!] She shouts into our link, making me wince and forcing it shut. If she wanted to talk, we can when she is dressed and in human form.

"So, give it to us straight. How is the defense?" Ariven asks as Dominic comes and settles beside us on the steps while we wait for his mate to return.

"Not bad, stronger than expected that's for sure. Fire did have a lot of fun wreaking havoc, though, so expect some suggestions to improve some more." He answers. Mika stands with the help of Lace, dusting himself off with an embarrassed look as he looks at Dominic questioningly.

"Dominic, Alpha of Blood Moon." He introduces with a carefree wave.

"Mika, Beta of Hidden Claws."

"Not the Alpha?" Amberle's voice cuts in as she exits the pack house and plops down beside her mate, snuggling into his side instantly.

"No, I handed the position over to someone much more suited to lead." He answers, a hint of pride in his voice. I can't help but smile, knowing that this one act of selflessness that Mika did to help grow his pack quickly.

"Who?" Dominic questions and Lace steps forward with a grin.

"Me. Lace, Alpha of Hidden Claws and Mika's little sister."

"Damn, and here I was hoping to kick Mika's ass as a bad Alpha." Amberle grumbles.

"There's still plenty of time for that." Ariven chimes in, getting a mischievous grin from the fire-haired she-wolf.

"As long as I can mess with the pack and help train them, that's all that matters. Taking care of two five-year-olds and a pack of my own can get boring." Once again, I chuckle as Lace walks past us into the pack house, with the rest of the group following. We have business to talk about before anything can be done.

Chapter 33 – Clashing Opinions

"I just want to say, thank you for coming to help." Lace starts, directing her attention to Dominic and Amberle. I see my friend beaming at the blonde Alpha Female, but Mika just has to ruin the moment by scoffing.

"What, you've got a problem with me coming to help, pup?" Amberle growls, glaring at my ex, who glares back at her. I frown, looking at Dominic, who sends me an exasperated look as we both get ready to play referee between these two.

"Yes, I have a problem! No one really asked you to be here!" Mika calls out in anger.

"Actually, I asked her to be here. Her adopted father was the one to come up with the theory of Soulless making an army, and Amberle has been researching it with the Temple of the Goddess for the last five years." I cut in calmly, raising an eyebrow and waiting for him to retort. Instead Lace gives Mika a warning look. To my surprise, he backs down and sulks in his chair.

"Sorry about that. My brother has been on edge lately." Lace sighs apologetically. Amberle shrugs it off not bothering to entertain a fight with Mika at this moment thankfully. Instead, she asks to have access to the computer where she promptly takes a USB drive from Dominic and inserts it. After opening up a few files, she turns to the five of us with a frown.

"So, as many of you may know, the Soulless problem gained our attention about six years ago. Five years ago, Forest Paw was dealing with a similar problem as Hidden Claws." She begins, pulling up a map of the nearest territories in Ontario.

"During that time, I had switched to being the Head Tracker of Blood Moon and our pack set off to help train just like Geminie did when she came here. That is when we noticed the attacks were organized as if someone was controlling them." My friend continues, pulling up notes from the meeting held at the now destroyed pack. It's been years since the mention of Forest

Paw, the pack destroyed by an organized Soulless attack days after Blood Moon pulled their support and alliance, a reminder to never turn your back on help.

"Blue, Amber's adopted father, actually came up with the theory of an army being formed. This led to us researching more attacks other than the ones from Moon Glade, Hidden Claws and Mountain Mist." Dominic chimes in. Amberle clicks a button, the map zooming out to include packs from Saskatchewan, Manitoba, and Nunavut.

"The attacks actually started in Nunavut, going after smaller packs back around one hundred years ago. The packs, being fed up, soon formed the Atuat Pack, the largest pack in Nunavut. From there, the number of Soulless decreased until there were none left in the northern part of Canada. Then comes Saskatchewan." She pauses, making sure we are following her as the map moves over to the northern part of Saskatchewan.

"Fifty years after the creation of Atuat Pack, Prairie Cloud, Creeping Trails, and Harvest Moon were facing similar organized attacks from Soulless." Confusion washes over me as I look at the trail, realizing there is a pattern, as the packs being attacked were weak, barely even holding fifty wolves.

"Amberle." I call out.

"Yes, Gem?" "Zoom out of the map and freeze the screen," I say, standing from my chair and walking towards the screen. Taking the electronic pen from the side of the screen, I ask Amberle to highlight the areas of the pack that were attacked, starting at the western part of Nunavut, and connecting each area to form a line. Looking closely, the Soulless had to cross part of the Northwest Territories to enter Saskatchewan safely without being spotted by humans. The line continues as I follow more recent attacks here in Ontario, and if I am correct, continue moving towards other packs until I reach the final one, the Royal Pack.

"What's the meaning of this?" Mika asks as I back away, the six of us staring at the screen.

"This army has been growing for years, not just one hundred years ago, if I am correct. Think Ira would have more mentions of attacks in Alaska or the Northwest Territories?" I direct my question to Ariven, my mate having lived in the Temple the longest.

"She might, I'll give her a call and see what she says." He answers, taking out his phone and moving towards the door.

"Also, ask for a list of the oldest living wolves that have connections to the Royal Pack." I instruct, watching him pause before nodding and heading into the hallway for some privacy.

"Why are you asking about the Royal Pack?" Lace questions, and I frown.

"If my hunch is correct, the Soulless Army is larger than we thought, and Lupus' end goal is the Royal Pack." I answer, a sinking feeling in the pit of my stomach. Lace suggests getting food and taking a break, the she-wolf leaving the room to towards the kitchen as Dominic's phone rings.

"Dominic speaking. Oh, Greg, you guys are here, give me a moment." He lowers his phone, directing his attention to Mika with a friendly smile.

"Think you can help me? My packmates finally arrived, and we need to know where to go."

"Yeah, we have a large guest house. Are you okay with sharing it, Gem?" Mika answers, directing the last part to me.

"Yeah, our packs are close, and I am sure the twins can't wait to torment Greg and Miles." I answer. The men soon leave after that, Dominic telling Greg to wait outside as he is on his way, while Amberle and I study the map in silence.

"Spill it." I finally state, seeing my friend fidget for a moment before letting out a long sigh and motioning me to the computer. She disconnects the computer's connection to the screen, pulling out a file from the USB drive and motioning for me to go through it.

Shock fills me as I stare at the image of a teenage girl with snow-white curls and prismatic eyes, the opposite of how I look. Her skin is fair, and a small smile plays on her lips as she stands to the side at a ball, with a tiara on her head.

"Who is this?" I asked, before noticing the necklace around her neck on a silver chain, the charm a moonstone so pure my eyes widen.

"Princess Crystalline of the Royal Pack and our future Queen. She is sixteen right now, but there is something about her that I can't place." Amberle answers, and I point to the necklace.

"She has the moonstone from the lost Princess." I state and Amberle nods, bringing up two more pictures. One is modern, of a baby holding the same necklace, while another is of a painting, one I have studied for hours as it is of the Lost Princess.

"They look so similar." I point out, seeing how the infant in both pictures has the same wispy, white hair and lively eyes, holding the moonstone and blanket wrapped around them in the same way.

"Gem, I think she is the Lost Princess."

Chapter 34 – Calling in Maverick

Lace returns quickly after Amberle and I discuss Crystalline being the Lost Princess, the true heir to the werewolf throne. Unfortunately, there is no way to know for sure, not without talking to her and having her hold the moonstone around my neck. Of course, we keep this between the two of us, wanting to discuss the topic with Mother and Ira.

After Lace and a few Omegas set the table with food and drinks, including coffee that I quickly down a cup of, much to Amberle's disgust. Dominic and Mika return followed by Ariven, a frown on his face.

"Ira says she will have to search through the archives. They have been digitizing everything to have backup copies of history, but she did confirm one thing." He states, taking my coffee from my hand and gulping down the hot liquid.

"What did she confirm?" Lace asks, worry in her voice.

"Lupus is one of the oldest wolves alive. No one knows when he appeared in Canada, but there are many pictures and paintings of him stored away. She will have everything about him sent our way soon in an email." My mate answers. A wave of unease washes over me, and I think back to the day when Alpha Sorus and Luna Reena were killed. Something in me tells me he killed them.

"Can I ask you two a question?" I ask Mika and Lace, turning to face the siblings.

"Shoot." Mika answers, his sister nodding in agreement.

"On the day your parents were killed, did you see any ice-blue eyes?" I ask, taking a moment to bring up the paint app on the computer and draw a mock design of what I remember being Lupus' eye colour.

"I remember blue lights, but my mind was focused on my mom." Lace answers and I motion for them to look at the computer screen. She gasps the moment she sees the image, slowly backing away from the screen and into her brother who holds her tightly, his own body trembling.

"I've seen those eyes. They are from a friend of Bastian's." Mika answers and I sigh. Taking my phone out of my pocket, I dial my father's number, waiting until someone picks up.

"Connor Starlight speaking; Maverick can't come to the phone right now—" A scream of pain cuts my brother's words off as I here him wince, causing me to roll my eyes.

"Connor, its me." I say right away.

"Hey sis, what's up? How's training that piece of shit ex's pack going?" His voice is nonchalant, as if the torture going on behind him isn't happening.

"Look, we can talk about that later, but I need to talk to dad now, it's urgent. Also, tell him to stop torturing the Blakes. We need a witch to walk through their memories." I hear Connor curse, his voice muffled as he shouts something. A few minutes of silence pass, until I hear the one voice I want to hear.

"Hi, sweetheart. Connor says you need to talk to me?" I smile at my father's voice. I start getting into the details of my theory of the Blakes and Lupus being in cahoots with them taking over Hidden Claws, starting with the death of the Alpha couple fourteen years ago.

"So, we need to have a witch walk through their memories." I end the explanation, getting a sigh from my father.

"Can you put me on speaker for a moment?"

"Yeah, one minute." I put the phone on the table, tapping the speaker button and letting out my own sigh.

"You're on speaker. Mika, Lace, Ariven, Dominic, and Amberle are in the room." I call out, seeing the unease on the siblings' faces.

"Hey, everyone. First off, Mika and Lace, I am so sorry for what my pack did to your parents. My wolves went AWOL and were not supposed to kill them. As such, I want to come back to sign an alliance with you two to help protect your pack." The sincerity in his voice is clear, causing the two to tear up and Lace letting out a small sob.

"I'd like that, Alpha Maverick." The she-wolf answers, getting a chuckle from my father.

"Just Mav or Maverick would do. Your parents were great wolves." I see the tension in their bodies leaves, finally getting some closure from my father for what his pack members did fourteen years ago.

"Second, at the time, we did receive an anonymous tip about Geminie being in your pack. That's why my wolves were dispatched at that time." He adds, a collective gasp running through the group.

"Do you know what form the tip came in?" Dominic asks.

"A note. The weird part is it had the smell of a Rogue turned Soulless but not yet Soulless at the same time." I frown and know what smell he is talking about.

"Lupus. That's his unique scent." I answer. My father sighs, a scream being heard from the background and I chuckle as everyone but Ariven, Amberle and I wince.

"Connor, tell them to stop torturing that wolf. I'm on the phone!" My father shouts.

"Sorry about that, some Rogue thought he could take over the pack and poison Connor with silver. He's fine, just pissed."

"Perks of being children of the Moon Goddess, immunity to silver." I point out, gaining a chuckle from my father.

"Yep. Surprisingly, Princess Crystalline has that same immunity. Anyway, I will get a witch in to walk through their memories and have the session recorded. We will know what Lupus wants soon enough." Amberle and I give each other a questioning gaze at the mention of the Princess before I say goodbye to my father and hang up.

"Seems like the Blakes did more than just "raise" you all." Dominic points out, motioning to Mika, Lace, and I.

"Seems like they wanted this pack to rule all by themselves as the only pack in Canada." I muse. With a sigh, I get up, needing to get fresh air.

"I'll be back. Amberle and Dom can go through the information with you all. I need to go for a run." Ariven looks at me with a questioning gaze, but I shake my head. I need to be alone with my thoughts for a bit.

Chapter 35 – Kidnapped

My breath comes in short pants as I push myself hard running through the forest, my head filled with the many thoughts of Lupus, the Soulless, and now Princess Crystalline. There seems to be too much to deal with in one shot.

[You safe, Gem?] Ariven's voice calls into our link. I slow my run to a walk, taking a deep breath as I take in the forest around me.

[Yeah. I needed a run.] I answer, leaning against a tree for support as I think of what to do next.

[I understand. That was a lot to take in.]

[It was. Amberle thinks that Princess Crystalline is the Lost Princess.] I spring the news on my mate as he has been helping me search for the Lost Princess and the moonstone necklace. Being as two-thousand years have passed since her disappearance, caused by the First Prince, I'm questioning if Crystalline is a distant relative of the Lost Princess.

[Any plans to return yet?] Ariven asks after a moment of silence passes through the link.

[Not yet. There is a place I have yet to visit.] Sadness seeps into my words while I stare in the direction of the lake where the troubles started fourteen years ago. I haven't visited their graves in years since my rejection, and now knowing I was partially the cause of their deaths means I own them an apology.

[I get it, darling. Stay safe and keep your link open.] Ariven calls out gently, and I smile, happy to have a mate that is understanding and caring. With an agreement to call for him if I need him, I start walking a familiar path that Mika, Lace and I walked with their parents years ago on that fateful.

The forest is calm, sounds of birds chittering, getting their last meals in before flying south for winter, while the scent of prey like deer and rabbits reach me. I should remind Lace to stock up for the winter. The pink water comes into view, and as I get even closer to the glistening water I see a statue sitting proudly overlooking the lake.

With a sad smile, I walk closer to the statue, made in the likeness of Alpha Sora and Luna Reena, a gravestone as they were buried where they were killed.

"Hello, Alpha and Luna." I call out softly, my voice cracking as I slowly kneel in front of their graves.

"I am so sorry for what happened to you. Your death was untimely, and you had so much life left to live." I start, holding back the tears. Losing these amazing wolves caused a domino effect on the pack, their pups' lives and my own. I start to talk about finding my identity, why they were killed when they should have lived a long life, my life after leaving the pack, and anything I could think of.

Every chance I can, I apologize, curling up in on myself until I am sobbing. I know they are well, Mother reassuring me that they hold no regret but, unfortunately, I cannot talk to them until my own ascension as the Moon Goddess. I could not help the sadness, grief, and guilt that has built over the years. The afternoon turns to evening, and then night.

[Gem, baby, are you coming back soon?] Ariven's voice brings me from the grief I am wallowing in, forcing me to open my tired eyes and let out a sigh. I felt better, finally saying my piece to Alpha Sorus and Luna Reena and now I have to finish training their children.

[Yes, I am coming back now.] I answer, standing and stretching my body. I must have dozed off as I cried, my body feeing heavy and groggy and the thought of walking back to the pack house not one I look forward to. Facing the lake, I watch the stars twinkling over the water for a moment until a twig snapping gets my attention.

[Ariven, I need back up!] I call out, the scent of Soulless reaching my nose. Getting ready to fight, I face the direction of the sound and notice a Soulless walking out, its blood-red eyes staring me down as they release a feral snarl. Then I feel it, the prick of a needle in my neck, and I turn to see my assailant. I am met with ice-blue eyes. Lupus.

[Riv... Help!] I call out once more before the world fades to black.

Chapter 36 - Lupus

I slowly open my heavy eyelids, feeling as if someone had glued them shut while I was unconscious. My body feels groggy, limbs unable to move. It feels like I had been rejected again minus the pain that had me wishing for death, but the mate bond hummed inside me, even if it is so faint I can barely feel it.

[Ariven?] I call out through our link, praying he hears me. In the end, nothing but silence answers my call. My senses are blocked, and my guess is wolfsbane. It's the only substance that can harm me in any way. I need to get away, heal, and find my mate. A door to my right opens, and the stench of rot and decay mixed with the scent of a Rogue wafts through. Someone has entered the room.

"Glad to see you are awake, Future Goddess." A man calls out. Fear takes hold of me, causing me to shiver as I recognize who has walked in. It's the man who is building an army. The man causing havoc in the werewolf world. The man who raped me as a child because of a debt Bastian had. Lupus.

"Release me!" I demand, turning to glare at the man who now stands beside my bed.

"No can do, Geminie." He chuckles with a smirk. I frown, the fear slowly turning to hatred when his eyes stare down at my body, his face a disgusting mix of lust and greed.

"Why? I should be nothing to you." Is my retort. I knew he was looking for me, and like an idiot I stupidly gave him an opportunity to take me.

"Because daddy dearest... Wait no... Bastian Blake promised me a mate." He answers slowly, changing the way he addresses Bastian towards me.

"You already knew I wasn't his daughter, didn't you?" I call out frowning.

"Of course I did. The daughter they lost almost twenty-one years ago was my pup. Bastian allowed me to have his mate a few times because of debt, just like he gave me you." Shock rocks through me, knowing that Bastian knew his lost daughter wasn't his. The abuse I was put through was all for naught for Bastian but was instead meant to make Jasmine feel better.

"Like I said, Bastian promised me a Mate, and since the day I got to have some fun with you, I knew I wanted you." He continues, trailing his fingers along my abdomen and touching whatever exposed skin he can. Disgust rippled through me as only Ariven should be the one enjoying the feel of my skin pressed to his, not this disgusting wolf. He already took far more from me than he should have as a child.

"The future Moon Goddess, Geminie, mated to the Soulless King, Lupus. Has a nice ring to it, don't you think?" He chuckles with a grin, leaning closer to my weak body and taking a deep breath of my scent.

"Besides, you may be the future Moon Goddess, but from my intel you still haven't shifted into your wolf form yet. You're still weak." I growl, pushing him away from me as best as I can, the wolfsbane making me as weak as a human child. My futile attempt just causes Lupus to chuckle, his hands holding me down.

"I can see you are mated, but once I'm done killing that mate of yours Mika, you'll be free and mine in a few days. So, stay in your cell, Little Wolf, and wait for the day I can fuck you senseless." He licks the side of my face after his little plan is revealed. In retaliation, I headbutt his nose and hear a satisfying crunch. A punch to my stomach reminds me of how weak I am right now, the breath leaving my lungs as I glare back at Lupus who holds a bleeding nose in his left hand - a bleeding nose with red blood. Shock fills me, the stench of a Soulless still prevalent on him but his red blood has me questioning his background.

"Breaking you and making you mine will be a lot of fun, Geminie. So just wait." He laughs maniacally, leaving the room and locking the door. Now alone, I slowly sit up on the bed, taking stock of my surroundings.

The room is made out of rock, a flickering light hanging overhead and swaying slightly, the only source of illumination in the room and keeping it from total darkness. Taking a deep breath as best as possible, the pain in my abdomen still present from the punch, I close my eyes and try my best to focus on my powers. It takes a few tries with the wolfsbane blocking my powers, but I am able to sense where I am for a brief moment, and what I see blows my mind.

Lupus has made a kingdom underground, the pathways extending as far as my limited powers could reach. It explains why no one could find him nor his army. He hid them well, but now we know how to flush them out like the infestation they are.

[Ariven, if you can hear me, call Father and get him to have Mother leave the heavens. Lupus' camp is underground.] I call out into the void that is our link, praying my mate can hear me in some way. But something inside me tells me it is impossible, and try as I might, I know nothing will reach Ariven right now no matter how much I scream into our link.

With a tired sigh, I lean against the rough wall behind me, happy for the small comfort of the bed below me and focus on metabolizing the wolfsbane in order to get it out of my system and return my power to full strength. I need to escape and soon, before Lupus can kill the innocent wolves in Hidden Claws.

Chapter 37 – Captive

Blood drips down the right side of my face, a throbbing pain from where Lupus punched me, his gloves cutting my flesh. Glaring at the man defiantly, I silently focus on removing the wolfsbane from my system, feeling the last of it almost gone thankfully. Escape will be soon.

"It's been a week and you still dare to defy me?!" He screams in anger. I want to chuckle but know that doing so will lead me to being stabbed with the knife held firmly in his hand. I can smell the wolfsbane on the blade, knowing full well one slice will cause my progress to go back, and I will be trapped here another week.

"I will never bow down to you, Lupus!" I yell, my head turning to the right as his fist collides with my jaw seconds after my statement. I growl, turning to face the man before me with immense hatred, wanting nothing than to destroy him right then and there.

"How about I take you right now and fuck you hard. You'll soon learn who you belong to after I fill you with my cum." He jeers, his free hand grasping my neck roughly as he leans closer to my body. But there is a flaw to this plan, and we both know it.

"You'd end up killing me just as you try to as I am already mated." I state, a smirk on my face. He can't touch me without me being unmated.

"You're right, Geminie. I guess I will have to kill Mika, then." A dark chuckle follows Lupus' retort. I keep glaring at the man before me, even as he pushes me back onto the bed and look over my body with a lust-filled gaze before leaving me in my cell. He has no idea that Ariven is my mate now, and I refuse to allow him that knowledge.

As long as my mark remains on my neck, I am safe from Lupus.

I sigh with relief once alone, wiping away the blood from my forehead and moving to the center of the bed and sitting in the lotus position. I need to finish burning the wolfsbane from my body by tomorrow if I want to escape. I focus hard, making sure to keep one ear open in case a servant of

Lupus walks in, as the amount of wolfsbane given to me should have kept me weak for a month, but seeing as no one reported to Lupus that I have powers and can shift gives me the upper hand on him as no one has dosed me a second time with the poison.

Come tomorrow with my escape, I will find a way to fight Lupus and have his head severed from his body.

A noise from the direction of the door catches my attention, and I quickly flop back onto the bed, pretending to be in a deep sleep caused by the wolfsbane weakening me. Seconds later, the door opens and the scent of two she-wolves fill the room.

"Are you sure she is the next Moon Goddess?" A quiet voice asks.

"Yes. Do you think she will help us if we help her?" Comes her companion's answer, with another question of her own following.

"She can shift, I've seen it. So, if there is anyone who can free us from the King, it's her." I sigh and sit up, seeing how these two are harmless now knowing their intent in coming to me.

"Help me escape tomorrow, and I will help you." I state, watching the two jump in fright while turning to face me. I smile friendly at the she-wolves, seeing a look of awe in their eyes.

They rush to tell me their story of how their father sold them to Lupus to repay a debt, that for the last five years they have been nothing but his playthings, unable to get free and find their true soulmates. I sympathize this them, explaining how Lupus raped me as a child, and the three of us form a plan.

"Just a quick question." I call out before the girls, Mira and Abigail, leave.

"What is it?" Mira asks, her skinny body looking relaxed after our talk.

"Where are we hiding right now?" I see a look of understanding pass between the sisters before Abigail turns to me and sighs, a look of guilt on her face.

"To be honest, we are at the base under the pink lake in Hidden Claws territory. Lupus has many tunnels leading to many bases under Canada. A tunnel is being built towards the palace as we speak, but the rocky terrain and mountains are making it difficult. We have no idea what his plans are, though." She answers and I nod in understanding. This information in valuable, something we can use to destroy this man once and for all.

I thank the girls as they leave, them promising to come to me before sunrise tomorrow, giving me plenty of time to finish removing the wolfsbane from my system.

Chapter 38 – Escape

[Gem? Geminie, can you hear me?] I groan as a voice fills my head, the effects of the wolfsbane finally gone and my body well rested and ready to escape.

[Geminie, darling, where are you?] Ariven! It is his voice reaching out to me. Bolting into a sitting position, I feel tears of happiness fill my eyes, an entire week of not being able to communicate with him taking its toll on me as the mate bond throbbed, needing the touch of my mate.

[I'm here, baby. I've missed you.] I call out, forcing myself not to cry. I want his warmth, to be held in his arms and hear his heartbeat beneath my ear as I lay against his chest. I need to have his scent envelope me, remind me I am safe.

[Gem, where are you?] I can hear the desperation in his voice, the pain of being separated from me without any contact clear as day. My heart breaks, wanting to rush to him and fall into his arms.

[Underground. Lupus made a base by the pink lake I told you about.] I answer, giving him a general direction where the entrance to the base is. I hear my mate curse into the link, asking to wait a few minutes to talk with the others before our link goes silent, but this hum of the mate bond is stronger than it has been the last seven days, making me feel complete with the small interaction.

[Geminie?]

[Still here, Ariven.] He sighs, and I can just picture the tension of not knowing where I have been these days seeping away.

[Mika, Lace, Amberle and Dominic sent their best to scout the area, we will know more within five minutes and be there at latest in thirty minutes. Do you think you can escape?] Ariven fills me in and I smile, seeing Mira and Abigail outside my door with scared eyes, as they look back and forth down the hall.

[Yes. I'll be bringing a few wolves with me too.] I reassure him. Hearing his deep familiar chuckles sends my heart fluttering.

[Why does that not surprise me? I'll see you soon, my darling. I love you.] I smile, closing my eyes to regain my composure. [I love you too, Ariven.] I reply before the link ends. We have thirty minutes to escape and escape we must. I have no idea what Abigail and Mira will face if we are caught. The door opens slowly, and I rush to the sisters waiting for me, their fear seeping into the air.

"Calm yourselves and take a deep breath. Your fear will give us away." I calmly explain, keeping my senses on alert for any chance of being discovered. The girls do as I say, their bodies relaxing with each deep breath they take until Mira looks at me, her eyes holding excitement, and I smile back at her.

"Lead the way, hun." I motion for Mira to take the lead, making sure not to touch and rub my scent onto the two. If by chance they get caught or questioned, not having my scent on them will save the sisters from being punished. We walk down the tunnel in silence, Mira in front, Abigail in the middle, and me taking the rear, our steps quiet as we each listen for an approaching wolf so we can hide quickly.

Suddenly, Mira stops just before we are meant to turn right, turning to look back at me with panic in her eyes. Ready to ask her what's wrong, I smell the familiar scent of Lupus and instantly grab the girls, making sure they stand flush against the dirt wall of the tunnel and activate my power. A dirt wall covers the three of us, the sisters thankfully staying silent as footsteps approach our hiding spot.

"What do you mean they are marching towards us!" Lupus growls, slamming his fist into the wall I have made. Mira winces in fright, and Abigail covers her mouth, trying not to say a word while I focus hard on keeping the wall solid and unshakable.

"Someone must have tipped them off to our location. It makes no sense how three days ago they searched just outside our base and gave up, only to be coming back ready to attack." A voice answers, his voice nasally and small. I smirk, thinking of my mate and our allies coming to destroy Lupus and his army.

"Your Majesty!" A she-wolf calls out urgently, her rapid footsteps stopping just outside the wall. I hold my breath, making sure that Abigail and Mira make no sound while we listen in.

"Your prisoner is gone! We went to gather her per your orders, and her cell is empty!" the she-wolf exclaims. Once again, the wall in front of me is hit as Lupus lets out an angry roar. Mira and Abigail are shaking with fear, but they stay silent. Their freedom from this cruel man is worth more than giving away our hiding spot.

"How did she fucking escape?! She had wolfsbane in her system and should have been weak!" Lupus roars, the tunnel shaking from the power of his anger. Something inside me clicks and I understand why this wolf has so much power and why so many wolves want to bow to him. He is a Royal!

"Sir, I think she had help." The she-wolf voices timidly. A tearing sound is heard followed by the scream of a woman and the stench of Soulless blood. I have a feeling that the she-wolf is now dead.

"Find my Queen now!" He orders, followed by a flurry of 'Yes Sir' and wolves frantically running around. We wait in silence as I allow a small part of the wall to open up, just enough to see what is happening. Abigail is shaking beside me, so I squeeze her hand, hoping to reassure the she-wolf that everything will be fine.

It takes a few minutes for the hallway to clear, many wolves running back and forth before affirming that no one is here in this section of the base before they go off searching in a different direction. I count to ten, not wanting to expose our hiding spot so early before lowering the wall and making sure that the surrounding do not look disturbed before turning to Mira who holds Abigail in her arms.

"We need to change our scents." I whisper, my eyes darting around to keep a lookout for any Soulless coming back to recheck this tunnel.

"I know a place. The clothes may stink though." Abigail voices, taking mine and Mira's hands and leading the two of us straight down the tunnel instead of turning right like we were supposed to. The halls are silent as we pass by different doors, some muffling growls and snarls coming from behind the heavy steel doors.

"Those are the Damned, Soulless the King releases to wreak havoc on unsuspecting packs." Mira explains and I nod, wanting nothing more than to put those wolves out of their misery and send them to Mother to heal their souls and send them on their way to rebirth. But they will have to wait.

Abigail ends our walk in front of a wooden door, using a key to unlock it, and pushes her sister and I inside before following after us and shutting the door. The smell of death and decay reaches me instantly, and it takes everything in me not to throw up what little substance I have in my stomach.

"Sorry about the smell. No matter how much the others assigned to laundry and I try to wash them out, the stench remains." Abigail explains, rummaging through the racks of clean clothing.

"How many Rogues are here?" I ask, curious as the sisters before I do not have the red eyes of the Soulless.

"Per base, there are one hundred Rogues either sold or captured by King Lupus and about three hundred Soulless at a time, give or take. When some reach the Damned state, they are either held back or released into the world to die or wreak havoc. Some Rogues turn Soulless because they lost all hope, and the cycle of having to find Rogues to do the chores or warm the bed of the King and his advisors begins again." Mira explains, taking the shirt handed to her by Abigail and changing into it without hesitation. Abigail sighs as she continues searching until she finds what she is looking for, a large, black hoodie that she throws at me.

I gag, wanting to throw it back at my new ally but instead put it on with a grimace and make sure to hide my white hair underneath the hood, allowing part of my face to be hidden. Abigail then changes into a baggy, long-sleeved dress and smiles at me as she motions for us to leave the room quietly.

"Mira and I can pretend to be showing you around," Abigail explains, locking the door again as we head down the tunnel we came from and make the correct turn to the exit. The two begin to talk about how the base works and its hierarchy from the lowest of the low to Lupus, explicitly explaining that she-wolves are used as bed warmers or maids. I shudder to think about this information, happy to have the sister on my side. They will bring perfect intel to the war Lupus is raging in the werewolf world.

"You three!" We freeze in our spots, recognizing Lupus' voice. Taking a deep breath, I turn towards him, his scent making me want to dig my claws into his neck, but I keep my head bowed in submission. I cannot blow our cover.

"Yes your Majesty?" Mira asks, stepping forward.

"Go outside and track Geminie down!" He orders, his eyes glancing over me, but instead, he turns and grabs a wolf with a hood covering his head as he frantically runs by—searching for me no doubt—pushing him towards me and forcing me to stop this small wolf from stumbling and falling.

"Take him with you and return by nightfall. If you return without my Queen, I will kill all of you." We bow in respect, the four of us rushing towards the exit and the tension of Mira, Abigail, and my escape seeping from our bodies. Of course, there is this extra wolf to consider and what to do with him.

[Geminie, we are in the area.] Ariven calls through our link and the bond hums. He is close, and soon I will be safe in my mate's arms. The teenage boy who had been thrown at me takes the lead, opening a well-hidden door that opens to reveal the lake before us, the pink water a welcoming sight. Rushing forward, I relish in the fresh air until my body is tackled, a scream leaves Mira's lips, and I am ready to tear into whomever it is above me until the wind blows the familiar scent of the person I call my home to me.

This idiot forgot that I was escaping.

With a chuckle, I calmly turn until I am on my back, Ariven's angry black wolf above me with teeth pressed against my neck. The hood falls back, revealing my white curls now dingy from the week being a prisoner, and tear-filled eyes as I stare back at my mate.

"Ariven, baby. It's me." I whisper, tears falling from my eyes. His angry snarls soon turn into whimpers as his snout pushes past the collar of the hoodie to my bare skin where he takes a deep breath. I shiver, wrapping my arms around his neck hands fisting his soft fur.

[I'm so sorry, darling. I just saw you all coming out of the tree, and you smelled like one of them.] He links, his small whimpers filling my ears as he licks my mark.

"I know, baby. Smelling like one of them was the only way to escape." I answer, burying my face into his fur and taking a deep breath. My tired body is relaxed, no longer in danger and now with my mate, my pack and my allies surrounding us and protecting me. I am safe once more.

"Theta Cross, are we going to attack?" A wolf calls out. I peek out to see John coming close. Ariven gives him a warning growl, and I chuckle, tugging on his ear and smiling at John, who looks at me with shock and happiness.

"Alpha!!"

"Hi, John No, we are not going to attack. They are still searching for me, so retreating would be a logical tactic right now." I answer, running my fingers through my mate's fur to prevent him from attacking our packmate and keep him calm.

"What do we do with those three then?" He nods towards the wolves I escaped with, remembering the teen who was pushed onto us. Pushing Ariven away softly, I stand and dust off my body, motioning for those guarding Mira and Abigail to back off and turning to face the teen who kneels on the ground with his hands on his head, eyes down and submitting to us. Good, this wolf is no fool.

"Did you link any of the Rogues in the base?" I ask, looking down at the wolf. He shakes his head no and I motion for mine to back away, spying Amberle, Dominic and Mika just a few feet away watching us. I smile at my friends before turning to look at the wolf kneeling before me, who seems to visibly relax without Maddie and Lena watching over his shoulders.

"I knew instantly who you were, Goddess Geminie, the moment that bastard pushed me toward you." The teen begins to say. Deciding to see if his words are true, I kneel in front of him and allow the wolf to continue.

"That bastard kidnapped me from my family ten years ago when I was six. He learned I could see the future from a member of the Rogue caravan we were a part of and kept me ever since." I place my hand under his chin, lifting his face to see his eyes looking calmly at me, eyes like a deep pool of silver without a ripple. He sends me a friendly smile and allows me to examine him. His skin is pale, even under the grime and dirt from being with Lupus for ten years, and his hair, although long and messy, is the colour of spun gold.

"You don't have red eyes!" I exclaim, smiling at the calm aura he releases and realizing just what he is.

"No. Even after trying to break me, I never gave up hope for escape. Lupus must have been out of his mind when he threw me at you, not realizing the two people he wanted to keep captive were escaping at the same time." He answers. I chuckle, standing and helping the kid to his feet before looking at Maddie and Matt who stand beside Amberle and Dominic.

Ariven stands with his fur a little on edge, and Mika sends me a knowing smile. I see the others in my pack give me a nod, and I know they approve of what I am about to do.

"Our pack is made up of Rogues looking for a second chance, a family or escaping from being rejected by their mates." I explain, motioning for Abigail and Mira to stand beside me.

"So what do you all say to having Abigail, Mira and..."

"Malachi." The teen answers.

"...And Malachi the Oracle join Silver Crystal Crescent?" I ask, seeing a shocked look on Malachi's face as my wolves cheer in acceptance of their new packmates. I smile and turn to Ariven before looking back at my three new members.

"I knew the moment I saw your eyes that you were an Oracle, Malachi. My mother told me about how rare you wolves are, and you will be in for a lot of training with me, my mother and Ira. Now let's go back to the guest house, get in a nice warm bath, and some tasty food." With that, I shift into my wolf form, not caring for the clothes torn apart, and trot to my mate, rubbing against his side and relishing in his touch as the group makes our way to the guest and pack houses of Hidden Claws.

We need to prepare for war, as I feel Lupus will be coming to take me back within the next few days after realizing I had indeed escaped with his unknowing help.

Chapter 39 – Intel

I sigh as the shower water turns cold, knowing that my time under the warm spray is up and that I have to face reality. We agreed to an impromptu meeting with Mika, Lace, Dominic and Amberle within three hours, giving Mira, Abigail, Malachi and me enough time to clean up, have a warm meal, and prepare for the meeting. Having these three around with important intel on Lupus will help turn the tide of the war that I have a feeling will be leading to something bigger, something that can change the werewolf world and expose us to the humans. We cannot allow that to happen. Secrecy of our people is necessary in order to keep everyone safe and avoid a war between humans and supernatural beings.

"Gem, darling, are you hungry?" Ariven's voice calls from the other side of the door. Climbing out of the shower and wrapping a fluffy towel around my body, I push open the door to the heavenly scent of pasta and garlic bread. Ariven places the food on the nightstand beside the bed before handing me a large bottle filled with a yellow liquid that I eye with a questioning look.

"Electrolytes. The doctor here suggested giving them to you and the other three." Ariven explains as I take the bottle and down its contents, feeling instantly better with a cold drink. My mate chuckles as he gently pulls me into his arms and plants a soft kiss on top of my head. I feel the bond hum happily between us while we just enjoy each other's comforting presence after a week of being kept apart. I can tell that Ariven wants to kill Lupus just as much as I do. Part of me wants to share the kill, and another part wants to hog the satisfaction of ending that disgusting disgrace of a wolf's existence.

"The meeting will happen in about an hour and a half. The three you brought here are being watched by Christian, Maddie and Matt, although I am positive the three are harmless." Ariven explains before scooping me into his arms and carrying me to the bed, relieved to know the three who helped me escape Lupus are safe and well, and shocked to know that Christian, Beta to Blood Moon, is here as well.

"I thought Christian's mate Camile was due any day now with his third pup!" I exclaim as we settle in bed and Ariven passes me the plate of food. "She is. She is also ready to kick his ass and the two pups' and told him to bring the pups with him for the experience. Having a twelve- and sixteen-year-old who know how to train pups have helped with training while searching for you." Ariven chuckles. He then explains how training has been, with the wolves from Blood Moon helping to train Hidden Claws while the rest went searching for me. Pride swells inside me knowing that instead of halting the progress made to focus on my kidnapping, my pack and my friends' helped to keep the training going. Hidden Claws will need to become stronger for the upcoming war.

"Do you think I have enough time to nap?" I ask yawning once full of food and feeling relaxed.

"Yeah, I'll wake you up before the meeting to get ready. Sleep tight, darling." I smile and snuggle closer to Ariven, his hand combing through my hair and helping me to fall asleep.

⋄⋄⋄

Sitting at the head of the table in the conference room, I watch as Lace and Mika argue about whether to attack the hidden base now or later. A headache forms while I think about who to hit upside the head first.

"He's been under our land for Goddess knows how long! We need to flush him out and kill him!" Mika yells, frustrated by his sister's calm and easy-going demeanour.

"No, we will wait for all the information and intel before we do anything. Maverick called yesterday saying the witch was finishing mind walking the Blakes, and we will have everything from them soon!" Lace exclaims exasperated with her brother. I look to Ariven with a questioning gaze and he nods. Whatever force stopped my father from coming and ripping the land apart to find me must have been strong, and for that, I am happy. I have enough on my plate and really do not want to deal with my father in "overprotective Alpha Dad mode" as Connor has put it multiple times since I reunited with my family.

"How about we let Malachi, Abigail, and Mira give us what they know, and we go from there first." Amberle suggests, walking into the room with the aforementioned wolves trailing behind her. Mika glares at the fire-haired wolf, who just shrugs and takes a seat beside me. I send her a grateful look, happy to have her stop the arguing as my three new pack mates take a seat.

"H-hi." Mira stutters shyly, trying to hide behind her sister.

"You know, after a shower, you two look really pretty." As if a switch is flicked, Mika goes from angry and annoyed to civil as he takes a look at Mira, something in his eye shining. I chuckle as I get the feeling my mother is having fun playing with a few strings of fates over in the dreamscape.

"Mika now is not the time for flirting. We need to gather as much information as possible on what Lupus has planned." Amberle chides the wolf as if talking to a pup. He rolls his eyes in annoyance at her words and takes a seat beside Lace, all the while glaring at the Alpha she-wolf who just ignores him.

"I am going to call my father and see if he has all the information ready." I declare, trying to diffuse the tension between Mika and Amberle. I keep an eye on the two, seeing Dominic give me a reassuring nod before I take out my cell phone. Once I am sure Dominic is ready to step in if a fight breaks out between my friend and my ex-mate, I dial my father's number and bring my phone to my ear, waiting for him to answer.

"Geminie, thank god you're okay!" I wince, pulling my phone away from my right ear and switching to the left.

"Was there a need to yell?" I question, rubbing my sore ear and rolling my eyes.

"Sorry, Gem, but I was so worried about you. Connor and your Uncle wouldn't allow me to rush down there to find you, and your mother was stopped by the Goddess of Destiny from descending down the dreamscape to Hidden Claws." I sigh, reassuring my father I am fine, uninjured, and ready to kill the bastard Lupus for kidnapping me. After a couple of minutes reassuring my father I am fine and will see him soon for my birthday, I place the call on speaker and put the phone on the table.

"We have Amberle and Dominic, Lace and Mika, Ariven and now three new members to S.C.C., Abigail, Mira and Malichi, here in the room. These three were once held against their wills by Lupus." I state so my father can address everyone properly now that the meeting is ready to commence.

"Hello, everyone." He calls out.

"Hi, Dad!" Amberle calls back jokingly. I roll my eyes as my father's chuckle rings through the room.

"Hi, Amber." There is a chuckle in the background after my dad replies, and I smile.

"Hi, Connor." Ariven calls out followed by Amberle yelling, "Hi, baby bro!" making me chuckle as well, happy to have this fiery wolf as a best friend and someone I consider a sister.

"Anyway, I am guessing this call is about the Witch's result in dream walking the Blakes." He continues.

"Yes. We need to know what the Blakes know both about our parents' deaths and the budding war with Lupus." Lace answers, Mika taking her hand in his as the sibling stare at my phone with a sombre look. The answers they've been looking for about their parents' death are now within their reach.

"Unfortunately, the answer is yes. The anonymous tip my pack received about your pack hiding my daughter was called in by Lupus. The Witch, Cassandra, walked their dreams and memories, and one thing is, Lupus is no ordinary wolf."

"He is a Royal, isn't he!" I state, everyone turning to look at me with wide eyes while I stare at my phone on the table. Everyone displays some form of shock, that is, everyone but Malachi. He stares at me with a steady gaze and I realize he already knew this information.

"He is. How do you know?" Connor calls out and I frown.

"When we escaped his base, he released his power. Everyone submitted to him but me. Instead, I felt something in my mind click, as if I should pay respect to him as an elder."

"So that makes him your some-what great grandfather?" Mika asks but I shake my head no. He is something else to me in my family tree. Now the question is what or who exactly is Lupus.

"Actually, he would be considered a somewhere-down-the-line great-uncle. He goes by Lupus now but his original name is Prince Coro, the first Prince of the Werewolf Lineage." No one speaks, too shocked by the information my father just released. Prince Coro is the sibling that caused the first Heir of the throne to go missing.

In the legend, Prince Coro is jealous of his twin sisters, one that inherited the power of the Moon Goddess and one that inherited the power of an Alpha King. He received neither power himself; he was the weaker of the three siblings in every sense, even with the twins only being a few days old. In the end, his jealousy got the better of him, and in the dead of night, he had a witch kidnap the Princess in order to kill her. He then became King years later, until his sister learned of the truth behind her twin's disappearance. He was removed from the throne and stripped of the King title, but unfortunately, without the true heir, Prince Coro's bloodline has continued to sit on the throne for years to come, including the current King, King Alexander.

"So that bastard is the First Prince, and he's doing all of this for what?" Mika shouts, standing to his feet and sending his chair crashing to the floor.

"He wants to kill his sister once and for all and claim the throne." Malachi's voice is quiet, but silence settles as everyone stares at him.

"His sister is missing, though. No one knows where the Lost Princess is—" Amberle points out, running a hand through her messy locks and giving an exasperated sigh.

"—Unless..."

"She is Crystalline Thorn and the current Heir to the throne." I continue, our eyes meeting as Amberle and I come to a quick understanding. The Lost Princess never died; someone hid her.

"So, what do we do now?" Dominic asks.

"He is still looking for Geminie, and by the sounds of it, all three entrances to his base are open and unguarded. If you wish to end him or cut down part of his power, now would be the time." Mira answers, her eyes glazing over. She must still be able to link with a few wolves from the Soulless Army.

"Then we attack at midnight when the moon is high, and Gem is at her most powerful." Ariven states, and I nod in agreement. We must do something to end Lupus, and tonight may be our best bet.

Chapter 40 – Flushing out a Disease Part 1

Ariven and I left the meeting room shortly after forming a plan to flush out Lupus and his Soulless and destroy as much of them as we can. For Rogues not yet turned Soulless, we will take them into holding cells and evaluate their mental, physical, and emotional state and help them find new packs to join or accept them into Hidden Claws, Blood Moon or Silver Crystal Crescent. Amberle even called a few Allies in Harvest Willow and Glacier to see if they could use new members once this operation is complete. They both thankfully say yes and ask her to inform them when these wolves are ready.

"Why not take a nap? I will wake you a few hours before the operation so you can get ready." My mate suggests, leading me up the stairs of the guest house to our room. I intend to dissuade this idea, but a yawn cuts me off, making Ariven chuckle as he climbs into bed and opens his arms wide—his way of saying come join him and cuddle.

Deciding he is right and that I need sleep, I climb in beside him and cuddle close to his side. His fingers comb through my hair gently, the soothing motion and the sound of his steady heartbeat quickly lulling me into sleep.

◆◆◆

I sigh as I stare at my reflection in the mirror. Tonight, we could lose some good wolves, all because Prince Coro wants to take the throne back by force. My hair is pinned into a bun, keeping it out of my face and harder to grab when the fighting begins. This fight will be pointless if I am caught.

"Gem, you ready?" Amberle walks into my room wearing a similar sleek black outfit as me, her fiery hair hidden under a black toque and her bright eyes filled with excitement and bloodlust. She, too, is itching for this fight.

"As ready as I can be." I answer, taking a deep breath.

"Is everyone else ready?" I question, turning to join my friend as she leans against the wall.

"Yes, although Ariven is having a hard time convincing Malachi to stay back." I sigh at her answer, motioning the she-wolf to follow me as we make our way down the stairs of the guest house. As we near the first floor, a commotion can be heard loud and clear, and a headache begins to form.

"For the last time, I want to come along too!" Malachi's voice is loud and clear, his anger radiating towards me in violent waves causing me to stumble back. I have never felt such hatred and anger from anyone, and it takes a moment to catch my breath before walking into view where Ariven and Dominic try to calm the juvenile down.

"Malachi, I can't allow you to come with us." I state as soon as I enter into his line of sight.

"Why not, Alpha?! I deserve some revenge as well!" He shouts, causing the others in the room to release a warning growl. I let out a growl of my own, directed at the adults in the room, silencing them before smiling calmly at the Oracle before me.

"Malachi, you are an Oracle and an asset to Lu—Prince Coro. If he gets his hands on you during the fight, we will not be able to rescue you." I explain calmly, pulling the teen into my arms and giving him a small hug.

"You've been through so much because of him. Stay here with the others and rest. You need it, hun, and we can't risk him getting his claws on you." His shoulders slump in defeat, his head nodding in compliance finally as he pulls away from the hug.

"I'll listen to you Alpha, but I don't like this. I have spent six years tortured by that vile man in order to tell him his future." Malachi states as he runs a hand through his hair. I sigh and pat his shoulder, reassuring him that Coro will receive his just karma. Lena - a tracker from my pack - volunteered to stay behind with some Warriors in order to protect Hidden Claws should this mission take a turn for the worse, and as she is about to lead the teenage Oracle away and to their pack house, Malachi grabs my hand his silver eyes pure-white and golden hair glowing.

[Be careful, Alpha. This battle will be one step in the war, but it will not end Coro. You need to come back alive for you and the pup inside you.] He links me, his mouth set into a grim line. Shocked, I intend to ask what the juvenile means, but he crumbles, and I reach out just in time to stop the kid from hitting the ground face first. When I look to make sure he is okay, I realize Malachi is in a deep sleep.

"What happened to him!" Mika shouts out as the rest of the group looks on in confusion.

"A vision, and an important one at that." Amberle answers before ordering Greg to help Lena with carrying Malachi to Hidden Claws' pack house. I stand still as everyone files out of the guest house, wrapping my mind around the revelation that I am pregnant. That bastard kept me locked away without any proper food and beat me when I defied him for seven days. My rage surges and the bloodlust becomes strong. I will kill Coro by any means possible for harming my baby and me.

"Geminie, darling?" A gentle hand is placed on my shoulder, the scent of my mate wrapping around me, calming the typhoon-like rage into a simmer.

"I'm pregnant." Shock fills Ariven's face, his eyes going between my face and flat stomach in confusion.

"How do you know?" "Malachi. He gave me a warning from the vision."

"How far along?"

"I'd say two to three weeks considering my heat was the perfect time to conceive." Running my hand across my face, I let out a shaky sigh.

For a few moments, we stand there in silence, accepting the fact we will be parents soon enough, then strong arms pull me towards the warmth of my mate, where he places a chaste kiss on my lips.

"I know you. I know you won't run from this fight. But promise me you will be careful. I can't lose you and our pup." I see the worry, the love, and the fear of losing us in this battle as Ariven states his words. He has already lost one mate and pup and the fear of losing another set is clear in his eyes. I am happy to know he will let me fight beside my friends and pack, and give him another kiss, this one longer than the first, and pour my heart and soul into it.

"I promise to keep our pup and I safe." I whisper, leaning into his embrace and taking a deep breath of his scent. No matter what happens, my pup and I will make it out alive. We allow ourselves another minute of holding onto each other, me knowing that Ariven needs this to calm himself, before I pull away and we join the group outside.

Amberle and Lace give me questioning gazes, and I just tell them I will explain later. Right now, I need to focus on the mission to either end Coro here and now or cripple his power.

"Everyone, before we leave, let me remind you all of a few things." I state, turning to face the crowd of fifty wolves all dressed for battle.

"Number one, all Soulless are to be killed. Unfortunately, their instincts have taken control and they are too far gone. Give them a merciful and instant death." Pausing, I allow the wolves from Hidden Claws, Blood Moon, and Silver Crystal Crescent to digest this information.

"Number two, for those in team A—all Rogues who surrender instantly are to be led out and handed to Team B, which will put restraints on them. Witch Cassandra will be here tomorrow to dream walk these surrendered wolves and decide whether they mean harm to the packs or are truly willing to find a pack to join." I look to Lace, Mika, Amberle, and Dominic, who all nod in agreement before addressing the wolves one last time

"Finally, do not engage in a fight with Lupus, who is the First Prince Coro. He has Royal Blood, and any command he gives when using his Royal Command will force you to do it. This may include killing your very own packmates. Run if you see him. Now, everyone, open your links to each other so we can communicate." With a resounding Yes Alpha, I join the other leaders while small nudges try to pry into the link. Closing my eyes, I pop each bubble, hearing a new voice pop in.

[Lena here, pack house is secured and ready to defend.]

[Greg.]

[Mason.]

[Mika.] Each voice answers as we accept each other one by one until everyone is linked. With a nod to the wolves involved, we stealthily make our way through the forest. Amberle and the Trackers take the lead in the trees, giving us warning of Rogues and Soulless on our path that we soon capture and knock out or give a quick and painless death. In minutes we make it to the entrance of Coro's base and prepare ourselves for this battle. It is time for the operation to begin.

Chapter 41 – Flushing out a Disease Part 2

Hidden just inside the treeline, I scan the surroundings of the base's entrance. Nothing is out of place since we escaped earlier today. Wolves run out of the entrance frantically searching for Malachi and me, a fearful look on these Rogues' faces, worried for the consequences of not finding one of us.

[Captured a Rogue and knocked her out as instructed. Handing her off to team B.] Maddie reports moments after a small she-wolf with deep olive skin and dirty, chocolate-coloured hair rush out of the base and towards my packmate.

[Copy. Make sure to treat that Rogue carefully until Cassandra can dream walk her mind.] Ariven responds.

[Greg, anything on your side?] Mika calls out.

[Nope. Malachi's friend came over, though, as promised. Only a few have gone out to look for Gem and Malachi, while the rest are cowering in fear of Coro.] Greg is quick to answer. A smirk plays on my lips as now is the right time to surprise the Rogues in the base.

[Remember, the base is underground, and some hallways are narrow. Don't die.] I call out. Taking a deep breath, I focus on heightening my senses before rushing out from the safety of the treeline and right to the entrance. It's time to attack. Rushing into the base, I soon discover a problem, as the entrance has been blocked by countless Soulless all snarling at us. No one can enter without battling these twelve beasts, but at the same time, there is no room for a battle.

[Surround me, I have a plan.] I link to my group as I close my eyes. The wolves around me quickly make my safety a priority as I focus my senses on the base. There are too many narrow hallways and too many hiding nooks. The only way to remedy this situation is to remove everything.

With my breath steady, I work my magic, using my power over earth to slowly shift the walls and force wolves out of hiding. I take the time to separate the Rogues from the Soulless, the women and children from the males, until nothing but a large cavern is created, with the entrance from behind us being the only way in and out.

[Greg and Maddie, get to the west side of the base quickly, I had no choice but to use my powers and separate the Rogues from the Soulless.] I link the Head Hunter of Blood Moon and my Head Tracker, sending a general location of where I need them to be. With a "yes Alpha" as their reply, I open my eyes and turn to the fifty Soulless now surrounded by my friends and allies. As usual, Amberle is enjoying the thrill of a hunt as she slices away at the Soulless who attack her, giving them a quick and painless death. Dominic chuckles as he stands beside me, protecting me while his mate has her fun.

"She saved me in a similar fashion when I first met her. Can't believe I am mated to her." He states as Amberle is thrown into the air, only to manoeuvre her body to where she lands on the neck of a Soulless, effectively snapping the bones and killing the poor thing on the spot.

Suddenly the scent of blood reaches me, not just anyone's blood, but Ariven's. Fearing for my mate, my focus shifts, and the cavern where the base once stood shakes, dirt falling from the ceiling.

[Ariven?] I call out frantically through our link, trying to regain control of my power and preventing the roof from caving in on the wolves fighting the Soulless.

[I'm fine, darling. Just got blindsided by a bastard of a Soulless, is all.] His answer comes after a pause of silence, and I feel my heart settle. Knowing that my mate is safe and alive helps me regain focus on the task at hand. I close my eyes and feel the earth, steadying the unstable cavern while my team dispatches the Soulless.

[Alpha, we are at the side you mentioned with wolves to escort these Rogues out. Open a door for us.] Maddie calls out, and I quickly oblige. I sense the wolves of our allies and from my own pack enter the side where I trapped the Rogues, feeling a shift in the earth as the males struggle as they are captured. My focus returns quickly to the fighting in the current cavern, the stench of death and decay growing stronger with each Soulless killed, causing me to become nauseous.

[Rogues are out, Geminie. You can close that section for good.] Greg calls out. I sigh with relief, my power retreating from that area as the sounds of a cave-in reach the battle. Now, I only have to keep the ceiling from falling and killing my friends in the current area. The sounds of a wolf rushing me causes me to create a barrier of stone in front of my body, and the cavern becomes unsteady.

[Darling?] Ariven asks through the link, worry etched into his words.

[I'm fine. Just had to protect myself and our pup from an onslaught of Soulless. Dom is ripping into them now.] I answer, the barrier falling as I watch Dominic shift into wolf form, his ice-like fur a blur as he quickly dispatches the Soulless that tried to kill me. The battle continues and, as I exert my powers to keep the cavern from closing in, I watch many Soulless die at the hands of my friends and allies, until finally the last of the Soulless passes away quickly.

[Everyone, time to leave!] Amberle calls through the link. An hour passes in a blink of an eye and with the continuous use of my power, I can feel exhaustion settle in. But the one wolf I want to find and kill was not inside the base. Wolves rush past me, with Dominic, Amberle and Ariven surrounding my body as we make sure to leave only the dead Soulless inside. This will be their final resting place. As the last of the wolves file out, I back away slowly, keeping the walls of earth up until the final three keeping watch leave, and I emerge from the base just in time for my power and body to falter from lack of energy.

"I got you, darling." Strong arms catch me before I reach the ground, and Ariven's scent wraps around me. I smile, relieved that this operation went smoothly, but have a nagging feeling, wondering where Coro is hiding.

Then I hear it, the long, slow howl that always sends shivers of fear coursing through my blood.

He escaped and is letting us know it.

He'll be gone like the wind in no time, untraceable to anyone, until his final plans are revealed. But today, we won the battle. Now, time will tell what awaits us in this war against the First Prince.

Chapter 42 – Witch Cassandra

I sit quietly in the prison under Hidden Claws' storage shed, watching Witch Cassandra dream walk through the tenth Rogue's mind. Her assistant takes the time they have during the dream link to write what they see while Ariven, Amberle, and Ira go through the reports. Four days have passed since the attempt to bring down Coro and his Soulless soldiers. We managed to weaken his power, but the war will rage on until his death.

"When you told me to come here, I never thought it would be to learn that Prince Coro is alive and that a war is starting." The Priestess states with a sigh, and I send an apologetic smile her way.

"It could be worse. We could be barging into the Royal Pack and fighting Alexander to give the throne to the rightful Queen." Dominic chuckles as he, Mika and Lace walk in with refreshments. I sigh, thinking about the next dilemma I will have to face soon. That sixteen-year-old Crystalline Thorn will have to be placed on the throne soon as the true heir, and Coro's line will have to end one way or another.

"We have two more years before Crystalline is eighteen and a legal adult. For now, we just watch over her as best as we can and send help when possible." Ariven adds as he hands me a glass of lemonade from the refreshments cart and pulls me to his side.

"I will bring up the idea of an alliance to Alexander in the meantime, stating that since we are from the Royal bloodline, we should protect and help each other." I suggest just as Cassandra finishes her dream walk and slumps in her chair. Her assistant hands Ira the newest notebook to go through as Mika hands the Witch a glass of lemonade to help the hardworking woman relax.

"Of all the dreams I have walked, I have never seen so many disgusting acts by one man." The black-haired woman states, her voice quivering with emotions that I cannot pinpoint. I sigh, leaning closer to my mate as I look to the she-wolf who Cassandra had just dream walked in, very skinny Rogue with signs of sexual abuse that only Coro would do.

"He's done similar things to me because of the Blakes." I admit, seeing the shocked look cross Cassandra's face.

"Well that man must die then. Centuries of tyranny in the shadows have been caused by Coro. If I am not mistaken, Alexander is being controlled by his some-time great-grandfather as well." The room grows silent as the sudden realization that Coro rules the werewolf world from the shadows brings one more problem to light. The possibility of him taking over from Alexander and regaining control of the nation something no one wants to come true.

"That means the true Princess will have to become Queen." Dominic chimes in.

"What do you mean by that?" The witch asks, staring at us with both confusion and hope in her eyes.

"We believe that Crystalline Thorn is not named after the lost Princess." Ariven begins, looking at me as if asking for approval to tell Cassandra the truth. I smile, turning to look at Cassandra, the hope in her eyes shining so bright that I feel a warmth of happiness radiate off of her in waves.

"Amberle and I believe that Crystalline is in fact the Lost Princess. If her brother Coro is still alive, then something happened to her that caused her to be suspended in time as a baby until the time was right." I finish, seeing tears build in the witch's eyes.

"Morai had a hand in that. The Goddess of Destiny protected the Princess like I asked all those years ago." She mutters softly. Hearing about Morai, I think back to a moment during training and how she mentioned a witch that has been her Patron and the protector of all Moon Goddesses.

"Are you the one who made this necklace?" I ask the witch, revealing the snowflake charm from under my shirt. Cassandra smile as she touches the moonstone before nodding.

"Yes. I had a feeling that the Moon Goddess Selene would hand this down to her descendants. Please keep this with you when you meet Crystalline. If she is truly my lost Princess, this stone will confirm the truth."

"I will." I answer, seeing the reassurance in her eyes.

"Now, how do we find that demented Prince who I wish I drowned as a babe?" Her voice is filled with venom as Cassandra speaks about Coro, and I realize she too wants to have a hand in his death.

"If I have learned anything about Coro, it's that he will be like the shadows and gone when light is shone on him. The only thing we can do now is plan for the final battle, and I believe that will have to happen once we have Princess Crystalline on our side." I voice my thoughts, seeing Cassandra nod in agreement. She soon asks to retire, her body exhausted from the strong spells performed, so Lace has a guard help the Witch to her rooms. With Cassandra the Ancient Witch on our side, the chances of winning this war are high. Of course, as I have learned through my life, destiny is not set in stone and Morai has many paths for us to follow.

"Why the grim look? Tonight is the last night for both your packs to be here. Let's go get cleaned up and enjoy the last bonfire of the night before you all have to leave!" Mika chimes in with his easy-going smile that I remembered as a child. I chuckle, motioning for him to lead the way as we all file out of the room with Dominic and Ira carrying the new stack of paperwork away. Tonight, we need a break.

Tomorrow, we can continue to plan for the war to come.

Chapter 43 – A Friendship Rekindled

I smile as I watch the wolves of Blood Moon, Hidden Claws, and my Silver Crystal Crescent mingle in the field outside of the pack house. Ariven and Dominic man the grill, the smell of burgers, steaks, sausages, and other delicious barbecue-worthy meats wafting in the breeze. Amberle is doing her best to get Lace drunk by the bonfire while some wolves sneak off into the night. I chuckle, realizing we may have to shuffle the packs around if my hunch is correct and some have found their mates.

"Gemmy." A voice calls out softly, and I turn to see Mika standing beside the table I sit at, a small smile on his lips and his hands holding two cans of cola.

"You think I can sit and talk with you for a bit? I brought you a drink." I chuckle, motioning for him to take the seat across from me and see a relieved look cross his face as he slides the cola in front of me and quickly sits before I could change my mind.

"What do you want to talk about?" I ask, cracking open the can and taking a gulp.

"I'm sorry." He blurts out, catching my attention. I stay silent, waiting for him to elaborate.

"I am sorry for not standing up for you when my parents were killed. I am sorry for standing by while Bastian abused you, and for abusing you as well. Most of all, I am sorry for rejecting you. I hurt you, and even when you came to help, I treated you like shit a few times." Shame and regret are coming off him in small waves. I can see his apology is sincere.

"To be honest, I regret the moment I rejected you. But Bastian scared the hell out of me. If we could go back in time to that day when my parents were killed, I would change everything." Mika continues, his fingers playing with the can of cola in his hands as he looks down. I sigh, reaching out and taking his hand in mine, causing the wolf before me to snap his head up in surprise.

"Unfortunately, we cannot go back in time. If things had been different and I had grown up with my father in Northern Snow, we would have met last year when I was twenty. But the Blakes fucked that up for both of us and changed our fates." He nods sadly, a small smile on his lips as he takes in my words.

"I am happy with how my life is now and I wouldn't change it for anything in the world, considering Ariven and I are expecting a pup and I have a pack of my own, a family that loves me, and friends who mean the world to me." I smile looking at the crowd of wolves that are celebrating our victory in our first battle with Prince Coro.

"Our past made us the better version of ourselves, and one day you'll have a second-chance mate. For now, know that you can always call me when you need a friend." I continue, feeling happy to end the pain and suffering caused by our past that is clouded by pain because of the Blakes. Ariven was right, I needed this trip to confront my past and move on.

"We're friends?" I chuckle at Mika's meek question and nod, standing from my chair as I spot Ariven giving me a questioning gaze.

"Yes, Mika, we are friends. You make a great Beta for Lace, but we both know that this won't last long. Trust me when I say your next mate will be kicking your ass in no time." With those final words, I give my friend a smile before walking over to Ariven who promptly wraps an arm around me and pulls me into a hug, his scent enveloping me.

"You okay, darling?" He asks, his free hand running through my hair.

"Yes." I answer, leaning into my mate and enjoying the sparks that ignite from our contact.

"Safe to say you're still mine." He chuckles. I smile, turning my head to nip at the mark I left on his neck.

"I'll always be yours. Nothing will ever change that, Ariven."

Chapter 44 – Lets Go Home

I groan as the sunlight from the window pours in, shining in my eyes and waking me from my sleep. My body is pressed to that of my mate as the sparks and tingles remind me that I am safe in his arms and that last night was the final night we spend in the guest house. Today, we can return home. Alex and Lizaria are at their wits' end with running a pack, and I need my family after all these weeks.

"Keep groaning like that and I will make sure to remind you how our pup was made." A deep voice rumbles and I chuckle, turning to see Ariven looking at me with sleep-filled eyes and a soft smile on his lips.

"Sorry, the sun woke me up. and I am not ready to be awake." I mumble, hiding my face in his chest and sighing. Another deep chuckle, and his strong yet gentle hands running through my hair have me slipping into sleep soon enough though.

"I'll make sure everyone is packed, darling, you sleep." Ariven whispers just before sleep consumes me.

◆◆◆

Soft kisses placed on my cheeks wake me once again. Ready to blast some form of air at the perpetrator waking me up, I open my eyes to see Ariven smiling down at me, a plate of food in his left hand and a mug of a steaming hot drink in his right.

"Sausages, bacon, and pancakes for breakfast, with a hot chocolate for you, darling." He chuckles, setting the food on the bedside table. I thank him, my stomach grumbling and needing the food.

"How long have I been asleep for?" I ask, taking a sip of the hot chocolate while Ariven lays on the bed with a groan.

"About four hours after we first woke up, it's eleven o'clock now. Everything is set to leave, though. Cassandra and Ira plan to stay for another week to make a list of wolves who wish to join our pack from the Rogues we captured." I nod, devouring the food and thinking of the buildings we will have to build to accommodate our new members.

"I was thinking, since we are mates and all, let's move into your cottage officially together." Ariven states, my hand pausing with a fork full of food between the plate and my open mouth. I frown, realizing that in the last few years since creating my pack, I never moved into the cottage officially.

It never felt like a home to me, being so empty and cold without the warmth of a family. I only used the moon pool to visit Mother on the Full Moon and meditate. After that, I would return to the pack house and sleep there, surrounded by pack members who did not have their own cabin yet. Sensing my hesitation, Ariven runs a hand through his hair and sighs.

"I mean, it would be nice to have our own home with our pup and hopefully even more future pups, raise a family together." He adds. Tears form and fall from my eyes at the prospect of a family, my own family and home, something I never thought of before. I did consider my pack house a home in some sense and my pack members family, but they have the choice to come and go, especially after finding their mates.

I focused more on becoming stronger and one day getting revenge. A look of panic takes over Ariven's face from my silent sobs, his mouth opening and closing like a fish out of water. I chuckle, placing the plate beside me and crawling into his lap to breath in his scent.

"Do you think we can get the cottage ready before the pup comes?" I ask through tears, feeling his arms tightening around me.

"Yes. Our pack loves you and would definitely do everything in their power to get a house, a proper house, ready for you." I smile at Ariven's answer. When we return home, we can build a future for ourselves, starting with our own cabin in the woods for our family.

For an hour, we stay like this, me sitting in his lap on the edge of the bed as he holds onto me, just talking about how we want our cottage to look like with Ariven wanting to raise chickens and grow a garden. I can just picture the sweet scene in front of me, with pups running around helping with our chickens or picking fresh vegetables from the garden. It's a scene I cannot wait to see come true. The door to our room opens, interrupting our conversation as Maddie and Matt walk in.

"Everyone is ready to leave, just waiting on you two." Maddie states, leaning against the wall.

"We figured if we didn't come get the two of you, our pack would be spending one more night here. Honestly I miss my bed." Matt adds, and I chuckle.

"We're leaving now." I answer, climbing off of Ariven and stretching for a moment. I see the excitement in the twins' faces, their happiness to return to our pack and see our friends and family again after weeks of being away. With a final look around and double-checking that our belongings were packed away, Ariven, the twins and I make our way downstairs and outside where we are greeted by our packmates mingling with Blood Moon and Hidden Claws in a final goodbye.

"Gem!" I turn to see Lace and Amberle making their way towards me, Mika and Dominic trailing behind the two Alpha wolves.

"I am going to stay behind and help Cassandra with sorting the Rogues. Lace also wants to have our packs train together." Amberle states before I can greet them.

"And after that we were thinking of having an annual meet-up. Next year, we can have Hidden Claws and Silver Crystal Crescent at Blood Moon, then we visit your pack, then back to mine." Lace continues and I smile, liking the idea of our packs starting a tradition.

"We could share training ideas, resources, and even have our pack members find their mates this way." I think aloud, noticing the two she-wolves nodding their heads like eager pups waiting to open their Christmas gifts. With an agreed-upon idea, I suggest we talk about this some more after the Rogues have been organized and settled into proper packs.

Finally, it's time to say goodbye as my pack climbs into their cars. I smile at the friends I have made on this trip, Hidden Claws no longer a place that haunts me, but now a place I look forward to coming back to. It will never be home to me again, but it can be a place I can escape to and see my friends. I notice Misbah and Lilly amongst the wolves coming back with us.

"They asked to leave last night. Lace and I talked to Ariven, and he agreed to let them join your pack this morning while you were asleep." Mika's voice sounds behind me and I turn to see him smiling softly at me. I return the smile before turning back and waving at the two Omegas who took me under their care when I was a pup, excited to have them be a part of my pack and with me once again.

"Thank you, Mika. This means a lot to me." Is my reply. He chuckles and looks to Ariven who waits by my car, giving Mika and I some space.

"You have a good mate there." He points out and I chuckle.

"I do. One day you'll have a mate too." I retort, seeing the sadness in his eyes as he looks at me.

"One day. For now, I think I need time to mourn our broken bond; even if I was the idiot that broke it." Without thinking, I wrap my arms around the wolf before me, giving him a tight hug. Just for a moment, I feel like a kid again, him and I curled up under that tree before tragedy struck Hidden Claws.

"Take your time. Just know that Morai has a destiny for you too, Mika." His arms wrap around me as he takes in my scent, sadness seeping into the air between us.

"Thanks, Gem. Have a safe trip home." With that, we pull away, Lace quickly pushing her brother aside to give me a hug as well, letting me know she will be at my baby shower when it happens and couldn't wait to meet my pup. After that, I make my way to my car where Ariven waits for me, wrapping me into his arms and placing a kiss on my forehead.

"Let's go home, Geminie."

Chapter 45 – Family

I smile down at the white- and curly-haired angel sleeping soundly in her bassinet, wondering if I will be a good mother to my newborn daughter. These last few weeks have been a blur but she is here safe and sound.

First, we returned home to announce Ariven as my mate and make sure that Alex did not do the "brotherly love" beating that Ariven would have won instantly.

Then came the announcement of our pup's impending arrival, which sent the pack into even more of a celebratory frenzy. After that, we welcomed the many new pack members and began our expansion, building new cabins and dorm buildings to accommodate my growing pack, with Ariven and I arguing many times over me helping with building, considering I am pregnant.

We then officially moved into my cottage I designed the day I claimed the land as my own, slowly feeling the warmth and love I longed for inside it, making me happy that I agreed to Ariven's request. As my pregnancy progressed, many pack duties soon became irritating and I found myself snapping more than usual as my hormones fluctuated. Thankfully the cottage became a sanctuary for us to relax after a long day, with no one to bother us up until my pup was born.

Then everyone came to pester me and the future-future Moon Goddess much to my displeasure and Ariven needing to shoo them all away before I electrocuted them.

Now, as I look down at Destiny, I wonder if I will be a good mother to her. Watching my pup sleep safe and sound and knowing my own upbringing, would I be able to raise her opposite to my own childhood? Can I really train her to take the place of Moon Goddess when her time comes?

"Penny for your thoughts, Little Wolf?" I turn and see Lizaria walking into the room with two mugs, the smell of hot apple cider wafting towards me.

"I'm just thinking." Meekly I reply. But this causes Lizaria to sigh as I take the offered drink and the Elf turns to look at my pup.

"I was never able to have children, but I'd like to think I raised you just how I would raise my own, to be strong and honest, but also know when they are wrong." She states, causing my eyes to widen with shock as she gently caresses Destiny's tiny cheek.

"I remember when I first started teaching you, every bump and scrape. I remember all the worry and pain I faced when having to see you leave, to return to those wolves who hurt you so badly. You are the daughter I always wanted." My eyes begin to tear as I think to the day when Lizaria first approached me. Snuggled up to the unicorns in the wildflowers napping with the foals, the Elf carefully woke me up with a smile, asking me if I was okay. It was another day of being punished by Jasmine, and the red mark of a handprint across my face was answer enough that I was not okay at all. Lizaria hugged me as I cried, combed my unruly hair into braids, and for once I felt safe in an adult's arms. The years of her teaching me about history, hand-to-hand combat, and then weaponry as I grew older are years that helped me to be the woman I am today. Lizaria is the mother who raised me.

"I love you, Mama." I whisper, leaning into the Elf beside me and getting a choked chuckle as a response from her.

"Will this pup call me Grandmother?" I look to see the tears falling from her eyes and smile, looking down to see Destiny watching us.

"Of course, you earned that title." I return to those thoughts about if I will be good mother or not to Destiny and smile. Because of Lizaria, I know I will be a good mom. Destiny and any future pups will always have a place to call home and a family.

"Ladies, if we were having a party in the nursery, why wasn't I invited?" I smile as my mother, Lisandra, walks in, coming to stand on my other side as she pulls me into her arms, hugging me tight.

"To think our daughter just had her own daughter." She states, looking over my head at Lizaria. The Elf chuckles and joins in the hug, her long hair blending into mine and my mother's.

"Yes, our daughter had her own daughter." Lizaria agrees. I smile, thinking about how horrible Jasmine was to me, but this led me to meet my chosen mother, Lizaria, and my real mother, Lisandra.

"Did you speak to Liz yet about your idea?" Mother asks as the three of us pull away from the hug and—with their help—walk over to the small sitting area Ariven set up in the nursery as a surprise for me.

"Not yet." I answer as a confused-looking Lizaria looks between the two of us. I smile, and link Ariven to bring the folder from my office and meet us in the nursery. Minutes later, he appears with a smile, passing me the folder before making a beeline for our daughter to coo over her. I chuckle and shake my head. The sight of the tall and muscular, tanned, tattooed man holding a small newborn wrapped in pink melts my heart, his long, black hair tied into a braid down his back. I wonder if a pup will look like him when we expand our family.

"The idea that Ariven, Alex, and I came up with is to allow the unicorns to roam the pack lands freely and have my wolves introduced to them." I state, looking away from my mate and handing the folder to Lizaria.

"All the wolves know you as part of the pack and my second mother, but they have no idea where you disappear to and why you cannot leave the land." I continue, Ariven coming to sit beside me with a sleeping Destiny in his arms.

"Gem, we talked about this. The pro—"

"Protection of the unicorns are your responsibility as they are the last herd, I know. But my pack will gladly take care of them with you and help lessen the burden. They all came here for a second chance and a true family, and you are part of that family." I see her hesitation as Lizaria looks through the folder of wolves who know about the unicorns and their letters pledging to protect them. Silence takes over the room while we sit waiting for Lizaria's answer. I can only suggest this idea to her and not force it if she says no.

"Okay." She finally agrees, closing the folder. I smile, turning to Ariven who nods in understanding. Tonight, we will have a pack meeting and place *Operation Unicorn* into motion. Lizaria needs a break, and as part of my family, I plan to help her like she has helped me.

Chapter 46 - Life Goes On

"Destiny, stop! You're going to hurt yourself." I sigh as I lift my three-year-old pup off of the pile of boxes that contain the rest of her playhouse materials.

With Ariven off on patrol and Lizaria on her first vacation in thousands of years, I am left alone to build the gift Mika and Lace sent for my pup's birthday, as the two went off to help spy on Alexander for Crystalline and I.

A war is brewing, but today, I just want to enjoy the warm weather with my pup.

"Gem, do you need help?" My mother walks outside carrying a tray with lemonade and finger sandwiches, placing them on the small café table with my father following behind her, arms full of food ready to be grilled.

"If you don't mind, could you hold Destiny while I put this wooden playhouse together?" I ask, seeing my mother chuckle as she takes the squirmy three-year-old from my arms and steps back to stand beside my father. With a smile, I close my eyes and focus on the boxes in front of me, picturing the built playhouse as the pieces fly out from the boxes and slowly begin to piece themselves together into a large, log cabin-style playhouse.

Finally, the small replica of the pack house stands before us, Destiny squealing in delight as she claps her hands in excitement.

"Again! Again!" Her little voice calls out, and I oblige, waving my hand where a limestone pathway slowly emerges from the ground and winds its way to the patio. Small gardens with wildflowers surround the playhouse and, as a last touch, I carve a large rock into a bench, fit for a growing child.

"Yay, mommy!" I chuckle at my daughter's excitement, my mother walking over and handing my pup to me. I promptly kiss her forehead and hug her tight.

"Would you like to go play, baby girl?" I ask, seeing her nod enthusiastically. Smiling, I set her down and watch her toddle down the path towards the playhouse.

"When will Amberle and Dominic arrive with their own pups?" My father asks. I sigh, taking a seat at the table while my mother hands me a drink.

"Soon, I hope. Alex and Missy should be here soon with their pups as well." I state, chuckling as my father tries and fails to get the grill going.

"You have to turn the valve open for the gas tank first, dad." I chuckle, seeing Maverick's confused face before he finally gets the grill lit.

"Crystalline unfortunately can't make it. But she did say she sent a gift all the way from Toronto." My mother states as she too watches my father try to get the barbeque working.

"Connor is also on his way with his mate. I cannot believe he is going to be a father soon." My father adds, a triumphant look on his face when he creates a large flame.

"Geez, these things get harder and harder to light. What happened to a nice fire pit or charcoal grill?" he mutters, causing my mother and I to laugh.

"Speaking of fathers, did you tell Ariven yet?" My mother asks through laughter, taking a sip of her own drink. I sigh, placing a hand on my flat stomach and shaking my head.

"Tell me what?" I jump, turning my head in the direction of my mate's voice as Ariven appears through the trees, his long black hair a mess from his patrol. Trailing behind him are Amberle, Dominic, and their three pups.

"Well, if my mother didn't say anything, I had this big plan to tell you tonight, but I guess I have no choice now." I mumble, watching as Destiny tries to climb onto her father.

"If you think Destiny is a handful, wait until her little sibling comes along." I state with a wide grin, a look of shock on my mate's face and happiness on my friends.

"You... You're pregnant?" Ariven stutters, handing Destiny to Amberle before making quick strides to where I sit and scooping me up into his arms. Letting out a surprised squeal, my lips are covered by his as he kisses me passionately, the sparks from the mate bond still strong even after three years of being together.

"Damnit! Ariven, that's our sister!" Someone protests, causing Ariven and I to pull away and see Connor and Alex standing just inside the door, a look of disgust on my brothers faces.

"Oh, shut it, Alex. Gem just told me we're having another pup soon." My mate fires back playfully.

"Doesn't mean you need to give us a preview of how this one was made!" Connor exclaims as he points to Destiny. I giggle, resting my head on my mate's shoulder. I may have gone through hell as a child, but I wouldn't change a thing if it meant the life I have now would disappear.

Looking at the friends I have made, the family I have, and the pack that I love which loves me back, I couldn't wish for a happier ending to my life.

No matter what is thrown my way, I will always remember that life goes on and that good days are ahead of the bad.

♡♡♡

Rejection is never the end, It's just the start of a new beginning...of a new life...of a new love

♡♡♡

Acknowledgement

I just want to thank my friends, beta readers and family that have supported me through my writing journey and keeping me motivated to keep writing. With out all of you, I would have never been able to become a full time author and build the life of my dreams without the amazing support.

I want to thank my niece and nephew for providing me much needed relief and amusement during my writers block though few and far between. How they always seem to know when I need a break to beat them at chess or cuddle during a Disney marathon.

Most importantly, I want to thank my fans and readers. Without all of you I would not be here, writing my fourth novel and second in a series. I would not be working on the third book excited to end the first series to the newly named "Moon-ivers" and I would not be so excited to continue writing in the new year. All the support and love I have received since joining Wattpad seven years ago led me to where I am today, so thank you all!

About the Author

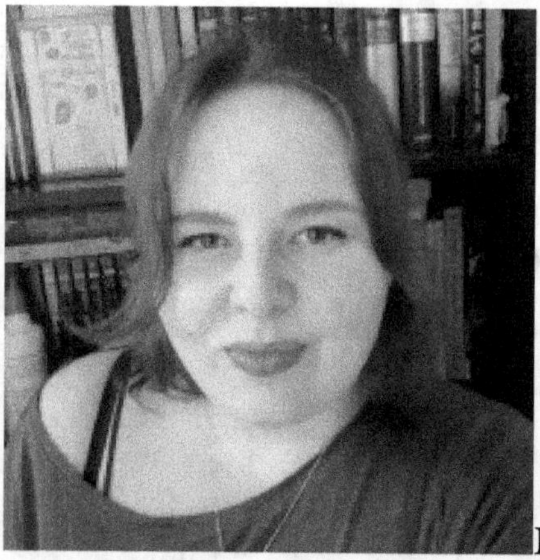

Born and raised in Brampton Ontario - also known at "The Flower City"- Alana Dyer started her relationship with books on a "Hate/Hate" relationship as a child that quickly became a passion for reading as she found that novels can bring you places never seen before.

From finding her love of reading, Alana Dyer soon began writing little stories as a child, and in 2015 with the discovery of Wattpad, Alana started writing seriously with the hopes of one day publishing. Five years later after writing for a loyal fanbase, Alana debuted August 30th, 2020, on Amazon with her first full length novel "The Runaway Breeder".

Now in 2023, Alana Dyer has published 6 novels and two Novelettes under the pen name A. Dyer and spends her days writing, playing with her many pets and planning to expand the distributions of her books.

REJECTING THE FUTURE MOON GODDESS

Rejection Series

Three she-wolves learn that life can take a turn for the worst and those who are supposed to love you can become your worst enemies. When the Moon Goddess and fate play a cruel card that shatters each of their hearts and a budding war is on the horizon can each one find their true strength that lie within and figure out just who is the mastermind in the war that will change the fate of the werewolf race?

Follow Amberle and her Full Moon Rejection in "Rejection on the Full Moon"

See if Geminie's soul mate regrets "Rejecting the Future Moon Goddess"

Can "Rejection to the Alpha King's Daughter" bring out the true Werewolf Queen in Crystalline

And will these girls be able to piece together the true Soulless Evil that hides behind his War?

ALANA DYER

Rejection on the Full Moon
Book 1

Soulless - werewolves who have turned rogue with no humanity left, giving in to their beastly urges.

Rejection - an act in which your soulmate rejects the mate bond, causing immense pain to the rejected.

These are the challenges Amberle Crest must overcome after becoming an outcast amongst the wolves her age due to an event outside of her control.

When her mate rejects her on her eighteenth birthday, Amberle realizes that living in a pack where the majority would rather use her as a slave than treat her as an equal is not worth the pain. She becomes the notorious wolf, Fire Foot, vowing that everyone would regret how they treated her, as she leaves her pack in the past.

Now a ghost forgotten by those that tormented her, Amberle does whatever it takes to survive as a lone wolf. A fateful day changes her lonely life to one full of happiness and hope—until ghosts from her own past call for aid in ridding their pack of the Soulless who threatens all wolf kind.

Faced with new friends, old foes, and the threat of a building army, will Amberle be able to fight the ghosts of her past to cherish the pack she has found or will an old mate claim her before a second chance mate can show her what being treasured by someone is all about?

Rejecting the Future Moon Goddess
Book 2

Soulless - werewolves who have turned rogue with no humanity left, giving in to their beastly urges.

Rejection - an act in which your soulmate rejects the mate bond, causing immense pain to the rejected.

Moon Goddess - the deity that created the werewolf race whom her creation worship

Omega - The lowest ranked wolf in the pack sometimes treated as nothing more than a slave or an object

These are the things Geminie Blake learns after being blamed for the tragic Deaths of her Alpha and Luna. With the pack turned against her and failing to shift as a wolf, Geminie faces challenges every day with the hope of one day gaining freedom or her mate saving her. But when her fated soul mate ends up being her ex-best friend and the son to the late Alpha and Luna rejects her, Geminie's life changes drastically.

Learning that she is not Geminie Blake - daughter to the Beta couple - but Geminie Starlite - daughter to the Moon Goddess and Future Moon Goddess herself - Geminie quickly faces the new challenges thrown her way as she navigates her wolf form and Goddess powers, creating a pack that rivals that of Blood Moon and building her life from scratch to one day take up the mantel as Moon Goddess becomes her priority.

Now, thriving and loving herself for who she is, Geminie forces the past behind her as she waits for her second chance at love. When her first mate requests help and aid from a threat created by Soulless and a potential Leader of the wolves that have lost their Humanity, Geminie is forced to face the wounds left unhealed and return to the place she called hell for eleven years of her life.

Will Geminie be able to overcome the scars left by years of abuse and find love once and for all, or will the panful wounds of her past and threat from the Leader of the army of Soulless ready to kill at a moments notice take the last bit of happiness this young Goddess has left.

Rejection to the Alpha King's Daughter
Book 3

Soulless - werewolves who have turned rogue with no humanity left, giving in to their beastly urges.

Rejection - an act in which your soulmate rejects the mate bond, causing immense pain to the rejected.

Moon Goddess - the deity that created the werewolf race whom her creation worship

Omega - The lowest ranked wolf in the pack sometimes treated as nothing more than a slave or an object

Alpha King/Queen - The rulers of the werewolf nation

Runt - The smallest of the wolf pack, usually ignored or bullied for being the smallest

Crystalline Thorn grows under the abuse by her father as she trains to take the throne one day and become the Alpha Queen, leader of every wolf in the werewolf nation. She dreams of the day when she meets her mate and be accepted as a strong Queen, especially since she is a runt.

But her dream is soon shattered when on the day of an Alliance her mate discovers her "weak" form and rejects her promptly leading to her father disowning her and her hopes to inherit the throne is dashed. But that is the least of her worries. Soon, with the help of Geminie and Amberle, Crystalline learns of a war that has been brewing for thousands of years, of a destiny that has been written in the stars by the original Moon Goddess - Luna - and the Goddess of Destiny - Morai - have placed upon her and her connection to the Lost Princess.

Will Crystalline be able to retrieve her throne?

Will she accept the mate that rejected her or chose the second chance mate?

Or will the weight of responsibility handed to her crush her entirely?

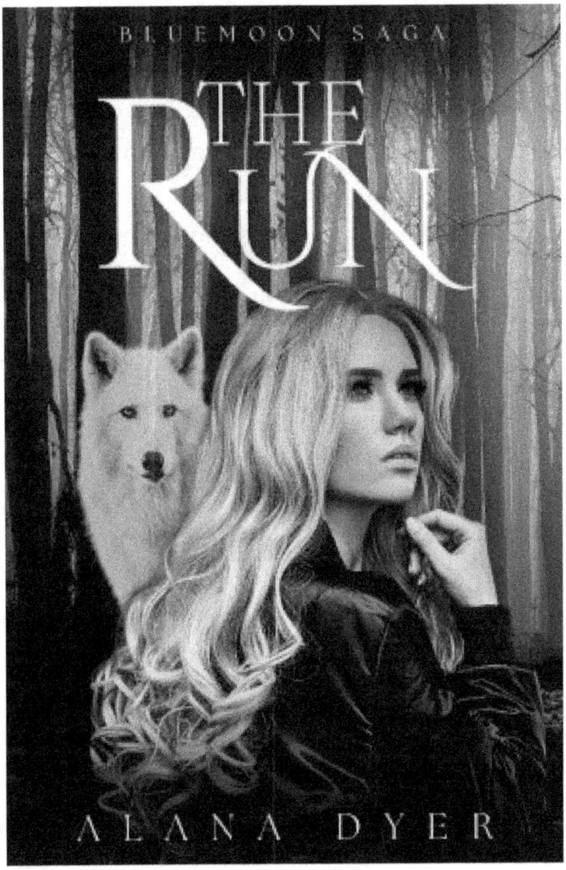

The Run

"The cage doors are released and I open my sapphire coloured eyes, dashing out of the prison and into the forest.

Seven days for the full moon to be blue.

Seven days from the starting line to the finish

Seven days, that's how long I had to make it to the lodge as an unmated female."

Legends of werewolves have gone back centuries. Always including the Moon Goddess and her blessing of soulmates to the beings she created. But the ugly truth is there is no such thing as soulmates. There is only The Run.

An event created centuries ago held twice a year during a blue moon where she-wolves run from their male counter parts. If they are captured, they are mated and marked, claimed by whoever captures them first.

No one is exempted from this event - not even Grace Harvest.

After being able to avoid attending the event since turning eighteen, Grace finds herself unable to find an excuse not to participate this time. With her last hope of remaining unmated until she can fall in love, she makes a bet with her Alpha. If she wins, he can no longer force wolves of his pack to participate in The Run and allow them to find love. If he wins, Grace will be mated, and her pack mates are forced to go no matter what.

But what will happen when she meets a golden haired wolf by the name Caden Wolfrain, who instantly captures her attention. Will she do all she can to win the bet, will Caden win her heart or will the secrets Caden keeps force her to cut ties with this golden haired wolf without a second thought no matter the heart break.

Books by the Author

CONTACT THE AUTHOR

alana.dyer.author@
hotmail.com

author.alana.dyer

alana.dyer

Alana Dyer
@alana.dyer.author

E-BOOK | PAPERBACK | HARDCOVERS

available where books are sold

Don't miss out!

Visit the website below and you can sign up to receive emails whenever Alana Dyer publishes a new book. There's no charge and no obligation.

https://books2read.com/r/B-A-LXGX-VOLOC

BOOKS 2 READ

Connecting independent readers to independent writers.

www.ingramcontent.com/pod-product-compliance
Lightning Source LLC
Chambersburg PA
CBHW070458260626
47161CB00004B/1352
* 9 7 8 1 7 3 8 1 0 0 4 4 6 *